DEADLY GUILD

DETECTIVE SARAH SPILLMAN MYSTERIES BOOK 3

RENÉE PAWLISH

Deadly Guild

Published by Creative Cat Press
copyright 2021 by Renée Pawlish

FOREWORD

I have exercised some creative license in bending settings and law-enforcement agencies to the whims of the story. This is, after all, a work of fiction. Any similarities between characters in this novel and real persons is strictly coincidental.

CHAPTER ONE

Teddy: *The Guild will now come to order.*

She read the line on the computer monitor, then put her hands to the keyboard and typed.

Marilyn: *Marilyn Monroe is here.*

She'd chosen her favorite actress as her pseudonym. She loved old-time movies, and she loved Marilyn Monroe. Monroe carried herself as few other females did. She was sexy, sultry, and yet she played hardball with the Hollywood studios. People thought Monroe was dumb, but she was smart and tough. The woman nodded. Yes, that name fit her well.

Her house was quiet except for the classical music that played in her office. She looked at the screen. Other members of the Guild said their hellos. There was Brad Pitt, well, not *really* Brad Pitt, but someone who said he liked Pitt's movies. She assumed Brad was a "he," but for all she knew Brad could be a woman. The whole idea was anonymity. That was key.

Daffy Duck, Pete Rose, and Joe Smith were there. She wasn't fond of Daffy Duck. Daffy came across as arrogant. Pete Rose. "That was someone who loved baseball, and was a gambler," she thought with a laugh. Joe Smith was really going for obscurity. She had no idea who they all were, and they had no idea who she was. That was the way the Guild worked. They were in a secure online chat room, where no one would be able to identify them. They all had secure internet connections, untraceable. They all had money, enough to buy that kind of secrecy and safety.

Teddy Roosevelt, the leader, typed again.

Please agree to the Guild rules. Everything said here remains here. Do not talk about a member's actions or plans to anyone outside of the Guild. We are the group, no new members will be allowed. We all have the resources to make you pay. Do not break the rules. Your word is your oath.

She thought it was interesting that Teddy always started each recitation of the rules with a polite "Please," but ended the rules with a threat. She frowned. None of them needed the threat. If one of them talked, they were all vulnerable, and none of them wanted to go to jail. Or worse. So no one would say a word.

The monitor lit up with a round of yeses from the Guild members. The woman dutifully agreed to the Guild rules as well. Teddy went on.

Does Daffy Duck have a report for us?

The woman rolled her eyes as Daffy Duck responded.

Did you all see the report about a drowning near Parker a few days ago?

A round of yeses.

Daffy Duck: *That was me.*
Pete Rose: *Proof?*
Daffy Duck: *Check the paper.*

The woman opened a browser. As she was sure the others were doing, she typed in the newspaper and searched for a man who'd drowned. She found an article and quickly read it. Then she came to the pertinent section. A silver necklace with a fake ruby had been found at the scene. Jewelry with a red stone was the proof. Innocuous to most, but proof for the Guild. She went back to the chat room. By now, Brad Pitt had responded.

Marilyn: *It's right there. The proof.*
Teddy Roosevelt: *That's correct.*
Pete Rose: *You did it.*
Daffy Duck: *I was a bit afraid at first. I wasn't sure I could go through with it. But then I hit him over the head, and the rest was easier than I thought.*
Brad Pitt: *Way to go, killer.*
Daffy Duck: *Ha ha. I've thought about this for so long, wanted to know what it would be like to actually do it. Now I'm part of an elite group of people.*
Brad Pitt: *Like Teddy and me.*

The woman felt a twinge of jealousy. Daffy Duck now had a kill, like the others. She wanted to know how it felt. Before she could ask him about it, Teddy cut into the conversation.

The next order of business, who is next?

The woman stared at the monitor, waiting to see if someone else might respond. When no one did, she put her shaking hands to the keyboard and typed.

Marilyn: *Me.*

Her breath caught in her throat. She was committed now.

Teddy Roosevelt: *When?*

She pondered that for a moment. For days she had been thinking how she would do it. And she'd formed a plan that she was sure was foolproof, where she could not get caught. It was time to forge ahead. She typed her response.

Marilyn: *Tomorrow night. Watch the news after that.*
Teddy Roosevelt: *Wonderful.*

She picked up a crystal glass and took a drink of Scotch to calm her nerves. She had to go through with it now. That order of business finished, the conversation with Daffy Duck resumed.

Pete Rose: *Daffy, you're sure you were careful?*
Daffy Duck: *Of course. Don't insult me.*
Teddy Roosevelt: *Just like the others. With the correct precautions, there won't be any problems.*

The woman nodded at the screen. Yes, they were all exceedingly careful. They had to be, or their lives would be ruined. No one could have that. The irony of their victims losing their lives was not lost on her. But that was the price that had to be paid for the Guild members to experience killing. And she wanted to know. She finally asked Daffy Duck what she'd wanted to ever since he said he'd completed his task.

Marilyn: *How did it feel?*
Daffy Duck: *Incredible.*

CHAPTER TWO

"How are you doing today?"

Dr. Feinstein looked at me, her eyes dark and curious. She crossed her legs at the ankles and glanced down at the notepad in her lap. She was a plump woman, maybe ten years older than my late thirties, with a matronly attitude about her, her eyes and voice full of concern. I don't know how the male officers who had to see Dr. Feinstein would've felt about her, but I was defensive. I didn't want to be here. No matter how motherly she might have been, it didn't take away the feelings I'd had about the shooting. Or the fact that she had to clear me before I could resume my normal duties again.

"I'm fine," I said, ignoring the knot in my stomach.

Her office was quiet, no windows, just a seascape hanging above a cluttered desk behind her. I glanced at a ficus in the corner near the couch where I sat. I caught a whiff of what I could only describe as a summery odor, as if a lawn had just been cut. I love that smell. It makes me think of the good times growing up, before things grew more complicated.

Dr. Feinstein contemplated me for a minute. "You're fine. That's a very non-specific answer."

"I don't have anything to say."

"This is our fourth session," she said. I stared at her, and she went on. "Would you like to talk about the incident?"

"We went over the whole thing before. I don't think I need to do that again."

"Sometimes it helps to talk through things multiple times. You might realize something now that you didn't before."

I took in a deep breath. "I don't know about that." I found a thread on the couch cushion, and I pulled at it. Growing up, I had a cat who would eat at a thread like that for a long time, until you redirected him to something else. I never knew why he did that. I knew I was trying to deflect her questions.

"Detective? What are you thinking?"

"About my cat."

She arched an eyebrow.

"It's nothing," I said.

Her eyes held subtle amusement at my deflections. She continued to prod. "Have the nightmares dissipated?"

I continued to evade. "Yes," I said, a little too quickly.

We engaged in an uneasy silence, as we had on previous sessions. Dr. Feinstein considered me again, then put her pen on the notepad, rubbed her brow for a second, and locked eyes with me.

"I know this is hard, Detective Spillman, and I don't want to make this process any longer than I have to."

I shrugged. "Then don't."

That brought a small smile. She had to be used to cops who kept their feelings locked up, had defenses higher and thicker than the Great Wall of China, and she took no offense. "How about you give me a little more than you're 'fine?' "

I thought for a moment. I didn't want to tell her too much. I rarely opened up to anybody, except maybe Harry. Harry Sousen and I have been together for over ten years, and even he would say that I have high walls and it takes time to penetrate them. Dr. Feinstein wasn't Harry, but I knew I had to give her something, or she wouldn't clear me to get back to my job. I suppressed a sigh. I had been on desk duty for a month now, since the shooting.

"What are you thinking?" Dr. Feinstein asked.

That was her favorite phrase. "It's nothing."

"You don't trust me."

She was perceptive, I'd give her that. My face had told her more than I'd meant to.

"I don't like to talk about myself."

"Not the first time I've heard that." She looked at her notepad. "You told me in scant detail what happened. I had to look up the report to find out what all happened that night. It doesn't tell me how you felt."

I raised my hands. "As I've told you before, I don't regret what I did. If I hadn't shot Carson Welch, he would've killed me." Knowing that hadn't eased the nightmares, though. Or the sleepless nights. I had still taken a life.

I wiped my sweaty palms on my slacks, then noticed her watching me and stopped. I stared past her and caught the cut-lawn smell again. This time, the scent took me back to that hot summer night not too long ago. Welch coming at me, the feel of my Glock as I pulled the trigger, the sound of the shot. His face twisting up, then him leaping at me with his knife raised. Dr. Feinstein cleared her throat, and my gaze went back to her.

"I had to do it."

She nodded. "You've said that from the beginning."

"And I'll continue to say that," I snapped. I felt my muscles tighten, and I tried to relax. "Look, I know we have to go through this process. I know you're only doing your job. I'd like to get back to *my* job. I'm not one for sitting at a desk, or going to community meetings."

"Community meetings?"

"It's a task force, to help foster positive relationships between the police and the community."

"Sounds like you read that out of a manual."

I couldn't help but smile. "Yes."

"You're not thrilled to be a part of it."

"One of the perks of the job," I said sarcastically. Then I shook my head. "Don't get me wrong. It's a great thing, I'd just rather be working. I need to be out there," I gestured with my hand toward the door, "finding the bad guys. That's what is going to make me feel better."

"Rather than explaining what you do to others," she finished.

"Right."

"Tell me about the nightmares."

I was defensive. "I didn't say I was having them anymore."

She wasn't fooled. She didn't say anything, but waited.

I shrugged again. "Since we talked last, I only had one dream, the other night." That wasn't completely true. I'd had fewer nightmares, but still more than just the few I'd told her about. "I'm chasing Welch up the stairs, and I can't catch him. I go into Diane's room, and he has the knife out. He slits her throat and runs out the door. I shouldn't leave my sister, but I want to shoot him. I run to the door, and he's there. When I pull the trigger, nothing happens. I can't stop him as he comes at me." I stopped talking, my hands pressed into my lap.

She finally asked, "What happens next?"

I looked away. "He comes at me with the knife. Right before he gets to me, he disappears. I go to the bed, and Diane's dead. Then I wake up."

She took a long time before saying anything. "Are your partners in the dream?" She glanced at her notes. "Ernie and Spats?

Ernie Moore and Roland "Spats" Youngfield, are great guys. I've worked with them for a long time, and yes, sometimes they can be protective of me.

"No," I said, then, "I'm not sure. It's like they're there, but not really. It's just Welch and me. And I couldn't stop him."

"You feel like you didn't protect your sister?"

My jaw tightened. "I did what I could, and yet ..." I blinked hard. "If I had figured things out sooner, he might not have attacked Diane."

"He didn't kill her, though."

"Right."

"You don't get along with your sister?"

I shook my head. "No, although I'm making an effort."

I hadn't told Feinstein too much about my relationship with Diane. That would take far too many sessions, way more than I was willing to do now. As I had told Feinstein, I wanted to get back to work, to resume my normal duties, which meant homicide investigations.

"She's okay?"

I nodded. "As well as can be expected after a killer almost rapes and kills you," I said. "She doesn't tell me a whole lot."

A wry smile crept across Feinstein's face. "Sounds like someone else I know."

I pursed my lips. "When it comes to Diane ... there's too much there to get into."

"Does she blame you for what happened that night?"

"She hasn't said it directly, but I think she's angry that I didn't find the killer before he attacked her."

"What could you have done differently?"

"I don't know," I snapped. She looked at me closely. I breathed hard. "I did the best I could." My decisions gnawed at me, though. If I'd put the pieces of the puzzle together sooner,

Welch might never have gone after Diane. There was nothing I could do about that now, and yet my guilt remained.

Feinstein jotted something down in her notebook. "You say the nightmares are happening less often. Are you feeling fearful?"

"No."

"Do you ever feel like maybe someone is around every corner, waiting to attack you?"

I shook my head. "No, I'm fine."

That word again. Dr. Feinstein raised an eyebrow. She had a habit of doing that.

"Fine?"

I was a little jumpy: Harry had noted that. But it was getting easier. I was hypervigilant, more so than usual. However, even if the doctor didn't believe me, I was getting better. I needed an investigation to fuel me.

"If you had to do it again," she said, "if a killer was coming after you, what would you do?"

I looked her in the eye. "I'd pull the trigger again. It's a split-second decision, and if my life is in danger, I'll act. It's part of the job, part of what I have to do."

"Taking another life can't be easy," she pressed.

I gnawed my lip. "No, it's not. I think about what Welch did to those women, though, how he raped and murdered them, and I feel better about my decision. I didn't want to do it, but he left me no choice. His actions dictated what happened. I wasn't in control of that."

Feinstein nodded.

"Did this investigation affect you more than other investigations?"

"No."

"How are things with Ernie and Spats? Would they feel you're ready to resume field work?"

"Yes." Again, a tad too quickly. I noted Dr. Feinstein's disapproval at my hasty answer and said, "They worry about me; they always have. Both can tell I'm itching to get away from my desk. They know I didn't do anything wrong." I didn't say that although I appreciated my partners' concern, I was ready for it to stop. That would mean things were back to normal, whatever that was.

She mulled over that, jotted down something else, and studied me. She chose her words carefully. "You do seem like you're more at peace with the shooting and the aftermath than the first time I saw you." Her brow furrowed wisely. "I know you're not telling me everything; nobody who comes in here for these brief sessions ever does. It takes too long. I know that you want to get back to doing what you do best. My job is to assess your fitness to resume your normal duties." She put her hands on top of the notepad. "From what I can tell, I think you're doing okay, so I'm going to clear you to go back into the field. I would agree that it's what is important for you, what's going to help you the most."

I nodded and held my excitement in check.

"I want you to know that the door is open to talk to me anytime," she said. "I know it's going to take more time, probably more than you even realize. I would encourage you to talk through your feelings more, if not with me, with Harry, with somebody. Don't bottle things up."

I breathed a sigh of relief, partly because she was going to clear me to get back to my job, partly for not having to talk to anyone about the shooting right now. I knew she was right, that I needed to open up about it, but I knew myself. I needed time. Right now I wanted to think about things other than what had happened with Welch.

"So we're done here?" I asked.

She contemplated me one last time. "I'll clear you to get back

13

to investigations. It may take a day or two for all the paperwork to be filed." She stood up. "Here." She took a card from her desk. "I gave you a card before, and I'd be willing to bet you don't have it."

I got up as well and took the card with a small smile. "Thanks for your time."

Feinstein stared at me. "I really mean it. Please take more time to talk through everything, with Harry. From what you've said, he will listen without any judgment. And I'm always available if you need me."

I walked out the door without a reply.

CHAPTER THREE

I left Dr. Feinstein's office and headed back to the station for the community meeting. It was a beautiful September day, the air dry, but with the hint of the coming winter. I stopped at a Subway for a quick bite, and I sat outside with my sandwich and mulled over my session with Feinstein.

I could compartmentalize things very well. I learned that skill as a kid. I'd lost my Uncle Brad, who I had been particularly close to when I was a kid. I'd never gotten along with my older sister, Diane, and Brad had seen that and had helped me when I thought the rest of my family didn't understand. I was stunned when he died of a heart attack, and I felt so alone.

I took a bite of my sandwich and thought about my sister. As I told Feinstein, delving into my relationship with Diane would take a long time. After years of avoiding the issue, I'd recently told Diane about the resentment toward her that I'd harbored for a good part of my life. It all stemmed from an incident in college, when Diane had messed up and done something illegal while she was in med school. I helped her out of the situation, but only by doing something illegal myself. I had desperately wanted my sister's approval, and I thought that by helping her, I would surely earn it. Not only did that not happen, she totally discounted my actions, even while I worried that what I'd done might cost me a career in law enforcement. Diane didn't seem to understand that at all, which didn't help our relationship. I needed to let that all go, but I was stubborn, and it was easier said than done.

I finished my sandwich without feeling much better. I glanced at my phone and realized I needed to get back to the station for the community meeting.

I did not want to make an appearance tonight. It wasn't that I didn't want to help, it just made me feel as if I couldn't do what I was cut out to do: investigate homicides. No one trusted me to do that at the moment. I crumpled up my sandwich wrapper and got up, threw it in a trash can, and went to my car. I used the drive time to try to get my mind into a better space. By the time I arrived at the station at Thirteenth and Cherokee, I'd managed to put on my game face. When I walked into the large conference room on the first floor, several people from the community were already there. I also saw Daniel Hackman, who's another homicide detective, along with a detective I didn't know from the robbery division, and Chief Duane Follett. Follett's over six feet tall, stocky, with a full head of gray hair, and a superior attitude that goes beyond his position. He's also a bit old school, and I get the feeling he thinks I can't handle my job. I frequently find myself biting my tongue around him. A couple of officers in uniform stood nearby, both rocking nervously on the balls of their feet. Follett nodded at me curtly and went back to a conversation he was having with a man in a business suit.

I had heard that the meetings had been started by a couple of big names in the community. One, Lawrence Ridley, was a well-known accident lawyer. You couldn't have the television on for more than a few minutes without seeing him hawking his firm's services. *If you've been in an accident, call us. We're fair, and we get the job done right for you.* Uh-huh. I'd never met him, but I'd heard people say that he was extremely nice and extremely smart. The other founding committee member was Ellen Scarsdale, the wife of a prominent local businessman, whose daughter had been beaten and raped. The assailant had never been found. At first Ellen had been extremely angry with the police, and then she decided to channel that anger, as she said, into something good. She felt it would be beneficial for the police to be more transparent in their operations, practices, and procedures. A delicate balance. The meetings were also a way for the police to let the public know what charitable things we did within the community.

People milled about, and the room buzzed with conversation as I took a seat at a long table in front of the crowd. Daniel looked at me with a grim smile.

"Don't worry, it'll be over soon," he murmured.

I smiled back. "How are things going?"

He shrugged. "You know, same old same old. Working on a tough case now. You?"

He knew I'd been on desk duty, and I didn't like the sympathetic look he was giving me. I tipped my head toward the audience. "I'm hoping to get back into the field soon."

"That'd be a good thing."

We tuned out the din of conversation and chit-chatted for a few minutes, and then at seven o'clock, one of the uniforms stood up and went to a lectern set on a long conference table. He raised his hands to shush the crowd, then spoke into the microphone.

"Thank you all for joining us at this month's meeting. I'm Officer Rodriguez. It's nice to see you all."

People took their seats and the conversations died down. Rodriguez introduced Daniel and me, then the others at the table, and ended with Chief Follett. Rodriguez paused for a smattering of polite applause, then he launched into an explanation of the meetings. After he spoke for a few minutes about a charity that the police force was working with, he reintroduced Chief Follett. Another tepid round of applause, and Follett got up and spoke for a few minutes and listed some of the concerns that the community had raised in past meetings, and how the department was addressing these. He talked smoothly, with a poised and purposeful manner, and when he finished, he excused himself, saying he had another engagement. I had no idea whether that was true. Regardless, he didn't sit through the rest of the meeting. After he left, the detective from the robbery division got up and talked in general terms about some of the crimes that had occurred in recent weeks, then raised some concerns about a rise in convenience store robberies in the north part of downtown. Then I was introduced again, and I went to the lectern. I obviously couldn't discuss any open cases, but I talked briefly about homicides in Denver, referring to some stats I'd pulled up earlier in the day. I'm not a fan of public speaking, and I was glad when I was able to sit down again. Daniel talked for a minute, and I stared in stoic silence above the crowd of faces. The minutes ticked by, and the meeting finally ended. I said goodbye to the people at the conference table, and as I was walking toward the back of the room, I was stopped by a woman and her husband.

"We saw you on TV." She smiled with perfect white teeth.

"The Welch case," her husband explained.

I drew in a breath and tried not to look perturbed. I didn't want to discuss it with them, or anyone else.

"That must've been so scary," the man intoned.

"It's part of the job, unfortunately," I said.

"It's a good thing you found Welch," he went on. "How many women did he kill?"

"I'm afraid I can't comment on open cases," I said. We knew Welch had killed at least five women, and we were working with other departments in Colorado and Ohio to see if he could be tied to more killings. However, there was no way I could share anything about my investigation with the public.

"I love to read the serial-killer books," the woman said. "It's fascinating to get into the mind of a killer."

"I don't know about that," I said with a forced smile. I had tried to figure out killers of all kinds. I never thought of it as "fascinating."

I thanked the couple for coming and continued toward the back. I was stopped by another woman who I guessed was in her sixties, decked out in an expensive white pantsuit and plenty of gold jewelry. Her long gray hair fell around thin shoulders.

"Detective," she said, her voice low. "I enjoyed your talk."

"Thank you."

She began asking me some questions about homicide investigations. "Are they anything like the television shows?"

"Not really," I said.

"I've heard that the forensics shows aren't accurate."

"There's some truth, some things are fiction. It's entertainment, though."

"I see," she murmured.

She asked a few more questions, and I answered them as briefly as I could, looking for the door. I used to work with the juvenile division, crimes against children. I'd also given talks to children at schools. They were an easier crowd than this. I was finally able to break away from her, and was stopped only one more time by another couple. I made it to the door and left before anybody could pepper me with more questions. Overall, the meeting hadn't been as bad as I'd anticipated, but I hoped that I wouldn't have to speak at one again.

CHAPTER FOUR

It was past midnight, and I was lying awake in bed, staring at the ceiling. Harry was snoring quietly beside me. It was Wednesday, a week since I'd last met with Dr. Feinstein. I'd finally been cleared yesterday to resume my normal duties, but so far nothing had happened. Harry had been pleased at the news. He knew how much my work meant to me, and yet I could tell he worried. I could lie to the psychologist, tell her that everything was okay, but I couldn't fool Harry. He could tell that although I was feeling a little bit better, I was still bothered about taking a life, even if it was a rapist and murderer. He had asked me about the nightmares as well, knowing they were still occurring. I told him I'd be okay. His frown told me he wasn't so sure. I wanted to tell him more, but every time I did, I stopped myself. I didn't want to relive that night again.

I lay for a while longer. The silence was deafening. Tired of not sleeping, but also afraid I'd have nightmares if I did, I carefully slipped from under the covers and donned a robe. I took my phone off the charger and slipped it into my robe pocket. I looked at Harry for a moment before tiptoeing out of the room. I went into the kitchen and poured a glass of wine, then padded on bare feet into the living room. It was tempting to turn on some music, but I didn't want to wake Harry, so I sat down on the couch and picked up a spy thriller by Brad Thor. After a sip of wine, I opened the book, and began reading. The words weren't sinking in and I finally put the book aside and picked up the wine glass. I slowly twirled the glass by the stem, but didn't take another drink. I stared at the red liquid and let my mind wander.

Images of Carson Welch flashed before me, and I shook my head to clear them away. I'd also talked to Diane this evening, and she had been a little cool with me. I wasn't sure why, but it bothered me. Was it about me not stopping Welch soon enough, or was it that I'd recently confronted her about that long-ago, unresolved situation between us? My phone vibrated in my robe pocket. I quickly set down the glass and answered the call. It was Ernie.

"Hey there," I said.

"You sound wide-awake." Ernie has a deep voice, one that gets your attention.

I looked at the clock on the wall over the fireplace. It was after one. I made excuses. "I just got up to go to the bathroom."

"Sure, you did." Ernie let out a wry laugh. I wasn't able to fool him, either. "You ready to get back to work?" He sounded a bit tired, stifled a yawn.

"What's going on?" I tried to keep my voice even, but I was excited.

"We got a dead body, a woman, found behind a motel on West Colfax," Ernie said. "She was shot. I don't have any more details at the moment."

"A motel on Colfax? Was she a hooker?" Many of the motels on Colfax were cheap and a draw for drug dealers and prostitutes.

"I don't know. I think they were going to give it to Hackman, and I said you should take it. Hackman's already working another case."

"They wanted to give it to someone else?" I sat a little straighter. "How do you know?"

"I just got off the phone with Rizzo," Ernie said. "He didn't sound too happy about you taking this one, something about the team rotation. But don't quote me on that."

Daniel Hackman had told me some about his other case at the community meeting. I didn't fault his skills, he knows what he's doing, and he'd be good on any investigation, but I didn't understand why Commander Rizzo wouldn't want me on this case.

"What's Rizzo's problem?" I voiced my concerns out loud. "All this time he's been backing me, saying he wants me back working actual homicides. Now he's bringing up the rotation?"

"I don't know. Anyway, you want to talk politics or you want to get over to the crime scene?" Ernie minced no words.

I stood up. "I'll be there in half an hour."

With that, I ended the call. I tiptoed back into the bedroom, went into the bathroom and splashed water on my face, then cracked the door for light while I got dressed. It didn't matter. Harry woke up anyway.

"What's going on?" he asked with a yawn.

"I'm sorry I woke you." I buttoned up a blouse while I talked. "Ernie called, I have to go." I told him what little I knew about the body found behind the motel.

Harry sat up and turned on the nightstand lamp. "You sure you're ready for this?"

I pulled on jeans, then got my gun from a box in the closet and put it in its belt holster. I finally turned to look at him. "I'm ready."

It would be cool at this time of night, so I grabbed a jacket with a DPD logo on it and slipped it on. I moved over to the bed and leaned down. I gave Harry a lingering kiss. "I'll be fine."

He held me close for a moment, then let me go. I stared into his dark eyes and wished I could wash away the apprehension. Before he could say more, I turned and left the room.

———

I RECOGNIZED Ernie's dark sedan when I parked on West Colfax near the Princeton Motel.

What a name for a sleazy motel, I thought.

I got out and glanced up and down the street. Colfax Avenue was once the main highway through Denver, and it got the nickname as the "longest, wickedest Main Street in America" because of stretches with shady motels known for drugs and prostitution. Right now, there was little activity on the street. The Princeton Motel was nothing more than a worn-down L-shaped building with several small rooms. At one time it had probably been a charming little place with a cute name, but as the city grew, it had faded into a dive for secret trysts. I looked toward the front of the motel, where a red neon signed flashed "Office" and didn't see anyone, so I walked past a few units with dark windows to the back of the building. Two uniformed officers stood at either end of a parking lot. A sole light on a building across from the hotel bathed the area in dim light. A stocky man in an out-of-date brown suit was bent down near a body sprawled near the door to a room. It was still the middle of the night, and besides police personnel, only a young-looking man and woman gawked at the other end of the lot. Other than that, it was quiet.

I walked up to the officer near me, and he noted the badge clipped to my belt. He gave me a curt nod as I told him my name and he noted my arrival in a notebook.

"No one's been in the parking lot since we got here," he said.

"Good." I left him on guard duty and cautiously walked up to the body, mindful of tainting evidence. The man in the suit straightened up.

"You look great, like you didn't even go to bed." Ernie brushed imaginary dirt off his hands and gave me an appraising look.

"I'm fine," I said.

He tipped his head and studied me. "Okay," he said slowly, the assessment continuing.

I shrugged that off and looked down at the body. The woman was lying on her side, faded jeans shorts hiked up almost to her rear. Her yellow blouse had smudges on it. A cheap black heel was on her right foot, her left foot bare. "Where's her other shoe?"

He shrugged. "Dunno."

"What have you got so far?"

Ernie gave me another little look, then squared his shoulders, acting as if all was okay. And it would be.

"Not much," he said. "She's probably late teens, maybe early twenties. You ask me, she had a rough life up to this point, so it's hard to say. Nothing in her pockets, no ID on her."

"No money?"

"Nada. Maybe she was robbed. And those two," he pointed to the couple hanging around at the other end of the lot, "say they don't know her. I don't believe them."

"Great," I muttered. I glanced around, then pointed at the couple. "You interview them?"

He shook his head. "Not yet. The officer talked briefly to them, told them not to go anywhere. I want a crack at them." He tipped his head. "Unless you want to question them."

"We'll get to them in a minute. Where's Spats?"

"He's talking to the motel manager. Up front. Did you see the office?"

I nodded. "Yeah, but not Spats. Who reported the body?"

"An anonymous call. The dispatcher said it sounded like a woman. She said there was a dead body behind the motel, gave the motel name, and hung up. The call came from a gas station down the street."

"Don't get involved," I muttered. "I'd like to find whoever called it in and see what she knows or saw."

"That would be helpful," he said dryly. "Dispatch sent a car here, and these two officers found her. They cordoned off the area and called in homicide."

"We'll need to interview whoever's working at the gas station, find out what they can tell us about the 911 caller."

"I'll stop by there later."

I crouched down and carefully put a hand on the ground. Even though the early morning held a chill, the asphalt still felt warm, and a faint oil smell hit me. I studied the body closely.

As Ernie had said, the woman looked as if life had been cruel to her. She was skinny, with a thin nose, heavily made-up eyes that didn't hide dark circles under them, and long, scraggly blond hair. Still, looking past that, there was something attractive about her. She probably had been cute in high school, then life had taken her down a dark path. Dirt was under gnawed fingernails, and a red ring adorned her right pinky finger.

"Did you see this?" I got down on all fours for a better look at the ring.

Ernie bent down. "Some cheap thing."

"Looks like plastic to me, brand new. Something she bought to make herself feel pretty?"

"She needed more than that. No other rings or jewelry, and not even a tan line on her finger, where she might normally wear a ring, even if she didn't have it on tonight."

"She's also got a tattoo on the inside of her left wrist." I looked closer. "What is that, a strawberry?"

"Looks that way to me. What did a strawberry mean to her?"

I leaned back and assessed her again, then moved in close so I could get a good look at her arms. "It looks like track marks there."

"Yeah, she uses." He stared at the motel. "How much you wanna bet she's turning tricks to pay for her habit."

I couldn't disagree. Most women in this particular night-life need some kind of chemicals to get by, something to ease the pain of the lifestyle, then something to ease the withdrawal symptoms. A vicious circle. I ran a hand over my face. "I won't bet. I'd lose." I shifted and stared at the back of her head. Her hair at the lower skull was singed, and I could see two small penetrations in her skull. She'd been shot. The gun had exploded so close to her head that it charred her hair, and there was gunpowder residue. Two point-blank shots. "Someone really wanted to make sure she died."

"Maybe a twenty-two? The bullets would rattle around in her head, but not exit."

I nodded and glanced up at him. "This looks like an execution." I gestured at the asphalt near her. "There's no blood. She was killed somewhere else and dumped here."

Ernie gnawed his lip. "I didn't want to say anything, see what you concluded. But yeah, that's what I think."

I looked at the woman again. "Who would want to execute a prostitute?"

"Good question. She pissed off the wrong person, they shoot her, end of story?"

"When we find out who she is and talk to her acquaintances, we might find that's true."

"That'd be a quick wrap-up to this case."

"Two shots to the head," I mused. "I don't know." Still careful not to disturb anything, I continued a close-up examination. "Look at the cuts here, on her elbow and her knee." I pointed to a couple of the gashes. "The one on her knee looks deep. Where did she get those?"

Ernie bent down. "They're not really bleeding, so I'd say these are postmortem. Did she get those wherever she was killed, or when she was dropped here? The coroner should be here any minute, maybe he can tell us."

"Is it Jamison?" I asked. Jack Jamison was the Department's coroner. He's a busy, but very thorough, man.

"I doubt he'll come this time of night. It'll be a backup."

I studied the cuts. "They don't look like defensive wounds. It doesn't appear that she struggled with her killer."

"Nope."

I heard voices and stood up. I swiped dirt off my jeans, then rubbed my hands together. A crime-scene crew had shown up, and they were being logged in by the officer at the end of the parking lot. I recognized Todd Siltz and walked over.

He looked past me, his blue eyes missing nothing. "A dead woman?" He surveyed the parking lot. "How'd she die?"

"She was shot," I said, then told him what I knew. "Probably somewhere else. I don't think you'll find much, but be thorough. Watch for anything that might tell us where she was killed. She has smudges on her clothes; maybe we can get something from that."

He brushed wavy hair out of his face. "You got it."

I nodded at the couple watching us. "And put up a barrier so those two can't see anything." The techs had a screen they could set up to shield the body from onlookers.

Todd and another tech I didn't recognize got to work, and I gestured for Ernie to join me. He lumbered over and we watched the techs for a moment.

"I don't think we're going to get anything," Ernie said. "It's a parking lot."

I let that hang in the air for a moment, then looked at the waiting couple. "You didn't talk to them?"

CHAPTER FIVE

Ernie stared at the man and woman at the end of the parking lot. "No. You want a crack at them?" He glanced at his notepad. "Steve Gibson and Madison McCann. They didn't see or hear anything." He grunted. "Right, and I'm the pope."

I rolled my eyes. "I'll work on them in a second." I pointed at the doors to the motel rooms. "Anybody knocking on doors?"

"Once I got here, I put an officer on it. So far, nobody heard or saw anything."

"Of course they didn't."

"I've got him checking the neighborhood."

I let my gaze rove around the parking lot, then spotted a woman with jet-black hair and close-set eyes peering around the corner of the building across the parking lot from the motel. "We have another observer," I said softly to Ernie. "Maybe the woman who called in the body?"

He saw where I was looking, and casually turned and gazed in that direction. The woman ducked behind the building. "She spooks easily."

"Hold on."

I hurried toward the other building, where I'd seen her. As I drew closer, she peeked around the corner again. When she saw me, her eyes widened in surprise. Her face was scarred, as if she'd been in an accident. That's as much as I noticed before she vanished.

"Hey!" I yelled. I raced toward the other building. "Hello?"

I rounded the corner and looked for her. She was at the other end of the building. I hollered at her again. "I just want to talk to you."

I ran after her, but by the time I got to the other side of the building, she was gone. I ran west and searched for her. I didn't see anyone around, so I tried the other direction. Nothing. I listened and heard a loud motorcycle on Colfax, nothing else. I put my hands on my hips in disgust. Why would she run away? Was she the 911 caller and couldn't afford to get involved, or did she know something about the body in the parking lot? I kicked a can. It rattled loudly on the asphalt. Then I trotted back toward the motel. The couple who had been watching everything snickered as I went by. I whirled around and fixed hard eyes on them as I caught my breath.

"That woman I was chasing. You know who she was?" I asked, my voice hard with authority and a veiled threat that said they'd better cooperate.

They were both young, with slack jaws and blank looks, as if they were high. The fear that leaped into their faces indicated neither one wanted any trouble. Both could've used a shower.

"We don't want no trouble," he said.

"Then answer my questions." I turned to the officer and gestured for him to take notes.

The young man stared at me, then finally answered. "I seen her around some." He was probably in his early twenties, with scraggly hair and a crooked smile with missing teeth. He wore tattered jeans and a T-shirt that hadn't been white in a long time.

He slouched and stared at me. "You won't get nothing from her, or anyone else."

"Why?" I asked.

He snickered. "Come on, lady. Nobody here wants to get into it with the law." He jerked his head toward the officer. "You got cops knocking on doors, ain't nobody coming to the door. Once the cops show up, people split or don't answer. They don't want their wives or girlfriends or whoever to know that they're here."

I couldn't argue with that, but I had to try. "What's her name?" I asked.

He shrugged, and so did the girl. I judged her to be in her late teens. They stared at me, and I cocked an eyebrow.

"I dunno," she finally said. Her hair was cropped short and dyed purple. She had a lot of piercings, some in places I knew had to be painful when she got them. She tugged at the sleeve of a loose-fitting striped blouse. "What's *your* name?"

"Detective Spillman, homicide. You're Steve and Madison?" That elicited slow nods. They both glanced past me and shifted from foot to foot. "You're sure you don't know who that woman is?"

Madison started to say something, and Steve snarled at her, so she bent her head down. He didn't want her talking to me at all, which she'd just done. I focused on her.

"Who is she?"

"Dunno," she whispered.

Steve glared at me. "Never heard her name."

"What do you know about her? What happened to her face?"

His eyes narrowed defiantly. "She was in a car accident."

I thought about pressing the issue, but decided against it. I gestured toward the other building. "You think she saw something?"

"How should we know?" Madison shrugged.

I narrowed my eyes at her. "You didn't talk to her tonight?"

She shook her head. "If she saw something, you think she's going to hang around? What if someone came after her?"

I glared at her. "Did you call the police about the body?"

"No way." Too forceful not to be true.

"Did either of you see anything suspicious around here?" I went on.

Madison gnawed her lip, and Steve scratched at a scab on his arm, probably needing another fix. Both finally shook their heads. I didn't believe them.

"You here to score something?" I asked, wondering if they were buying drugs here.

"No," Steve replied quickly. His serious expression didn't hide his lie. If he wasn't buying, he was selling.

I kept prodding away at him. "The woman with the scarred face, does she buy from you?" He hesitated, and I snapped at him. "Quit dancing around my questions and tell me what you know or I'll haul your asses downtown and we can discuss this there."

He stood straight, scared. "Yeah, she buys some from me. A lot of the women around here buy from me." He pointed at the motel. "They get with somebody, they make a few bucks, and I hook them up."

The officer grunted. "Lovely," I muttered. "Was she here earlier tonight?" I repeated the question to see if I'd get a different answer.

He shrugged, and I glared at him. He held up his hands. "I don't know. I didn't sell her anything tonight, if that's what you want to know. Maybe she was around, maybe she wasn't."

"How long have you two been here?" I asked.

"Not too long," Madison said. "We were at The Easy Bar, and then we came by here." She stared at me. "You can even ask the bartender."

The Easy Bar was a dive not far down the road. I smiled without humor. "I will."

She gulped, probably wishing she hadn't told me that. Having cops sniffing around asking about them would ruin their drug sales.

Steve glared at her, then pointed toward the screen that shielded the body. "She was murdered?"

I didn't give him anything. "That's what I'm trying to find out. Do you know who *she* was?"

"Dunno," Madison said.

"What's her name?" I barked.

"Pixie." Steve's slow demeanor vanished. He wanted to be believed, and he wanted the interrogation to end. "Just Pixie. I haven't seen her around much."

"Did you see her tonight?"

"No"

"You sell to her?"

He hesitated. "Once or twice, that's it. I don't know who she is."

"What'd she tell you about herself?"

"Nothing."

"Did she have an accent, like she wasn't from around here?"

"No."

"So you left the Easy Bar and came here," I went on. "What'd you do?"

"We sold to a couple of people here, then sat in my car." He glanced toward Colfax. "We stayed there until we saw the cop cars."

"You didn't see anything else?" I asked. "Any johns? Cars?"

"A car or two."

"What make or model?

"I don't know. One car, one truck."

"Did you see the drivers?"

He shook his head. "No."

"License plates?"

"I don't pay attention to stuff like that."

I studied him closely. He looked me in the eye and seemed to be telling the truth.

"Man, it's cold," Madison said. "You wanna let us go?"

I figured I'd gotten all that I was going to out of both of them. I looked at the officer. "You checked their IDs, got their phone numbers and addresses?" He nodded. I turned back to Steve and Madison. "I don't want to see either of you around here again, you understand?"

They nodded their heads vigorously. "We don't want no trouble with the law." Steve was back to his slow manner. He put his arm around Madison's shoulder. "Come on, let's get out of here."

Both looked relieved that I was letting them go. Maybe they assumed I was going to arrest them, and I probably could have, but I had more important things to do.

"You get all that?" I asked the officer.

"Yeah, I'll write it up and put it in my report. Charming couple. So helpful."

"Right, a great conversation."

I thanked him and went back to Ernie.

CHAPTER SIX

Ernie was talking to Todd, who was fussing with his camera when I came over.

"What do you think?" Ernie asked. "Do they know anything? Were they involved?"

"No and I don't know," I replied and filled him in on my conversation with Steve and Madison. I glanced over my shoulder. "They could've killed her, I guess."

"They have some kind of beef with her, so they shoot her?"

"Then hang around and tell us they don't know anything?" I wasn't buying it. "Anything's possible. My gut says no, but I won't dismiss it. We need to run background checks on them later. And when we're asking around, check on them, see if anyone can verify when they arrived here, and if they stayed in their car like they said they did. And we'll want to check with the bartender at the Easy Bar to see if they really were there."

"Alrighty," Ernie said to me. "I was just asking Todd about getting some prints off the body."

Todd nodded and held up his camera. "I've taken pics of the body and the area around her. Also some video."

"Let's get her prints then," I said. "Then we can run them and see if we get a match."

Before Ernie could reply, a tall man with a television camera came around the corner, along with a woman in dark slacks and a jacket with one of the local news logos on it.

"Oh, good Lord," I muttered.

"Listening to police scanners," Todd said.

"That's Deborah North, from Channel Seven," Ernie said. "I swear, she has some kind of homing device that attracts her to the dark deeds in the underbelly of the city." Sarcasm oozed like oil from his voice.

I stared at him. "That's very poetic, in a disturbing way."

He didn't laugh, just continued to frown at the news people. "I hear she's ladder-climbing, but this story won't help her. It's a prostitute: no one cares. It won't make the nightly news. The best she can hope for is the noon broadcast."

Ernie went to tell the reporters to move back around the building where they couldn't see, and Todd got to work. I was about to join him when Spats came around the corner of the motel and waved as he approached.

"Speelmahn," he said with a big grin. Why he pronounced my name like that, I'll never know. "Rizzo let you take this one?" he asked. Spats usually wore a suit and tie, but now he was uncharacteristically dressed down in khakis and a polo shirt. He had gotten his odd nickname from a former partner who thought the style of suits and ties Spats wore were reminiscent of a gangster from the Thirties, the type with flashy clothes, wing-tip shoes, and yes, spats. I'd seen Spats wear the flashy clothes and even wing-tip shoes, but never spats. And I rarely saw him as casual as he was now.

I nodded. "What's going on with the motel manager?"

Irritation flashed in his eyes. "I've been talking to him. Well," he threw up his hands. "He doesn't want to say much. I started asking him questions, and then he was interrupted with a phone call, and he made me wait. Can you believe that? When I finally got back to questioning him, he just kept telling me he didn't know there was a problem until the cops arrived, that he didn't see or hear anything, and no one told him about a body out back. He went to look and saw the woman, but he had to get back to the office. I haven't run across anybody that obstinate in a long time."

Ernie had sidled up. "Obstinate. Now that's a good word."

"Yeah, it's from my word-of-the-day calendar." Spats smirked.

"Let's stay focused," I said. Inside though, I was feeling good. I missed this kind of banter.

"I tried with the guy, but he's staying tight-lipped," Spats went on.

"Distrust of the police?" Ernie asked.

"I think he's from somewhere in the Middle East," Spats said.

"So much government and police corruption there, so it doesn't surprise me you got the reaction you did." I pointed over my shoulder. "Spats, you take over here. The forensics team is working the area, and I don't think they'll find much. Do you have a portable fingerprint kit with you?" He nodded. "Get prints of the vic so we can run them through the system, see if we can ID her. And the coroner should be here soon. Then we can get the body out of here."

"It's obvious how she was killed," Ernie said. "The coroner's just a formality now."

I gestured at him. "Let's talk to the manager."

Spats nodded. "I'll handle things here. Good luck with that guy."

Ernie and I started toward the front of the motel, then I turned around. "What's his name?"

"Ahmed." Spats spelled it. "He's got a thick accent. I hope you can understand him better than I could."

Ernie hefted up his pants and we headed to the motel office. On the way, Ernie pulled a cheap cigar from his coat pocket, bit off the end of it, and jammed it into the corner of his mouth. He rarely ever smokes the cigars, just chews on them.

"I thought you were quitting," I said.

He shrugged. "It's hit-and-miss. Right now I need to think, and the cigar helps me."

I had heard that before. As far as I was concerned, if it kept him focused, I was fine with the cigar.

"How do you want to play this?" he asked. "I don't think good cop bad cop is a good approach, if he's fearful of the police."

"True. Why don't you take the lead, be nice. I'll hold back and see what he does. Let's hope he doesn't get obstinate."

"Obstinate." He wagged his head. "Word of the day."

I grinned. Then Deborah North stalked toward us as we neared the front, and my smile vanished. She shoved a microphone in my face, and her cameraman focused on me.

"What can you tell us about the body found in back of the motel?" she said in a serious tone.

"No comment," I said.

"Who was the victim?"

"No comment," I repeated.

I rarely said anything to the press unless instructed by Rizzo to do so. The department had people to handle the press. If I talked, it would only lead to trouble. Deborah pleaded one more time for something, and Ernie growled at her and told her to back off. She finally stepped away from us.

At the front of the motel, the neon sign above the office doorway lit up the sidewalk. We walked inside where a dark-complexioned man sat at a stool behind a counter. An old coffeemaker and cups sat on a small table in the corner. Loud music blared from a laptop nearby, something with a Middle Eastern flare with strings and percussion. When he saw us, he frowned. He quickly tamped out a cigarette and waved away smoke.

"I don't want trouble," he said. As Spats had said, his accent was thick.

Ernie pointed at the laptop and spoke loudly to be heard over the music. "Would you mind turning that down?"

Ahmed quickly complied and tapped the laptop. The music abruptly stopped, the silence refreshing.

Ernie eased up to the counter and smiled. "Ahmed, right?" Now his voice was soft, no threat in it.

The man nodded, ran a hand over curly dark hair turning gray, and stood up. He was tall, probably at least six-six, and bigger than he had seemed when he was perched on the chair. Ernie looked up at him, then made a motion with his hand. "Nah, sit down, make yourself comfortable. I'm Detective Moore, and this is Detective Spillman."

Ahmed eyed him, then sank slowly back onto the stool.

Ernie put an elbow on the counter. "Do you have a few minutes?"

"I tell that other man, I don't know anything," Ahmed said.

Ernie nodded knowingly,

"I hate to bother you again, but the thing is," Ernie said, "we need to have some questions answered." He drew in a breath and let it out noisily, as if he didn't want to talk to Ahmed at all. "I don't want to cause you any trouble, and I'd like to get out of here myself, go have a cup of coffee."

Ahmed glanced at the coffeemaker, but didn't offer any to us. "I tell other man everything."

"Which was what?"

Ahmed remained quiet. Ernie glanced at me, and I stepped forward.

"I think we'll be able to wrap up our investigation quickly, as long as we know what went on. It looks like that woman's body was dumped in the alley. However, if she was killed in one of the rooms, I'll have to get a forensics team to go through every room with a fine-toothed comb. That could take a lot of time and attract a lot of attention."

That touched a nerve. Ahmed didn't want any attention himself, and I'm sure he knew that whoever owned the motel wouldn't want the attention, either.

"I only know what other police tell me," Ahmed said. "A woman is dead out back. That's it."

I didn't buy it. I made a show of looking around the tiny office. The walls cried out for a coat of paint, the Formica counter had pieces peeling from it, and two chairs next to the door were threadbare. The overhead light was dim, but it couldn't hide the despair throughout the room.

I put my hands on the counter and immediately regretted it. I removed my hands, subtly wiped grime off them, and put them in my pockets. "Did you know the woman, the one in the parking lot?"

"The dead one?" Ahmed pointed out the door. "I told other man I don't see or hear anything until cop cars arrive."

I nodded slowly. "You did go out back to look, so you saw her?"

He shook his head. "Just her hair. She's a blond. Lots of women around here are blond."

"You didn't recognize her clothes or shoes?"

Another head shake. He crossed his arms. "I tell the truth."

Ernie took a turn, his manner still easygoing. "Have you heard the name Pixie?"

Ahmed's eyebrows shot up. "That is who it is?"

"Describe her to us," Ernie said.

Ahmed hesitated. "I don't know her good. A lot of women come and go."

"Give it a shot," I said.

"She have the blond hair." He raised a hand to his own head, as if running his hand through longer hair. "She skinny, too. Like so many that come here, she don't look good."

His description probably fit a lot of women that hung around the motel. "What else?" I asked. "Anything to set her apart from other women?"

He pointed at the inside of his left wrist. "She have a tattoo there. I can't tell what it is, a rose, maybe."

Ernie and I exchanged a glance. Ahmed caught it.

"It is her," he said.

"What do you know about her?" I asked.

He gave me a blank look. "I know nothing."

Ernie's easygoing manner slipped a little. "You have to know something about her. What's her last name?"

"Dust."

Ernie scowled. "What?"

The look on my face must've been priceless. "Her name is Pixie Dust," I said skeptically.

Ahmed hesitated. "That's how I know her. They don't use real names."

Ernie laughed at the name. "You've got to be kidding."

Ahmed shrugged. "These women, they don't want people to know them."

"You've never heard her called by any other name?" I asked.

Ahmed glanced between us. "Tell me," I pressed him. He knew more. "And we'll let you finish your shift in peace."

He held up his hands. "I think one time I hear another girl call her Nicole."

"No last name?" Ernie said.

Ahmed shook his head. "I tell you, I don't know any of them. Usually men pay for a room, and they stay for a little while. Later on, I see women leave the rooms, go back to the street, and the men drive away. You know how it is."

"What about a woman with a scarred face and black hair?"

He shook his head and averted his eyes, and I could tell he knew her.

"Tell me about her," I said.

"She around, that's all." He clamped his jaw shut.

"What about the other girls around here?" Ernie asked. "Do you have names of anybody else we could talk to, someone who might know more about Pixie or this other woman?"

Ahmed hesitated, and I gave him a sympathetic look. "She was murdered. Don't you want to find out what happened to Pixie? Don't you want justice for the poor girl?"

Ahmed wasn't moved by that. "I don't want trouble."

"Then help us out," I said, equally as matter-of-fact.

He shook his head. "I stay out of it." He gestured at the door. "I let them do their thing, I don't pay attention. It's better for them, for me."

"So you won't give us names of other women who come around here?" I asked.

Ahmed stared at me blankly.

Ernie took a turn with Ahmed. "Don't you know anything about Pixie? Does she have family, friends?"

His face remained expressionless. "I don't know."

Ernie tapped the counter. "Was she in any kind of trouble? Did someone want to hurt her, you know, like enemies?"

"Enemies?" he asked. Then he answered his own question. "How would I know that? I don't talk to her, I just see her around."

"Did she drive here? Take a bus?" Ernie fired off the questions.

"I don't know," Ahmed repeated.

"You don't know much," Ernie said sarcastically, his cool gone.

Ahmed blinked at him. "No." He wasn't insulted by it, he knew it was better to not know.

"Did you hear anything?" I asked again. "A gunshot?" A head shake. "Did you see someone or a car that made you suspicious?"

Ahmed tapped the laptop. "I have music on, and I read."

If he had heard or seen things, he was accustomed to not making note of it. It was better for him to stay out. I wasn't sure whether he was telling the truth, so I continued to press him, hoping if I rattled him, he might give us some answers.

"Do you know if Pixie went to a room with anyone tonight?"

Ahmed shook his head. "I don't know she's around until this whole thing." He frowned. "You can't look in rooms, okay? It will scare customers away."

"Not right now." I'd have to get a warrant to search rooms, and I didn't have reason enough to ask for one. I had no idea whether Pixie had been in a room or not.

"Is there anybody she sees regularly?" Ernie asked.

Ahmed shrugged. "I don't pay attention."

"And even if you did, you wouldn't tell us, right? That way you stay out of trouble, you stay safe," I said. He didn't respond to that. "I get it, but I wish you'd help us. That girl has a family who needs to know what happened."

Ahmed locked eyes with me, and even though I'd tried appealing to him emotionally, we both knew I was right: The less he knew or said, the better off he would be. If word got around that the manager talked to the police or anyone else, customers would vanish. A place like this stayed in business by being safe for all the illegal activity that went on.

"I don't want trouble," Ahmed said. "I can tell you no more. I don't know."

"You don't know?" I repeated, then shook my head. "This poor woman deserves your help." One final try that went nowhere. His expression didn't change. Ernie and I glanced at each other. At this point, we were wasting our time.

"What's your contact information, in case we need to talk to you again?" I pulled out a little notepad. I was old-fashioned and didn't use my phone to take notes.

Ahmed told me his last name, and he gave me his address and phone number. I thanked him for his time, and Ernie and I headed out the door.

CHAPTER SEVEN

"Oh, thank you," I said as Ernie brought a cup of coffee to me.

"We're going to need it." He sat down at his chair, and the chair did its usual squawking at his bulk. He pulled himself up to his desk and logged onto his computer. He bit into one of the breakfast burritos that he'd bought from a vendor outside the station, and talked as he chewed. "Let's see what we can find on Pixie Dust. We won't get very far without knowing who she really is, and we can't contact any next of kin, either."

"Lord, you'd think she could've picked a better name than that," I said. I unwrapped one of the breakfast burritos he'd given me, and bit into it. I was famished, and it tasted delicious, with plenty of jalapenos and cheese.

"Like Bambi?"

I raised eyebrows. "Choosing an orphaned deer? His mother was shot, you know."

"And why would a female prostitute choose a male name?"

"Good point, unless it's a male prostitute?"

Ernie looked down his nose at me. "You ever hear of a male prostitute named Bambi?"

"Um, no. It should be Bam-bo for a guy, something like that."

He laughed. "Oh, it's good to have you back."

After we had finished questioning Ahmed, we'd left Spats along with the officers to canvass the neighborhood to see if anybody had seen or heard anything suspicious near the motel, and to see if anyone had information about Pixie Dust. They were also going to find out what they could on the woman with the scarred face, and on Steve Gibson and Madison McCann. The Easy Bar wasn't open yet, but I'd have someone follow up on that later to verify that Steve and Madison were there when they said they were. Even though it was the middle of the night, time was critical. I didn't envy Spats having to wake people up, but it had to be done.

In the meantime, Ernie had stopped at the gas station where the 911 call had originated. The man working the counter had told him a woman with a scarred face had come in and begged to use the phone. The man let her, but he denied knowing who she called. Ernie tried to get the surveillance video, but the employee said he didn't know how to operate the equipment, and that he'd have to check with his boss before he could let the police view the video. I put that on a list of things to follow up on in the light of day.

I had wrapped up with the crime scene techs, who hadn't found anything noteworthy in the parking lot. The coroner had preliminarily determined that the woman had died from the gunshot wounds. As we thought, he also surmised as we had that she may have been killed somewhere else and dumped in the parking lot. Beyond that, he wouldn't say much. It was typical of a coroner not to make conclusions. I'd have to wait for a full autopsy to know more. After he had left, I had come back to the station to see what we could learn about Pixie Dust. Ernie was working his way through a couple of breakfast burritos while he went through our arrest records, searching for women with the alias Pixie Dust, who had a strawberry tattoo. I was investigating Steve and Madison. I typed Steve's name into a database and immediately found arrest records.

"Well, shocker," I said. "Steve has been picked up several times, mostly for petty drug charges, and he also has a few petty theft charges." Ernie glanced at me. "No gun charges?"

I shook my head. "If either was the killer, they could've easily bought a stolen gun."

"True."

Some other detectives walked by, just beginning their day, and I waved at them, then turned back to my computer. "Madison doesn't have an arrest record; she's clean."

Ernie snorted. "Well, clean of charges, maybe. That woman had a serious relationship with drugs."

My laugh held no humor. "No doubt about that." I sat back in my chair and finished the burrito. "Back to Steve and Madison. I don't figure either one of them as murderers. I *do* think they know more than they're telling."

"If you want, I can question them again, put the heat on them for more information."

"Let's see what we can find about their whereabouts last night and go from there."

"Sounds good."

I poked around on the internet a little more and found old social media accounts for both Steve and Madison. Neither one posted much, but knowing they had a social media presence might come in handy later. I gulped more coffee and yawned.

"Here we go," Ernie finally said. He waved me over.

I stretched and came around to his desk, then looked at his monitor.

He tapped the screen. "Pixie Dust, real name Nicole Lockwood."

I studied Nicole's arrest picture. She had stringy blond hair, stark blue eyes that had a lost look in them, and full lips turned into a pout. Smudges of dirt were on her left cheek and neck.

"She looks rough," he said.

"Look at her arrest records." I stared at the screen. Nicole had been arrested for prostitution five times, a Class 3 misdemeanor in Colorado. Each offense could've cost her up to six months behind bars and a fine up to $750, but I doubted she'd spent much time in jails, which were too crowded already. She also had a few misdemeanor drug possession charges. Those had been older convictions, as local law enforcement was getting lax on charging people who possessed small amounts of drugs.

"You think she would've learned how not to run afoul of the cops," Ernie said. He popped the last bite of burrito into his mouth and washed it down with Diet Coke.

I nodded. "Let's see what else we have on her."

Ernie scrolled down the screen. "She was only twenty. Wow." He has two daughters, one in high school, the other in eighth grade, and I'm sure reading about Nicole hit home for him. "Her last known address was on St. Paul Street. Or that's the address she gave the arresting officer." He pulled up another web browser and googled the address. "I've been there before. Those are some cheap apartments."

"I wonder if she still lives there. I'll follow up on that. Maybe someone there knows her."

He nodded. "I'll text you the address."

I tapped the monitor. "Print her picture for me."

"Sure."

He maneuvered the mouse, and his printer soon spat out Nicole's picture. He handed it to me, and I stared at it for a second. "What a waste," I finally said.

I went back to my desk and gulped down the rest of my coffee. I was wired from working on a new case, but at some point that would wear off. I needed the caffeine to keep me going. I googled Nicole Lockwood and found information on her family. "Her parents are Kara, with a K, and Jason. It looks like they're divorced. I only see an address for Kara. Let's go talk to her and maybe she can tell us where to find the father."

Ernie glanced at his watch. "Bad news this early in the morning ..."

"I know."

"Oh, my aching feet." Spats walked in, looking weary, his face long and dejected. He went to the coffee machine and poured a cup. "I've been hoofing it around that motel for a couple of hours. I've talked to more prostitutes tonight than I care to admit. Don't tell Trissa that," he joked as he gulped some coffee. At least I hoped he was really joking.

Spats had recently told me that he and Trissa, his live-in and mother of their baby boy, were having problems related to his job, the long hours and time away from home. His joking seemed to be a good sign, though, especially since he'd just worked through the night. Spats also has an eleven-year-old daughter from a previous marriage. He has a lot on his plate, and I sometimes think that his careful attention to his wardrobe is a way to control some of his life.

Spats went on. "What I found out is that Pixie was nice, and she had a heroin addiction. One other prostitute named Alice said she saw Pixie fighting with a man a few days ago, they were screaming and yelling, but Alice didn't know who the guy was. He was clean-cut, and Alice didn't think he would've killed Pixie, for what that's worth. No one else knew of anybody who would want to shoot Pixie execution-style. Or any other style." Spats looked between us. "What'd you find?"

"Pixie's real name is Nicole Lockwood," I said. I told him

what Ernie and I had discovered. "We were about to go talk to her mother."

"Maybe she has an idea of who might have wanted to kill her daughter," Spats said.

Ernie scrunched up his face. "I kind of doubt that, but we can hope."

Spats went over to his desk, gulped more coffee, and sat down with a sigh. Then he got on the computer. "I've got to meet with the DA on another case this morning, and I don't know how long I'll be. I need to review my case notes."

"Spats, let me know when you're free." I double-checked where Kara Lockwood lived and grabbed my car keys. I gestured at Ernie. "Let's go."

CHAPTER EIGHT

The house was quiet. After Marilyn had gotten home, she had been a jangle of nerves. She was glad her husband was out of town, so no one was there to pester her with questions. She'd fixed herself a drink and went outside to the back porch. She saw the stars, could hear the occasional car or two in the distance, but otherwise it was peaceful. Her hand shook as she sipped her drink. She sat down at a lounge chair, stretched out her legs, and leaned back. Then she went over everything that had happened. As far as she could tell, the deed had gone flawlessly. No one had seen her, and even if they had, they wouldn't know it was her.

Perfect.

As it should be. After all, she'd been plotting this out for weeks. She'd known a while ago that she was going to choose a prostitute. Selecting a vulnerable victim was another part of the Guild rules. It had to be a stranger to you. No revenge murders. That way, less likelihood of the murder being traced back to a member. She was sure she wouldn't get caught. Her plans were too well thought out.

It was now almost dawn, the sky morphing from black to a lighter hue, and she finally was feeling tired. Now, she could finally relax. The fear she'd felt earlier was gone, replaced by exhilaration. Just as Daffy Duck had said, it was incredible. She sipped more Scotch, its slight burn soothing. She had wondered if she could really go through with it, but when the time came, it had been easy. She closed her eyes and went over the whole night again, making sure she hadn't missed anything. She concluded she hadn't. Her eyes flew open and she stared into the yard. She smiled broadly. This could be a perfect crime. She didn't see how she could be tripped up, and, on the off chance she had made a mistake, she was prepared for that. She would never go to jail.

The sky was turning pink and orange when exhaustion finally overtook her. And yet, she wondered if she could sleep. She couldn't wait to tell the group. They would meet later, and she had better be alert for that. She went inside and put her empty glass in the dishwasher. Then she went into her bedroom, set an alarm, disrobed, and slipped under the covers. Within seconds she fell into a peaceful sleep.

CHAPTER NINE

"What is somebody doing visiting me so early in the morning?" Kara Lockwood said.

Ernie and I stood on her small front porch of her tiny house in Commerce City and talked to her through the screen.

"Are you Nicole Lockwood's mother?" I asked.

"What's she done now?" She wore leggings that showed ample curves, a wrinkled yellow blouse, and no makeup. Her shoulder-length blond hair was going gray, and her voice was low and harsh. *Close to sixty, at least,* I thought. I cocked an eyebrow at her, and she said, "Yes."

"I'm sorry to be the bearer of bad news," I said. "But your daughter is dead."

She put her hands on her hips and looked off into the distance. "Well, I can't say I'm surprised." She had the trace of a Southern accent.

I wasn't sure what to say. I sensed Ernie stiffen, and I knew he was taken aback as well.

"I know that's not what you expected me to say," Kara went on. "But it is what it is. I suppose you have questions." She let out a big sigh, then held the screen open for us. "You might as well come in." Ernie and I stepped into a tiny foyer and waited as she closed the screen. She waved a hand at us. "Come into the kitchen. Would you like coffee?"

The house wasn't much, just a living room big enough for a couch, a worn coffee table, and a small entertainment center. A poster from a jazz festival hung on one wall, the others bare. Down a short hallway were a few doors, probably a couple of bedrooms and a bathroom. The kitchen was decorated in kitschy knick-knacks displayed on a cheap bookcase. A dog calendar was taped to the refrigerator, nothing else.

She went to the coffeemaker on the counter, then eyed us.

"No thanks," I said. Ernie shook his head.

She poured herself a cup and topped it off with a splash of Kahlua. "I'm off today," she said in explanation. She took a seat at a small round Formica table and indicated that we should join her. Ernie and I slipped into seats across from her.

"What'd Nicole do to get herself killed?" Kara asked she picked up a pack of cigarettes. She shook one out, lit it, and took a long drag.

"She was murdered," I said.

"Well." She tapped ash into a glass ashtray on the table. She blew smoke and looked at us.

"You don't seem surprised," I observed wryly.

"That girl's been in trouble since junior high," Kara said. She dragged on the cigarette and blew another long stream of smoke. I resisted the urge to cough. The room reeked, the walls gray from years of accumulated smoke.

"Nicole was an okay kid, did all right in school," Kara went on as she sipped coffee. "She was no scholar, but she got by. Then, when my husband left, things went downhill."

"Where is Kara's dad now?" Ernie asked.

"Oh, he's dead. Which is probably just as well."

There seemed to be no love lost between her and her ex. "What happened to him?" I asked.

"He worked for the railroad, got into some kind of an accident near the railroad tracks, and got himself killed. Serves him right. He wasn't a nice guy, not to me, and not to Nicole. Although she thought he was great." She sneered. "But that's what kids do, right? They idolize one of the parents, blame the other for everything. She did with him and thought I was the mean one."

That explained some of her aloofness to her daughter.

"He was abusive to Nicole?"

She shook her head. "Just mean when he was drunk, far as I know. Then he'd take her for ice cream or something the next day, and she'd think he was too cool."

"How bad were things with your husband?" Ernie asked.

She pinched up her face in disgust. "Drew and I were high school sweethearts. Although, truth be told, there wasn't a lot of sweet in our relationship. He was hot, though, and boy did we have a lot of fun. Then I got pregnant the end of our senior year. So much for going on to college or anything like that. Drew and I thought we were in love, and we got married." She swore. "I was all of eighteen years old and I was married with a kid. We tried to make it work, but we liked to party before Nicole was born, and we partied after. It was a rough time, and money was always tight." She sucked on the cigarette, her cheeks concave. "I know I made mistakes, but I did clean things up as Nicole got older, and we moved here from Tennessee. It was supposed to be a clean start for us all, but it wasn't long before Drew was drinking and drugging again. He had a decent job, and I was afraid he was going to lose it, but he managed to keep that. He couldn't keep me, though. He worked too much, and then I found out he was sleeping around. I finally booted him out." She tapped ash into the ashtray with a hard finger. "Nicole was mad at me, because all she saw in her daddy was somebody who spoiled her. He would never raise a hand to her, didn't yell at her, and I had to do all the disciplining. That made me unpopular. The few times he would get mad at her, she would blame me, and tell me that it was my fault that he was mad at her. After he left, Nicole started to get in some trouble. I think she was drinking and probably smoking some pot. When Drew died, she got even worse. She started ditching school, and some nights she wouldn't come home at all. I tried a few times to get the police involved, but they never did much, said she was a runaway and she'd come home soon. And I couldn't do much, either. I had two jobs, had to keep things going. Drew didn't have any life insurance, and even if he did, I'm sure he wouldn't have left anything to me, even though we never divorced. As it was, he didn't leave a thing for us. Anyway, it went on like that for a while. One time, I read a few of her texts, and I got the impression she was seeing an older guy, maybe somebody in college."

"What was his name?" I asked.

"I don't know. I asked her, and of course she said it was just some guy at school. I didn't believe her, but what could I do? I tried to talk to Nicole about her behavior, and she just got mad at me. She blamed me for her father leaving, and she blamed me for him dying. What was I supposed to do?" she said defensively and swore again. "That was what, six, seven years ago? I was only thirty-three and a widow. Too young for all the drama."

I did some quick math, and realized that Kara couldn't be more than forty. I glanced subtly at Ernie, and I could tell he was thinking the same thing. She looked a lot older than that. Her drinking and smoking really had taken their toll. I also wondered if she was telling the truth about Drew not abusing to Nicole.

"Then what happened?" I asked.

The cigarette started toward her mouth, but this time she didn't take a drag. "One night, she just didn't come home. She was sixteen. Between her sophomore and junior year. I called the police again, after a few days, thinking that maybe she had been kidnapped or killed, and they put out a missing person's report and left it at that. A week went by, and then she showed up. She didn't look that good, and at that point I could tell that she was doing some kind of harder drugs, meth, heroin, I don't know what. She told me she was sorry for running away, and that she'd try to do better. But she didn't. I think she mostly wanted to come home, to get a few meals and clean up, and then she was gone again. I tried to talk to her, told her that she needed to clean up her act, and that just made her madder. Then she was gone again, this time for a lot longer. I didn't bother calling the police that time, I knew she was out doing who knows what. That time she was gone for a few months. When she came home, she looked even worse. The second I told her she needed to clean up her act, she yelled at me, and went through the blame routine. I told her to get out."

If there was regret, I didn't hear it. Ernie shifted uncomfortably in his chair. I'm sure he couldn't imagine a situation where he'd do that to one of his daughters.

As if she sensed our thoughts, Kara said, "I know what you're thinking, that I'm cruel, and that I should've helped Nicole. Well, I tried. I didn't have money for rehab or anything like that, but I encouraged her to go to AA or NA, things like that. I told her that she ought to try something. All she would do is tell me that I should mind my own drinking." She sniffed at that. "I don't have a problem, she does. Or did."

I didn't say anything to that. "You haven't seen her since she was sixteen?"

Kara shook her head. "Oh, she came home a few times, here and there, when she needed money. But that was it."

"When was the last time you saw her?" Ernie asked.

She thought for a second as she sipped more coffee. "It

must've been in the spring. She looked like hell. And of course, she just wanted money, some food. We talked a little, and I fixed her dinner. She didn't outright say it, but she was hooking, trying to pay for her drug habit that way. That's what she was doing, right?" Ernie and I nodded.

"It looks that way," I said.

"How did she die?" Kara finally asked. She hadn't been curious up to now.

"She was shot twice in the back of the head," Ernie said. "Almost like an execution." He didn't tell her anymore.

Kara looked past us for a moment. "Oh god. That's terrible."

"Do you know of anyone who would want to do that to her?" I asked.

"I told you, I barely saw my daughter. I have no idea who would kill her. I thought you'd say she died of an overdose, or maybe some guy got too rough with her, something like that. But shoot her? I don't know."

I put my elbows on the table. "When she came around, did Nicole talk about any friends?"

"No, not that I can ..." Then she paused. "One of the times when she was here, when I told her I wouldn't give her any money, she started yelling at me about it, and she said something about that's how Lola said I would react." She finished the cigarette and forcefully crushed it out. "I don't know if that's a friend of hers or not. I have no idea who Lola is. Whoever she is, Nicole would've told her all kinds of bad things about me."

"Lola's not one of her friends from high school?" Ernie asked.

"No, her only good friend from high school was Tracy. I have no idea if Nicole sees her anymore or not."

"Do you have Tracy's contact information?" Ernie pulled out his notepad.

Kara swiped a hand across the table impatiently, clearing crumbs. "Are you kidding me? They were friends years ago."

"What about a last name?" he asked.

She shook her head, then held up a hand. "Hold on." She got up and disappeared from the room.

"Man," Ernie whispered. "I can't imagine having *no* reaction after hearing your child had been murdered."

"I know."

I didn't say more because Kara returned with a yearbook. "I cleared out Nicole's room a while back, but I kept some of her stuff." She sat down at the table and opened the book. "Let's see ... Tracy." She began flipping through pages, then stopped and put a finger on a picture. "This is her. Tracy Sheppard." She took the yearbook and turned it around for us to see.

Ernie and I looked down at Tracy. She was a cute girl, with long brown hair, dangling earrings, and a wide, toothy smile that didn't try to hide her braces.

"I have no idea where she is now," Kara said. "Her family used to live about a mile from here. Nice family, met them a time or two when I'd drop Nicole there or pick her up. Nicole went for sleepovers there."

I tapped the yearbook. "Do you mind if I look at Nicole?"

"Help yourself." Kara smoked while I flipped through the yearbook. I found Nicole's picture, and Ernie and I studied it as well. As I'd thought back at the motel earlier this morning, Nicole had been pretty. At the time the picture had been taken, the hard life hadn't gotten her in its grip yet. I saw where a few of her classmates had written things in the yearbook. "Have a great summer! You're a great pal, stay cool. You rock!" Kara may have felt little for her daughter, but I suddenly felt sad. Such a waste of a life.

This was a hard part of the job, one of the things I hadn't missed.

"When she was here the last time, you didn't get any indication that she might have been in danger?" I asked.

Kara shook her head. "The only danger I was aware of was her being a prostitute. I can't imagine that that's safe."

"Did she leave anything behind?" Ernie asked.

Kara sneered. "She didn't stay long enough to leave anything. We argued again, I refused to give her any money, and she left."

I glanced around the room, so stark and bare, so lacking in comfort and love. I could in some small way understand why Nicole might've wanted to escape, although she ended up in an even worse situation.

"Do you know where she was living?" I went on.

"At one point, she told me she had a place with some girls on St. Paul Street, but I don't know if she was living there the last time I saw her. For all I know, she could've been homeless."

That matched with the address I'd gotten on her latest arrest report.

"Have you heard of the Princeton Motel?" Ernie asked.

She shook her head. "Where's that?"

"On West Colfax," he said.

"Figures," she muttered. "Was she hanging out there?"

"Something like that," Ernie replied.

Kara drained her coffee cup, got up, and went to the counter. "Are you sure I can't get you a cup?"

Ernie and I both shook our heads. I didn't want to extend the conversation longer than I had to. Kara poured another cup and topped it off with more Kahlua, and came back to the table.

"I'm sure you thought this conversation would go differently," she said. "I watch enough cop shows to know how they think things should be. I'm sorry, but I wasn't close to my daughter, and I don't know what happened."

Something popped into my head that I was curious about. "She had a strawberry tattoo. Was there any meaning in that?"

"She loved strawberries, and her daddy said she was his little strawberry."

Some people would've thought that was cute, but apparently Kara did not. I couldn't think of anything else to ask, and I really wanted to get away from the smoke and the depressing feeling that surrounded us. I pulled out a business card and slipped it across the table.

"That has my contact information. If you think of anything else that might be important, please call me. And if anybody happens to call you about your daughter, would you please let me know?"

She took the card and nodded. "I wouldn't count on anything."

I held up the yearbook. "Do you mind if we take this? I'll return it when our investigation is finished."

"Sure," she said indifferently.

"I'm sorry for your loss." It wasn't a rote statement for me, but something I meant. This time, it fell on deaf ears.

CHAPTER TEN

"That's a helluva mother," Ernie said as we were driving away. He pulled a cigar from his coat pocket. He bit off the end and blew it out the window, then stuck the cigar in his mouth.

"Don't light that," I joked.

"Ha ha."

"I don't get it," I said. "Kara's awfully bitter toward her daughter, awfully callous. Given everything she told us, was the tension between the two of them because of the struggles Kara had financially and otherwise? Or did the tension stem from issues with Kara's husband?" I turned the corner.

"You're thinking she would murder her daughter over animosity toward her ex?"

I thought long and hard about that. "I don't know. That's awfully cold as well. *Someone* was angry enough at Nicole to execute her. Is Kara that angry?"

"That would mean she lied to us left and right," Ernie said. The cigar rolled as he gnawed it from one side of his mouth to the other. "What would Kara's motive be to kill Nicole? I don't buy that she'd kill her just because she's angry at her." I shrugged. He worked the cigar for a moment. "Are you saying she knew where her daughter was, went down to the motel and picked her up, then shot her and brought her back to the parking lot?"

As we sat at a traffic light, I worked on that theory. "Honestly, no. But we can't rule out anything. I got the impression Kara was lying about Drew being abusive. Maybe Nicole and Kara fought about that. Here's another theory. Kara hired someone to kill her daughter." I held up a hand before Ernie could protest. "I know, it all sounds crazy. I don't see Kara having enough money to hire anyone, even if people will kill for precious little these days."

"Me, neither."

"For that matter, anybody could've paid to have Nicole killed."

"The question is who?"

That hung in the air for a minute.

"When we get back to the station," I said, "I want you to track down Nicole's high school friends. The yearbook should help with that. You're good with kids, so you might be able to find out something to help us. Nicole might've recently been in touch with someone she was friends with, someone who might know if anyone had a beef with Nicole."

"Enough to want to kill her."

"Exactly. Check the yearbook and see if you can find Lola, too, or if anyone you talk to knows who she is."

"Will do."

"I'll send Spats back to Colfax to canvas the neighborhood again, check with the businesses in the area to see if anybody has any video cameras pointed toward the motel, or if anyone at the all-night gas stations in the area heard or saw anything. Let's see if we can find who came to the motel around the time her body was discovered, and who left. He needs to look at the gas station video to see if he can find out more about the 911 caller."

"His to-do list is getting longer."

I laughed. "Oh, and one more thing. He needs to verify that Steve Gibson and Madison McCann were at the Easy Bar when they said they were, and if anyone saw them waiting outside the motel."

"Makes sense," he said. By his tone, he knew it could be a long day of running around town.

I dialed Spats and put him on speaker.

"Hey," he said, then yawned. "I think I'll be here all morning. The DA has a lot of questions. What do you need?"

I told him what I wanted him to do. "And if you happen to run into any prostitutes while you're out and about, which I'm sure you will, see what they know about Nicole, or a woman named Lola."

"I'm sure I'll run into some hookers," Spats said. "They shouldn't be called 'ladies of the night' anymore, since they're out and about twenty-four-seven."

"Right." I continued. "In the meantime, I'm going to see if I can track down Nicole's friend, Tracy. It's possible Nicole kept in touch with her."

Spats rang off. By now, I'd arrived at the station. I dropped Ernie off by his car, then parked and went up to the second floor where my desk is. It was quiet, no one around. I grabbed a cup of coffee, then got on the internet.

A people-search told me that Tracy Sheppard lived in Commerce City with her parents, not too far from where Kara lived. After a bit more searching, I found a phone number for the house and called. It was now getting close to nine, and I wondered if anyone would be at home. I lucked out when a woman answered.

"Hello?" The voice was mid-range and soft.

I identified myself, then asked for Tracy.

"She's not here right now."

"Are you Mrs. Sheppard. Tracy's mother?"

"Yes." The tone went frantic, her words tumbling over each other. "What's this about? Is Tracy okay?"

"It's about Nicole Lockwood," I said. "She was killed last night. I was hoping to talk to your daughter about Nicole. They were friends in high school, correct?"

Dead silence for a moment, then, "When you said you were a homicide detective, I immediately thought about my daughter. I haven't heard Nicole's name in ages. What happened?" Her voice went up, curious. After my conversation with Kara Lockwood, I pictured Mrs. Sheppard. She sounded pleasant and actually caring and motherly.

"It's an ongoing investigation, so I can't tell you much. I will say the death is suspicious. Tracy and Nicole were friends in high school?" I prompted her.

"Yes, that's true."

"What can you tell me about Nicole?"

"When I knew her, she was a sweet girl, at least initially. She was shy and didn't say a lot to me, but she was very nice. My daughter took a liking to her, and I think in some ways felt a little sorry for her." She let out a sad breath. "I don't think Nicole had the best home life. There were problems with her mother."

"What kinds of problems?"

"From what I could gather, they fought a lot. And Nicole would say that her mom wasn't too concerned about her. Nicole was upset about her father's death, too. Beyond that, I don't know a whole lot. My daughter might be able to tell you more. She hung around Nicole a lot, and kind of helped Nicole with some of her classes. Nicole struggled in school."

"Where is your daughter? I'd like to speak with her in person if I could."

"She's taking classes at Metro. She has a psychology class at ten. You might be able to find her down there. Or she'll be home later tonight."

"I'd like to talk to her now, if possible. Would you be able to get hold of her and have her meet me somewhere?"

"I can try. Let me see if I can reach her. Can I call you back?"

"Sure." I gave her my number, ended the call, and stared at my laptop monitor. I was feeling tired, and while I waited for Mrs. Sheppard to call back, I took a moment to stretch and clear my head. The time at the beginning of an investigation is critical, so I tend to go non-stop. It's also when things make the least sense – too much information that's disconnected. Having a fuzzy brain wouldn't help me.

I walked around the room, then sat back down and googled Kara Lockwood. She had no arrests and no traffic tickets, basically a clean record. A bit more research told me she was active on social media, and that she'd worked as a manager at a Bed Bath & Beyond for several years. I found a high school reunion website, and a few people had made some comments about her, how she used to like to party, but not a whole lot else. I couldn't find anything to indicate she was in any kind of trouble, legally, financially, or in any other way. If Kara had killed her daughter, I was likely not going to find a motive for that online. I was sipping coffee when I heard a familiar voice.

"Sarah, can you come to my office?" It was Commander Calvin Rizzo standing right beside my desk. He's tall and seemed to tower over me.

I like Rizzo, I get along with him, and feel like he is a fair boss. He's tough when he needs to be, compassionate when it's warranted, and he's smart and knows how to help us. And best of all, he lets me do my job. Which is why it had puzzled me to hear that he didn't want me on this investigation. I found myself resentful about that now. My stomach knotted up, and my palms began to sweat. I didn't want to talk to him right at the moment, but I had to.

I got up and followed him into his office, my steps forceful. He went around his desk and gestured for me to close the door. He sat down and rested his hands on the desk, a seeming concilia-tory move. I glanced over his shoulder at awards and pictures of him with local dignitaries, then focused on him.

"I'm sure you heard by now that I was going to have Daniel Hackman take this investigation instead of you," he said.

Yes." My voice was clipped, and knew it held more anger than I wanted him to hear.

He tipped his head, indicating I should sit down. I hesitated, then took a seat across from him. He hadn't closed the blinds on the window behind me that looked out to the detective corp. If he was going to dress me down, I wished he would. He stared at me and said, "It's not what you think."

"What is it about?"

"What did you hear?" he deflected my question with one of his own.

I marshalled calm and began. "I don't get it. I'd just been cleared to resume my normal duties, and you'd backed me this whole time I was on desk duty, said that whenever I felt ready to get back out there, you'd support me. When Carson Welch was killed, you said you had my back, that you knew what I did was justified."

I went for another breath, and he held up a hand to stop me. "What you heard isn't correct," he said. I stopped talking. "I knew you were mad at me." He rubbed his forehead and groaned, then went on. "Have you heard anything about Oakley's investi-gation, the death of a homeless vet?"

Ed Oakley is another detective in the department. I don't know him very well, just that he's from Boston and he'd recently been promoted to the homicide division. I'd heard he was smart, but I couldn't say from personal experience. We crossed paths on a recent investigation, and I didn't have any issues with him.

I shrugged. "Only that he hasn't gotten very far with the investigation. He's been working on it since last week?"

Rizzo nodded and leaned back in his chair. He didn't look happy. "You're correct. The case has been open for a while, and Oakley hasn't come up with anything. I'm not faulting him, he's a new homicide detective and he's doing the best he can. The problem is that the victim's father is Carlton Hall." I quickly tried to place the name, but couldn't. Rizzo continued. "He's a good friend of Chief Follett."

Now I remembered Carlton Hall. "The lieutenant governor's son was murdered?" I was beginning to see what was going on. Politics at play, just as Ernie and I had speculated. Just not in the way I'd originally thought. Rizzo was getting pressure to run the investigation according to Follett's wishes.

Rizzo could see I was putting things into place. "Yes. We haven't talked to the press yet because Hall doesn't want people to know his son was homeless. And I've got Follett pushing me to get the case resolved ASAP. He wants someone else to step in and help Oakley, and I suggested you. Follett wasn't keen on that because your last case involved a shooting, justified or not. He also wasn't happy to hear you were cleared for the investigation you just got this morning. I actually had to fight him, telling him you would be the best one for your case, and to help Oakley. Speaking of your investigation, what do you have so far?"

"A dead hooker," I said. "We've been on it for hours, and I'll stay on it all day."

He did the hand thing again, shushing me. "I don't have any problems with your skills. But I need you to assist Oakley as well. I want you to get together with him. I know it's going to be tough with what you've got going on, but talk to him and see if you can help move his case forward. That way we get Follett off our backs. Oh, to complicate things, Carlton Hall now wants the press to know. He hopes going public might get someone to come out of the woodwork with information on his son's killing. There's a news conference at three. You need to be here for it."

I sucked in a breath. "That'll bring us attention we don't want."

"It's out of my control."

I didn't argue that. "What do you know about Oakley's investigation?"

"Jonathan Hall, Carlton's son, was homeless, and his body was found on the South Platte River, an apparent drowning. Not a lot to go on, and on the face of it, it didn't look like much. Get together with Oakley for all the details. I told Oakley you'd call him. The scrutiny on this one is intense, so we need to find his murderer, and fast. And don't forget the press conference at three." He glanced at a clock on the wall. "As the saying goes, the clock is ticking. Give me some results." That was Rizzo's way of dismissing me.

I got up and headed out of his office, feeling somewhat vindicated. My life had suddenly gotten more complicated, but I was okay with that, because I knew Rizzo hadn't lost faith in me.

CHAPTER ELEVEN

I had no sooner sat down at my desk than my phone rang.

"Hi, it's Jill Sheppard. I talked to Tracy, and she said she could meet you after her class. It's in the Central Classroom Building on the Auraria Campus. Are you familiar with the campus?"

"No, but I can figure it out."

"She told me to tell you she's wearing white shorts and a blue blouse, and that she has a black backpack."

"Thanks, I'm sure I can find her. I appreciate your help."

"I'll do whatever I can. I haven't seen Nicole in a long time, but I feel really bad about this. I do hope you find out what happened to her."

I thanked her for her time and ended the call. I got back on the computer. Metropolitan State University is a state school near downtown on the Auraria Campus, and I looked up the campus and located the Central Classroom Building. It would be easy to find. I called Oakley next. He didn't answer, so I left him a message to call me. I took a bathroom break – too much coffee –

and as I returned to my desk, my cell phone buzzed. I looked at the text. It was from Harry.

I HOPE your day is going well. I have faith in you. You're a great detective. I love you.

I SAT BACK AND SMILED. Harry is a wonderful man. We've been together for over ten years, but we've never gotten married. During the Welch investigation, I had thought more about why that was. I realized most of it had to do with me. I had put up walls between us, kept him at a distance. I didn't know if I could make a marriage work. Some of it was not trusting myself, but I had to admit that secrets from my past held me back, too. I'd finally told Harry about the long-ago stuff between Diane and me – the illegal things we'd both done, my stupidity in the risks I'd taken to protect her and curry her favor, and her selfish ingratitude about the whole thing. It had left our relationship strained, and it had also left me doubting myself. I wondered, though, if I was reaching a point where I could let all that go. Was it time to commit to Harry once and for all?

I texted him back, telling him I loved him, too, and that I wasn't sure when I'd be home. He's used to my erratic hours, so I wasn't surprising him. I pocketed my phone and spent a little time on the computer, submitting a report about my community outreach meeting. By the time I left, I still hadn't heard from Oakley.

TRACY SHEPPARD WAS SITTING at a long table in an open area in the Central Classroom Building. She had a Dazbog coffee cup in one hand, a book in front of her. When I approached, she looked up with a tentative smile.

"Are you Detective Spillman?" she asked. She was as described, in white shorts and blue blouse, and she looked similar to her yearbook picture, a little older, her hair a bit longer, still with all the world before her. She frowned and blinked a few times, then shifted nervously on her seat. Morning sun from high windows bathed us in warmth.

I slid onto the bench across from her, laced my fingers, and put my hands down on the table. "Your mom told you about Nicole?"

She nodded, then closed her book. "Yeah, she did. She said you can't tell us how it happened." I shook my head, and she went on. "I can't say that it was a total shock, knowing how much trouble she seemed to be getting into. But it still makes me sad." She glanced down at the table. "We sure had some fun, a while back. I hated to hear this."

Although there were no tears, it was still a stark contrast to Nicole's mother. Tracy looked around. Other students milled about, but nobody paid any attention to us.

"Tell me what you remember about Nicole," I said gently.

Her face lit up. "There was a point in time where we had a lot of fun, just screwing around. And it wasn't the drinking and drugging that she eventually got into. I was never much interested in that. I mean, yeah, I drank some, and smoked pot here and there, but it wasn't any big deal. I've always wanted to do well in school, and had even tried to get some scholarships to some bigger colleges. That didn't happen, so I started classes here and I'm hoping at some point to transfer to a university. I'd like to go to Notre Dame." She gulped a little coffee. "So anyway, even though I could cut it up here and there, I still stayed focused on my schooling. I want to be a lawyer."

"You know how the saying goes. If you work hard, you can achieve it."

"Thanks." A small smile. "Nicole wasn't really like that, into school. She never talked about what she hoped to do. You know things weren't good with her mom, right?" I nodded. "They didn't get along at all, and fought a lot. Mrs. Lockwood just wasn't that interested in Nicole, didn't really encourage her to do anything. It was kind of sad. My mom and dad don't have a ton of money, but they always push me to do better, and tell me that I can get a good education and make something of myself. They're really encouraging that way. Not Nicole's mom, she didn't care that much. Then Nicole got in with a rougher crowd, and she stopped caring about school at all. She started partying more, and I saw less of her. I tried to stay friends because she was nice, but it didn't last." She shrugged.

"Her mom said something about her hanging out with an older man. Do you know anything about that?"

Tracy hesitated, her gaze darting around the room.

"You can tell me."

"I don't know ..." Not to my question, but to whether she should answer.

"Please, it might help us find who killed Nicole."

She wrinkled her brow and thought for a moment. "I never knew his name, just that she met him late one night, when she was on her way home. It sounded like he was in a car, and he stopped to talk to her. At first I thought the guy was in college, or something like that, you know, closer to our age. But the more she talked about it, it sounded like he was older than that, like someone with a career." She glanced away.

"Please tell me what you know. Even little things might help with our investigation."

Tracy finally looked at me again. "I think he was a cop."

"She was seeing a cop?" I repeated. That would be big, a law enforcement officer seeing an underage girl. I could see why Nicole would want to keep that a secret. My guess was the cop had to have been pressuring her not to say anything as well. I tried to keep my voice neutral so I wouldn't frighten Tracy into not talking about it. "You're sure?"

"Yes. She said something about him looking hot in a uniform, and I asked if the guy was in the military. She said not that kind of uniform, but he did carry a gun." She shrugged. "I asked her if she meant a cop, and she wouldn't tell me. But that's the impression I got."

"You're sure she never slipped and told you this guy's name?"

"No, she was super-careful, and told me I had to keep it a secret. She was afraid of getting in trouble." She shook her head in disgust. "Her mom wouldn't have cared that much, but whatever. I told Nicole she was crazy and she should stop seeing him, but she just ignored that. She said he was a great guy, and they had fun together. I tried to get her to tell me what they did, and she wouldn't say. I think it was mostly sex, and you could tell she was crazy about him." She frowned. "It's funny, I'm in a psych class and learning about relationships and stuff. I think maybe Nicole was looking for a father figure. You know her dad died, right?"

"Yes, I heard that."

"She missed him, and maybe this guy was kind of a replacement for her dad. But that cop would get in a lot of trouble, dating an underage girl."

"You got that right. Are you sure she never gave you anything that might tell us who he was?"

A conversation at another table grew louder, and Tracy put her elbows on the table and leaned closer to me. "No, not at all. She was really careful."

I considered what she'd said. "Once Nicole started partying a lot, you lost touch with her?"

"Yeah, I'd see her around school some, until she dropped out. I haven't heard anything from her since. Somewhere I heard she had gotten into some pretty heavy drug use, but I don't know any more than that. Until my mom called me."

"Who heard she was doing heavier drugs?"

"You mean names? We had another friend, Yolanda Ortiz. I'm still friends with her. Maybe she knows more about what Nicole was doing, although she probably would've said something to me. You could still try her. She's a nanny, so she might have some time to talk to you." She pulled out her phone and scrolled through numbers, then gave Yolanda's number to me.

I jotted it down. "Do you know of anyone or any reason why someone might want to kill Nicole?"

"I don't. When we were in school, she was generally well-liked. Before she started partying, she was quiet, not into sports or anything. Both of us were the type that would fade into the background. But people liked her. I think she was bullied here and there, and I was, too. Then she got into the partying and was popular with some of that crowd. But nobody was mad enough at her to do anything. Besides, that was a few years ago. I don't know about now." She shrugged. "I wouldn't have any idea."

"You mentioned issues with her mom. Was there anything going on there that would have her mom so mad she'd want to go do something to Nicole?"

Her jaw dropped. "You don't think Mrs. Lockwood did anything, do you? I mean, they didn't get along, but I don't see her mom doing *that*. Mrs. Lockwood was nice enough to me. Nicole said her mom had kind of a rough background, and I know she was young when she had Nicole, but I don't think she would do anything to her."

"Do you know if her mom was in any kind of trouble, or in any bad relationships with men?"

"Oh, you mean like a boyfriend that would've gone after

Nicole?" She mulled that over, then shook her head. "No, nothing like that. To my knowledge, her mom never really dated after Nicole's dad left, and I never heard Nicole talk about other men around the house."

"Anything else you can think of? Anyone in Nicole's past who might've wanted to kill her?"

She glanced at her phone. "No, I can't think of anyone. I feel really bad about all of this, and if I think of anything, I can let you know. I haven't talked to Nicole in a long time, and I don't know what she was up to, or who her friends were. Sorry." Another glance at the phone. "I have to meet somebody for a study session. I have to go."

I gave her my card. "I really appreciate your taking the time to talk to me right away. And if you do think of anything else, please give me a call."

"Yeah, I will. Nicole got in with the wrong crowd. I always wondered if something bad would happen to her. And it did."

Her eyes grew wet and she swiped at them. She stuffed her book into her backpack, got up, and hurried away without another word.

CHAPTER TWELVE

As I was walking back to my car, Oakley called.

"Hey, returning your call," he said briefly. His voice is a little nasally, and even though he's lived in Colorado for some time, he still has a bit of a Boston accent, where he drops his 'r's.

"Rizzo said to give you a call." I wasn't sure how he was taking the directive to get my help, so I was careful in my approach. "He said you're taking some heat from Chief Follett on your homicide investigation."

"Yeah, this thing has kind of exploded on me." He didn't sound too happy. I heard noises in the background, then he said, "Hey, it's almost lunchtime. You want to grab a bite to eat somewhere and I can fill you in?"

It was a little after eleven, and his question made me realize I hadn't eaten anything in hours. "Lunch sounds good. I'm at Auraria now, where are you?"

"I'm not too far from there. How about we meet at Brewery Bar II? It's off Santa Fe. Turn west on Third and go partway down the block. You can't miss it."

"Perfect, I'll see you there soon."

"If you get there first, get a table. It can get busy at lunch."

"Will do."

I ended the call and hurried to my car. The sun was high in a cloudless sky and it was getting hot, which was making me sleepy. The walk in the fresh air was helping, but I would need more caffeine soon.

The Auraria Campus isn't too far from the brewery Oakley had suggested for lunch. I hopped on Kalamath Street and headed south. It only took me a few minutes to get there.

"Welcome to Brewery Bar II," a hostess said with a big smile. "Will you be dining alone today?"

"No, I'm meeting someone."

"Okay. I can show you to a table now if you'd like, or you can wait in the bar."

"A table would be fine."

She grabbed menus and walked with perky steps to a table in the corner. I wished I could steal some of her energy. A waitress came by and I ordered coffee, then sat back and looked around while I waited for Oakley. The bar had a southwestern flavor, from the adobe walls outside to the rich, reddish-brown painted walls. Mariachi music played softly overhead. While I waited, I called Yolanda Ortiz. After a few rings, a soft voice answered.

"Hello?"

"Yolanda?"

"Yes?" In the background, a little girl talked. "I'm on the phone, hang on a second."

"This is Detective Spillman."

"Oh, Tracy texted that you might call. She told me about Nicole." Before I could begin questioning her, she said, "I haven't heard from Nicole since high school. Tracy said you'd be asking all kinds of things."

"Well," I said, but couldn't finish.

"I didn't have a clue what Nicole was up to in high school," she said. "I told Tracy if I did, she'd hear about it, and she figured that was true." The little girl asked something else, and Yolanda gently shushed her. "I knew Nicole was screwing things up, the partying was getting out of control, but beyond that, I don't know what she was up to."

"You don't know anything about her seeing an older man."

"Nope. I heard that from Tracy, never from Nicole."

"And you have no idea who might've wanted to kill Nicole?"

"Nope," she repeated. "Nicole got in with a different crowd, and we hardly talked anymore. I don't even know if she graduated."

"Do you have any other friends who might be able to tell me what Nicole had been doing recently?"

"Nuh-uh."

At least that was different from "nope." Just to be certain, I ran through the rest of the questions I'd asked Tracy, but Yolanda didn't know anything that seemed helpful. I thanked her for her time and ended the call. I nibbled on chips and salsa that a busboy dropped by and watched the door. Oakley walked in a minute later, greeted by the perky hostess. Oakley's of average height, stocky, with the beginnings of a paunch around his middle. He looked around and saw me, shook his head at a question the hostess asked, and walked over. He pulled out the chair and it screeched loudly on the tile floor. He sat down before saying anything.

"I suppose I should say thanks for meeting me, but I'm not too sure what's going on," he said.

I nodded. "I get that. No one likes to be told they're not cutting it."

"Man, I'm hungry." He loaded a chip with salsa and popped

it into his mouth. "This is a great little place. Good Mexican food. They have great chili rellenos."

"I have a favorite Mexican restaurant, but I'm always willing to try someplace new." Carson Welch had worked at that restaurant, Tres Hermanos, and I hadn't been able to go back there since the night I'd killed him.

The waitress came over and Oakley ordered a Coke. She left, and he jammed more chips into his mouth. After an awkward moment, he looked at me.

"You must think I don't know anything," he said, wariness in his eyes. "To be told you need assistance ..." He left the rest unsaid.

I nodded slowly. "Let's get this out on the table. I've heard good things about you, that you're smart, and you know what you're doing. As far as having another detective pulled into your investigation, it happens sometimes."

He loaded another chip with salsa. Some dripped on the table. He finally took a bite, and chewed slowly. "Thanks." He swiped at the spilt salsa with a napkin.

We waited for a moment. The waitress brought his drink, we ordered rellenos, then I said, "Tell me about your investigation."

He gulped some soda, then said, "Male, thirty-five years old. His body was lying next to the Platte River, near some bushes. I was called in, and it looked pretty straightforward." He scowled, his dark eyes angry. "Drowning of a homeless guy. How easy could that be? He didn't have identification on him, no money. I have no idea if he'd been robbed or what. It happened late at night, but the body wasn't discovered until early the next morning by a jogger who runs the bike path that follows the river. By the time I got to the scene, I couldn't find any witnesses." He grabbed another chip, shrugged. "I thought that was it, didn't put too much time into it. Then I find out that the guy was actually the son of Carlton Hall, the lieutenant governor."

"... whose friends with Chief Follett," I interjected.

He swallowed hard and took a sip of soda. "Yep. What are the odds? I told Follett that it was open and shut, the guy drowned, but he didn't believe me." The scowl remained.

"What happened next?" I asked softly.

He pushed the chips away. "I got the autopsy results. Turns out, there was some bruising on the back of the vic's neck. He also had a couple of broken fingernails." He let that sink in.

"So now it looks like it's not an accidental drowning, but a forced drowning," I said.

"Yep." He snapped his fingers. "That fast, we went from an accident to a murder. And I hadn't given it much thought, had dismissed the case and was ready to move on."

"It happens."

"Sure it does, but this one goes all the way up to the Chief of Police. He's not happy with me at all."

"He's not too happy with me, either. Not that that would make you feel better."

He chuckled. "I heard he wanted Hackman to work with me, not you. No offense."

"I did, too. But you're stuck with me."

Now he smiled. "You have time for it?"

I nodded. "I'm finally back in business, and I'll make the time. Tell me more about the murder. You said the body was found on the Platte, but where?"

"There's an overpass at Mississippi Avenue. The body was about ten yards north of it, on the east side of the river. Some of the homeless people sleep down there, and that's where he was."

"You said there weren't any witnesses?"

"Correct. I don't know if somebody was around and saw what happened, and they don't want to talk, but we spent the better part of a day questioning the people who hang around that area. We couldn't find anybody who would admit to being there that night. Near that overpass, it's mostly businesses, and we checked for surveillance cameras, but didn't come up with anything. Then, when I found out we had a murder on our hands, I went back and spent more time talking to people around there. No one saw or heard anything."

That sounded similar to everyone we'd talked to around the Princeton Motel. No one knew anything. "Where exactly was his body found? Describe the scene to me."

The waitress arrived with our food. We both ate for a moment, then he went on.

"His head was lying in the water, the rest of his body on the bank. He had on old jeans, a ratty T-shirt, and a flannel shirt. Old shoes. Nothing to note, really. Like I said, a jogger called it in about six a.m. She was pretty shaken up, and a cyclist who rode by stopped and stayed with her until the police and homicide arrived. We interviewed them extensively, and I think they're exactly who they say they are. They didn't have anything to do with it. It's all in my report. I'll email it to you."

"How'd you identify the body?"

"Fingerprints. We matched them to his service record, then found out who he was related to." He finished his rellenos and gulped some Coke. "I had to tell the lieutenant governor and his wife. That wasn't fun. She could barely talk to me. He was both shocked at the death, and clear that I was to keep the death out of the public eye. He didn't want anyone to know his son was homeless. I guess the son was pretty smart, ex-military. They thought he would go places, but he served in Iraq and that messed him up."

I mulled over everything he'd told me while I finished my lunch. "That was good." He nodded. "What evidence was at the scene?"

He wiped his hands on his napkin, then dropped it beside his plate. "There was some trash around, nothing that gave me any clue to a murderer. Again, it's in the report. You can check it out, tell me if you see anything noteworthy. Other than that, nothing." He glanced toward the door, as if hoping he could escape. "As you can see, I'm completely at a loss."

"Once you found out it was the lieutenant governor's son, what did you do? Where did your investigation lead?"

He grabbed a napkin and fiddled with it. "We talked to his family and friends. No one could understand who would want to murder him. They don't think he had any enemies. He didn't have any trouble when he was in the military."

"You think another person living down there would've wanted to drown him?"

"It's possible. I went to some of the homeless shelters to see whether anyone recognized his picture, or could tell me somebody might've had a beef with him. Nothing came of that. Homeless people can be territorial. Maybe he encroached on someone else's spot, and that led to a fight. I don't know."

"I'm dealing with a similar situation, where no one knows anything." I told him about my investigation.

He'd taken to tearing at the napkin, and he had a small pile of shreds on the table. "Yeah, only you're just starting with your investigation. I've had time, and I'm not coming up with anything. And I've got the Chief breathing down my neck."

"Don't worry about him," I said. "Let me take some time this afternoon to go over your case notes, and I'll see what I can come up with. Between the two of us, I'll bet we can figure this out." I put more confidence into my tone than I felt.

He nodded. "Thanks, I appreciate it." He got out his wallet. "You heard there's a press conference at three?"

"Rizzo wants me there." I started to get money out to pay, and he waved me off.

"This is on me." As he waved for the waitress and handed her his credit card, he said, "The lieutenant governor wanted his son's death kept quiet, but now he wants everyone to know, see if someone will come forward with information. We'll get a bunch of useless leads, that's what I think."

I couldn't argue with that.

CHAPTER THIRTEEN

Nicole's arrest record said that she lived on St. Paul Street, so I went there next. The neighborhood was full of old houses built decades ago, most with long covered porches, and a few apartment buildings. Nicole had lived in a three-story nondescript brick building set close to the street. This neighborhood had been run-down when I was a kid, but had been through a gentrification. Even so, the apartment building was out of place among all the nicer homes. This time of the day a lot of people were at work, and I was able to park in front of the building. A school must've been close by because I heard the shrill yells of children playing. The sun filtered through the leaves of towering oak trees and shaded the front entrance to her building. She had lived in 203, and I entered a small foyer and pressed a buzzer. A moment later, the lock on the door clicked, and I entered. Was someone in that apartment expecting a visitor? They'd be surprised to see me. I took carpeted stairs to the second floor, then walked down to 203. I knocked and waited, then knocked again. I was not going away. The door finally opened.

"About time you –" The woman stopped short. As I

surmised, I was not who she was expecting. She put her hands on her hips. "Who're you?" She was young, with long red hair pulled into a ponytail, circles under her eyes, and a freckled face. She wore tight-fitted shorts and a green T-shirt with a high school logo on it. She yawned, then her eyes went to the badge clipped on my belt loop. Her brow crinkled with apprehension and she dropped her hands to her sides. She didn't invite me inside, just stared at me, mute.

I introduced myself, then asked, "Do you know Nicole Lockwood?"

She licked her lips, hesitant, as if she wanted to lie but knew she shouldn't. She still played it cool. "Who?"

I raised my voice. "You want me to create a scene here, because I can."

She leaned out and looked up and down the hall. "Hey, I'm sorry, okay? Chill out."

"Don't tell me to chill out," I snapped.

She grew flustered, not sure what to say, but she sure as hell didn't want anyone to see us. "Look, um, Miss ..."

"Detective Spillman," I said with emphasis on the first word. "I'll repeat. Do you know Nicole Lockwood?"

"Sure, I've seen her around. She got herself into trouble again? I didn't have anything to do with it."

I shook my head. "She's dead."

She took a step back, and it took her a second to form words. "What happened?"

"You haven't heard?"

She shook her head, puzzled. Her reaction seemed genuine, not like the faked expressions of surprise we sometimes see, the ones with the exaggerated wide eyes or a dropped jaw. You can always figure those folks are lying. "Not a thing, I swear."

"She was killed outside the Princeton Motel last night." I

watched her closely. Her face was blank. "You haven't heard anything about that?" I repeated.

"No," she whispered. I smelled cigarettes and a greasy odor. She tugged at her shirt. "I was out late, and I didn't see her last night. I got home early this morning, and I've been sleeping. How'd she die?"

"She was murdered."

She sucked in a breath, her eyes wide. "Wow."

"Does Nicole live here?"

"Nah, she hasn't lived here in a while."

"Why not?"

She scratched her arm. "She couldn't pay her rent. We got three of us here now, and it's tight. Rent's high. She couldn't pay her share, so we had to get somebody else in here who could."

"Why couldn't Nicole pay?"

She frowned, looked for an excuse and settled on, "You know how it goes." She went silent. I waited. "She spent more of it on drugs, okay?"

I tried for a glimpse of the apartment again. "Three of you live here?"

"Yeah."

"You all work the streets?"

"Um, well ... come on," she whined. "You're not going to hassle me, are you? I haven't done anything wrong."

"Not if you cooperate."

She sighed. "We don't cause any problems here, okay?"

I wondered if the landlord knew hookers lived in the building. "What's your name?"

She hesitated. "Rachel."

"Rachel what?"

She looked everywhere but at me. I waited her out. "Ingalls," she finally said. "You don't have anything on me, do you?"

I shook my head. "Just trying to find out what I can about Nicole. Do you know if *she* was in some kind of trouble?"

Somewhere back in the apartment, a door opened and closed. Rachel took a peek over her shoulder, then looked back at me. "I don't know. She hasn't lived here in a while. I've seen her around, but I hardly talk to her. If she had something going on, I wouldn't know."

"That's the truth?" I snapped, trying to keep her off-balance so she hopefully wouldn't have time to lie.

"Yes!" she wailed.

I pointed into the apartment. "Who's there?"

"Nobody." Her voice was soft.

I glanced behind her "If it's somebody who might be able to tell me more about Nicole, I—"

"It's nobody," she interrupted. "Just a friend. We're partying."

I got it. It was a guy. "Would he know anything?"

"No, I didn't pick him up at the Princeton."

I could hassle her some more to let me talk to the guy, but beyond that, I couldn't force her to do anything. I frowned. "If your roommates are home ..."

"They aren't here, and I don't think they knew Nicole. You can come back and talk to them later. They'll probably be around this afternoon."

"What're their names?"

"Misty Chandler and Gwen Pruitt."

I wrote down the names and tried a different tack. "If someone is going after hookers, wouldn't you want to get him off the streets?"

She went pale. "You think we need to be watching out?"

"Of course you do," I said. "At this point, I don't know if this was a random attack or not."

It may have been a little dramatic, but I needed to get her to cooperate. "I don't know anything."

"Did Nicole have any issues with a particular john, that kind of thing?"

"Not that I'm aware of. Most girls aren't going to tell you much, anyway. They want to be left alone."

I left that as is and went to something else. "There's someone else I'd like to talk to." I described the woman that I'd seen and chased near the motel, and pointed to my face. "She's got some scarring here. You know who I'm talking about?"

"Yeah, that's Lola."

"Is that her real name?"

"I don't know, and before you ask, I don't have a last name. I just overheard someone talking about her, and they said her name is Lola."

"Where can I find her?"

She shrugged. "I don't know where she lives."

I crossed my arms. She was holding back. "Give me something more than that."

"Hey, I'm telling the truth. I think she might work at some strip club on Evans. The Diamond Club. Near the Platte."

I'd heard of it. It was a dive.

"She's there, and she turns tricks. You know how it goes." She looked over her shoulder again. "You need anything else? I gotta get going."

"Do you have ID?"

She muttered under her breath. "Yeah, hold on." She partially closed the door and went to a table in a small nook close to a kitchen, rummaged in a dark-colored purse, and came back. "Here."

I verified her name, then handed the ID back. "Thanks." Then I eyed her carefully. "I hope you're telling me the truth. I'd hate to have to come back."

Footsteps sounded on the stairs, and an older woman with long gray hair came down the hall. She slowed as she approached, gave me a quick onceover, then threw a small smile at Rachel.

"Hello," the woman said. "Is everything okay?"

"Yes, no problems, Mrs. Spruce."

The woman continued to her apartment and glanced at me as she unlocked the door. After she disappeared inside, Rachel looked at me, her big eyes were pleading. "I'm telling you the truth. Please, I need to stay out of trouble."

I met her gaze and held it for a moment before pulling a business card from my pocket. "If you think of anything else that might help me find Nicole's killer, you be sure to call me, okay?"

"Of course."

She shut the door, and I knew I wouldn't hear from her again.

CHAPTER FOURTEEN

On the way to the strip club, I made phone calls, starting with Ernie. "Have you found out anything from Nicole's friends?"

"Not so far. I'm having a hard time tracking them down. You know, a yearbook is a great resource for names, but it's been a few years. Some have moved, others are working, or in college."

"I get that. Keep on it." I told him about the lead with Lola and that I'd be going to the strip club.

"I hope Harry is understanding about that."

"He knows I don't eat from the other side of the buffet."

He was still laughing when I disconnected.

I called Spats next. "Have you seen the surveillance video from the gas station of the 911 call that was made?"

"Not yet. The guy on the day shift wants me to talk to his boss, which is proving a hard thing to do."

"Don't worry about it. I've got a bead on her. Her name's Lola."

"Lola? Like the Kinks song?"

"Yes. I'm going to see if I can talk to her now."

"All right. You know I'm going to be hearing that song in my head now, don't you?"

"No need to thank me."

THERE WERE several cars in the Diamond Club parking lot when I drove up. It was early in the afternoon, but that didn't stop the desire for sex. I received wary looks from a couple of men in business suits as I got out of my car and walked into the building. The foyer was gloomy, and loud music with a heavy base greeted me, along with a tall bouncer with thick arms and an equally thick mustache. He stared at me as I walked up, not overly surprised that a woman had walked through the door. I flashed my badge at him. That elicited little response as well.

"Does a woman named Lola work here?" I asked.

"I don't know," he said. His voice was surprisingly high, almost comical compared to his burly form.

"Come on, Lola's not a common name."

"I don't know," he repeated.

I let out a slow, dramatic sigh. "I really don't want to do this."

"Do what?" He crossed his arms and stared down at me.

"I don't want this to be a thing."

He was still lost. "What?"

I leaned against the wall. "I don't want to end up having to hassle you, threatening to bring the police in here to see what you're doing that might not be legal." I pointed past him toward the main part of the club, where I could see some men at tables. "I'm sure there's something going on in here that shouldn't be. Drugs being sold? Maybe sexual favors? Who knows? I would hate to have to shake this place down, which would make your customers unhappy, and I would think that would make your manager *very* unhappy. And do you know what would make your manager even more unhappy?"

"What?"

"When I tell your manager that the shakedown didn't need to happen," I extended a finger at him, "except that you wouldn't cooperate with me."

His lips twitched under the mustache.

"It's a simple question," I said.

He finally relented, not happy to do so. "Lola works here, but she's not here right now."

"How about you get your manager to confirm that."

"He's busy."

We were back to obstructive. "Make him un-busy."

We engaged in a staring contest, and he lost. He broke eye contact and reached for a phone on the wall behind him. He spoke into it for a moment, hung up, and stared again with fire in his eyes. Then another man in a black suit, tie, and gold cuff links materialized out of nowhere.

"I'm the manager, Victor Golic. I understand you want to talk to one of the women who works here?" He was being exceedingly polite. If he thought that was going to make me go away, he was wrong.

"As I told your bouncer here," I pointed at the big man, "I need to speak to Lola."

He put his palms together. "She isn't working here right now."

"When's her next shift?"

He glanced at a gold watch. "Not until five."

"Perfect." I smiled. "And what's Lola's last name?"

"Tyndale." He spelled it.

"Thank you," I said.

"You're quite welcome." He gazed at me, waiting for me to

leave. I held back for a moment, just to make him uncomfortable. He cleared his throat and waited some more.

"I'll see you soon." I had no choice but to believe they were telling me the truth, which meant I had to leave.

I went outside and got into the Escape. I was close to the South Platte River, so I decided to stop where Oakley's murder victim had been found. I got onto Santa Fe and drove north to Mississippi Avenue, then hunted around until I found a parking place on a side street. I walked toward the overpass where Oakley said Jonathan Hall's body had been found. The afternoon was warm and pleasant, a beautiful late summer day. I waited at a stoplight, then crossed Mississippi and walked onto a bike path which led down underneath the street. Shadows overtook me, and it was cooler, although the traffic sounds were barely muted.

Jonathan Hall had been found near some bushes about ten yards north of the overpass, so I continued down the path, then veered off it toward the Platte River. This section of the Platte is really more a creek than a river, the name somewhat of an embarrassment to real rivers like the mighty Mississippi. The South Platte forms southwest of Denver, but in the metro area, it's smaller, with some wider sections and areas that flow over rocks, but where I was it's quite a bit narrower. I made my way through taller grass that was brown and thirsty, stepping carefully on the steeper slope. As I got closer to the edge of the river, it grew rockier. Once I reached the river, I walked slowly toward some bushes, then stood and listened. Santa Fe's a major north-south road, running on either side of the Platte, and at this time of the day there was no shortage of traffic noise. I tuned out the sound, squatted down and looked around the rocks, and didn't see anything. Whatever evidence might have been here that Oakley could've missed was probably long gone. I stared at the ground and wondered why a homeless person would venture down close to the river in the middle of the night. Was he relieving himself, or had he heard something? Had he been lured there by his killer? I pictured someone holding Hall down. It would have to be a fairly strong person, and the killer would likely have been on his hands and knees on the rocks. That could've hurt. And if Hall had struggled, had the killer been injured, or bruised his hands and knees? I listened to the water, then finally stood up and brushed off my pant legs. I carefully checked around the bushes and didn't see anything, not even trash. I could see how Oakley could dismiss the murder as some kind of fight between homeless people, or a robbery gone bad. Not much else made sense. I looked up and down the river, hoping for some kind of inspiration. None came.

I turned around, and to my surprise, I saw a homeless man crouched beneath the concrete barriers of the overpass, watching me. I climbed back up the slope to the bike path and walked toward the overpass. The man followed my movements. I was alert for any trouble. In the last few years, Denver's homeless population has grown, and there have been more problems with crime than have been reported in the news media. When I reached the overpass, the man took a few steps down from his perch. He wore tattered jeans and a flannel shirt, a threadbare blanket draped around his shoulders. He reeked of booze and body odor, even from a distance.

"Hello," I said. He was older than I first realized, with a wizened face, gray hair, and a scraggly beard.

"Whatcha doin' lady?"

I glanced back toward the Platte. "Just looking around."

He slid down the slope toward the bike path, a hand on the ground to steady himself. He took a few more steps toward me, walking with a weird shuffle because his shoes were too big. As he drew near, I saw that he was short, a good five or six inches under my five-nine. He stared at me with beady eyes. "You looking where Shooter was."

"Shooter?"

He pointed toward the Platte, where I had been. "Shooter."

"You mean Jonathan Hall?"

He squinted up at me. "He was down there by the river. I seen him."

"Who?"

"Shooter," he repeated.

"What's he look like?"

His lips went in and out. "He's big, and he's losing his hair." He guffawed.

"What color?"

"Brown."

I had no idea whether he meant Jonathan Hall or not, but I ran with it anyway. "When did you see him?"

He gave me a toothless grin. "Who are you, lady?" Then he saw my badge, and he crinkled up his eyes. "I don't want to talk to you."

He started to turn around.

"Wait!"

He stopped in his tracks and slowly turned around. His eyes twitched nervously. "If I talk to you, something bad will happen. That's what happens when you talk to people. Bad things happen. Bad things."

Like many of the homeless, he wasn't in his right mind. I treaded carefully.

"What did you see?"

"He was down there." He pointed with a dirty hand to the river. "Then the bad stuff happened, and he was in the water. His face was," he clapped his hands together, "right in the water. You can't live with your face in the water."

My pulse quickened. Had he seen Jonathan Hall's murder? "What bad stuff happened?"

His eyes twitched. "If I tell you, it could happen to me."

I shook my head. "No, it'll be okay. I'll make sure. You stay around here?"

"He'll come back."

"Who?"

He pulled the blanket around his scrawny shoulders. He lowered his voice. "The man. He was scary."

"What did he look like?"

He scrunched up his face. "He was spooky. Dark clothes and a hood." With the traffic noise, I strained to hear him.

"You saw him?" I tried to hide my excitement so I wouldn't scare him.

He flapped his arms and pointed again. "Over there, where you were."

I tried hard to ignore his stench. "What happened?"

"He talked to Shooter, and they went down by the river. I heard noises and splashing. I didn't want to look. I was scared. You know bad things can happen."

I nodded sympathetically. "Yes. Then what happened to Shooter?"

"He didn't come back. His face was in the river. You can't live with your face in the water."

"What about the man in the hoodie?"

"Hoodie?"

"The man in dark clothes and the hood?"

"He walked that way." He gestured south. "He was breathing hard. I could hear gasps, like a monster."

The killer being out of breath would make sense if he'd struggled to drown Shooter. "Did the man say anything?"

He shook his head, his eyes twitching again. "And I wouldn't say anything to him."

"Of course not. What happened next?"

He stared at me for a moment, not sure he wanted to answer.

I wondered if I could get him to say more. "I went down to Shooter," he went on. "He was dead, you know."

I nodded. "Yes, I heard that."

"I didn't know what to do. And I didn't want to see anyone. I don't want to go to jail."

"You won't get in trouble."

"Yeah, but I took something."

"What?" I said hurriedly.

"His shoes." He glanced at his feet. "They're bigger than mine, but my feet are warmer now. He didn't need them. You think he'll be mad at me for stealing them?"

I shook my head. "I'm sure he'd be glad that it's helping you out."

A big toothless grin at that. "I took this, too." He reached into his jeans pocket and pulled out a large folding knife. "It's pretty, right?"

"Yes, it is. That belonged to Shooter, too?"

He shook his head. "I never seen him with it. It was on the ground near him. And I took his money, he had three dollars on him. I bought some food with it."

"The knife didn't belong to Shooter?" I clarified.

"I think the monster dropped it."

I couldn't be sure about that, but I wanted the knife regardless. "Do you think I could have it?"

He pulled his hand back defensively. "No, it's mine."

"Yes, it is. And it looks really cool. What if I bought it from you?"

He pursed his lips and thought about that. "How much would you give me?"

I reached into my pocket and pulled out a twenty. "I have this." I showed it to him.

It was probably more money than he'd seen in a long time. "What if the knife is worth more?" He was a shrewd negotiator.

I shrugged. "It's all I have."

He squinted and thought about that. It was too much temptation. "Okay." He took a few steps toward me and held out the knife. I walked over with the twenty, his smell almost overpowering. He snatched the money from me, and I grabbed the knife, both of us wanting to get the transaction done before either one changed our mind. I wanted to look at the knife more closely, but I didn't want him to ask for it back, so I pocketed it. It might be nothing, but it could be something as well.

"Did you see anything else?" I asked.

"The cops came. I had to stay away. I don't want them to take me anywhere. I've been in places, and I don't want to be locked up."

That would explain why Oakley hadn't seen him.

"Was anyone else around when all this happened?"

He shook his head. "It was just me. Shooter and me hang around here. He kept everyone else away." As Oakley had noted, homeless people can be territorial.

"The man in the hood," I went on. "Did you see his face?"

He shook his head. "I was hidden. I didn't want him to do something bad to me." He did the nose-wrinkling again. "I got to go now," he said. He held up the twenty, then smelled it. I hoped he would spend at least some of it on a good meal.

"You take care of yourself," I said, feeling sorry for him.

"I'll be fine." He turned around and did the weird walk-shuffle down the bike path. I watched until he disappeared around a bend, then hurried back to my car.

CHAPTER FIFTEEN

Teddy: *The Guild will now come to order.*

The members announced themselves.

Teddy: *Please agree to the Guild rules. Everything said here remains here. Do not talk about a member's actions or plans to anyone outside of the Guild. We are the group, no new members will be allowed. We all have the resources to make you pay. Do not break the rules. Your word is your oath.*

Everybody agreed to the rules. Marilyn was irritated. Must Teddy recite the rules *every* time they got together? Even though her mind tingled with weariness, she was giddy with anticipation.

Teddy: *Marilyn, I think you have some news for us.*

A satisfied smile swept across her face. She waited just a moment, then put her fingers to the keyboard and typed.

Marilyn: *Did you all watch the noon news?*

Teddy: *No, I didn't have a chance.*

Daffy Duck: *Yes, I watched. The prostitute. Was that you?*

Marilyn: *Yes, that was me. I did it last night.*

Brad: *There was no mention of the jewelry. How do we know it was you?*

Marilyn sometimes found herself not liking Brad Pitt, and it figured that he would be the one to doubt her. He'd had his turn, and he seemed to think that made him an expert. Well, maybe he'd done his deed, a lot of deeds perhaps, she didn't know. She still didn't like his attitude. She listened to her favorite symphony, so soothing, then picked up her cup of coffee and sipped it as she formed a response. She'd only gotten a few hours of sleep before the meeting, and she needed the caffeine to focus. The Guild met on an erratic schedule, Marilyn assumed, to make it harder to trace their online activities. She couldn't miss this meeting, though. It was her big moment. And she was glad to meet soon after her deed, she just *had* to tell someone what she'd done. And this obviously wasn't something she could tell her husband or friends. The house was quiet; no one was around. She was going to enjoy telling them.

Marilyn: *It was a prostitute, not something that's going to make the evening news. It's a catch-22, don't you think? You choose a vulnerable person because it's easy to do the deed, but no one's going to care about them, either. You have to take my word for it about the prostitute, that was me.*

Pete: *No, we don't have to take your word.*

Teddy: *It's okay, I have ways to validate this. Marilyn, did you leave proof?*

Marilyn: *A ring with a red stone.*

Teddy: *I'll confirm that the jewelry was at the scene. We have no reason to doubt Marilyn, though.*

Pete always wanted the proof, too. Marilyn didn't doubt Teddy would verify her deed. She wondered how he would find out. He must have connections somewhere. She stifled a yawn. The few hours of sleep might not be enough to carry her through the day. Not like when she was younger, when she could last forever. Now, she had to act as normal as possible. The cleaning lady had shown up, and Marilyn had a friend come over as well.

She'd had to cut that time short because the Guild had agreed to meet at this time, and she had to make her announcement.

Joe: *Marilyn, how did it feel?*

She thought about it for a second. She'd been through a range of emotions since the deed. One thing she hadn't felt was anything for the prostitute. She was a pawn in the game, no more. Marilyn thought longer. What did it most feel like? She pursed her lips. Once she'd gotten past the initial fear, she'd felt powerful. She'd never felt like that before. She also knew she was in an elite group. Few people had done what she had. That meant she had to be careful. Like the others, she could not get caught. She had a contingency plan, she knew she would never go to jail, but she hoped she never had to do that. She put her fingers on the keyboard.

Marilyn: *Just like the others have said, it was exhilarating.*

Brad: *It was for me, too.*

Daffy Duck: *Yes! I would love to have that feeling again.*

Marilyn stared at the screen, lips pursed. Would any of them do the deed again? Could she? Her heart quickened at the thought. She'd planned so much on her one deed ... could there be another? She shook her head and focused on the chat. Those who had gone before talked in general terms about their deeds, and Marilyn felt that sense of power again. She was part of a special group. She sipped her coffee and chatted with the others. After a while, Teddy took control again.

Teddy: *The next order of business. Who will go now?*

Marilyn watched the screen, waiting.

Joe: *I'm ready to go.*

Teddy: *When can we expect this?*

Joe: *Tonight.*

Teddy: *So soon after Marilyn? I'm not sure this is wise.*

Joe: *It's another vulnerable person. No one will know. I know what I'm doing.*

Teddy: *You have to be extremely careful. Everything is contingent on extreme caution.*

Daffy Duck: *We all know we have to be.*

Joe: *Don't worry, I've planned this well. I won't get caught.*

Teddy: *Good. I will reach out soon about our next meeting.*

The members chatted for a few minutes longer, and then Teddy ended the chat. Marilyn wished she could talk to them longer, but she also needed to freshen up before her husband came home. She felt a little sad as she logged off the computer and left the room.

CHAPTER SIXTEEN

By now, it was time for me to head back to the station for the press conference on Jonathan Hall's death. I drove back downtown, and wasn't even able to sit down at my desk before Chief Follett saw me. He was in Rizzo's office, and he waved for me to join them. I looked around and saw no escape. When I'd returned to my car after talking to the homeless man, I'd put the knife into an evidence bag. I discreetly dropped it in a desk drawer, then did the gallows walk into Rizzo's office. Follett shut the door with a bang.

"Have a seat, Detective." When he spoke, it was clear it wasn't a suggestion. As much as I didn't like the man, and didn't want to have to obey him, I sat down across the desk from Rizzo.

Chief Follett smoothed a hand over his gray hair and paused just long enough to make me uncomfortable. I'm not bothered so much that he's gruff; I'm bothered by a sense that he has reservations about me and my skills. And that fed right into the long-held doubts I had about myself. Follett leaned on a bookcase against one wall, crossed his hands over his midsection, and stared at me. I waited.

"Calvin tells me he wants you at this press conference," Follett said.

I nodded, taken aback by Follett's use of Rizzo's first name. "Yes," I replied.

Follett's lips formed a thin, disapproving line. He paused a long beat, just enough to make me feel even more uncomfortable. "I'm not sure that's a good idea. You have recently been reinstated after an officer-involved shooting. I'm not sure it makes sense to have you in front of the cameras again."

Rizzo came to my defense. "She'll be fine."

"I'm not so sure."

"I have full faith that Detective Spillman can handle this with the utmost professionalism." Rizzo talked in a formal manner; he wanted Follett's attention. "She needs to know what's shared with the press."

Follett took us both in with his gaze, then made his decision. "I want to be absolutely clear that if you get any questions about your previous case, that you'll say nothing about it, understand?"

"Of course," I said. That went without saying, and I didn't like his implication that I wouldn't know that. But, I tried to let it go.

Follett had second thoughts. "Better yet, don't answer any questions, leave that to me."

"Fine," I said.

Rizzo held up a hand. "Sarah can handle herself."

Follett didn't answer that, whether because he didn't want to, or because he doubted me, I couldn't be sure. "How much do you know about the Hall investigation?" he asked.

"Not much," I said honestly. "I met with Oakley a couple of hours ago, and he told me what he's uncovered so far. That's about it. I still need to go through the case notes." I didn't tell him about the homeless guy I'd talked to or the knife, because I wasn't sure if either one had anything to do with Jonathan Hall's murder. If it turned out they were unrelated, it would only lessen me in Follett's eyes. I didn't need that.

Follett glanced at his watch. "I guess that's fine, since you won't be saying anything. Let's get downstairs for the conference. I want this on the five o'clock news, see if we can stir things up and get this investigation moving forward."

He strode out of the office. I glanced at Rizzo, and he gave me a reassuring nod. I followed Follett, and we picked up Oakley at his desk. He looked as if he'd just eaten some really bad food. His face was pale, and he swallowed hard when Follett barked at him. Then we all went downstairs and outside to the front steps of the building.

"I've never been front and center at a press conference before," Oakley whispered to me. Perspiration popped up on his brow.

"Let Follett handle it," I murmured. "Silent and stoic."

He nodded subtly. Several reporters from the local stations were waiting with camera crews, along with Deborah North, from Channel Seven, plus a reporter that I knew from the *Denver Post*, the local newspaper. Deborah gave me a slight nod. I did as I'd told Oakley, silent and stoic. There was a buzz among them as we waited. Someone had alerted them that a big announcement was being made. Follett wore a dark blue suit, white shirt, and blue-striped tie, his shoes polished. Nothing like looking good for the press. Promptly at three o'clock, he stepped up to a microphone that was set up on the steps.

"I'd like to thank you all for coming today," he began. "I'll say a few words, then take questions. Last week, a man named Jonathan Hall was found dead near the South Platte River. This was initially thought to be a drowning." He glanced, not too subtly at Oakley, then back to the cameras. Oakley worked hard not to grimace as Follett went on. "We now suspect that Hall was murdered. I'm sure some of you are familiar with the name.

Jonathan Hall is the son of Carlton Hall, the lieutenant gover-nor." A crackling energy went through the small crowd, and reporters started firing questions at Follett. He held up a hand impatiently to stop them. "I'll get to your questions in a moment. Carlton Hall is a close friend of mine, and he's devastated that his estranged son died under mysterious circumstances. We are requesting that anyone with information about his son's death call our hotline." He glanced at a piece of paper and read the number, then repeated it. "As you can imagine, it's important to me as well as to the family to find out what happened to Jonathan." He cleared his throat, then said, "I'll take questions now."

The reporters immediately and loudly peppered him with questions, thrown out in staccato fashion.

"Do you have any suspects?" one woman asked.

"No comment," Follett said.

"Where on the South Platte?" another asked.

"Near Mississippi Avenue."

Follett gestured at another reporter. The questions began to blur for me.

"What clues do you have so far?"

"Was the victim robbed?

"Is there a motive?"

Follett answered what he could, but kept out pertinent details of the killing that only the murderer would know. A couple of the reporters called out to me, asking about Carson Welch's case. Follett glanced at me and I did exactly as he'd instructed, and I stayed quiet. After fielding a few more ques-tions, someone asked, "Why isn't the lieutenant governor here?"

Follett stared at the reporter, then held up his hands. "He's busy now. That'll be all, thank you."

We turned to leave and more questions kept coming. Follett

opened the station door without looking back. We went back inside, and their voices died off. Follett loosened his tie.

"That ought to buy us some leads," he said.

"And plenty of crap to deal with too," I said softly.

Not softly enough, as Follett said, "You know how this works, Detective. Sift through the garbage until you find what's helpful. I have to meet with the lieutenant governor soon, so give me something to tell him. If I go to him emptyhanded, that won't look good." Without another word, he turned on his heel and disappeared into the elevator.

"He's worried about his job," Oakley said.

I nodded as we took the stairs to the second floor. We got to my desk, and Oakley perched on the corner of it while I sat down.

He rubbed a hand over his face. "I'm worried about my job, too."

I nodded. "The pressure is definitely on, but don't let it get to you. No one's going to ask you to resign over this."

"I emailed you the case file," he said. "Have you had a chance to look at it?"

I shook my head. "I had a couple of stops before I got back here, and then Follett snagged me the minute I walked in. I'll read it now."

"Thanks."

"And," I picked up a pen and fiddled with it, "I stopped by the Platte, where you said the body was found. There was a homeless guy there who was hanging out under the overpass. He was older, with gray hair and a scraggly beard, and he wore jeans and a flannel shirt. Does he sound familiar?"

"He sounds like a lot of the homeless guys I talked to."

"The thing is, he seemed to know some of what went on with Hall, like he saw Hall being drowned."

Oakley's jaw dropped. "Where was he when I was looking for witnesses?"

"He was pretty scared, and he isn't in his right mind."

"Did he see the murderer?"

"Somebody in a hoodie, that's all he said." I glanced around, put the pen down, and pulled the knife from the desk drawer. "He says he picked this up near Hall's body. We need to see about forensics on this. It may not be anything, or it may belong to the killer. I bought it off the homeless guy, figured we should have it, just in case. It's going to have my prints on it, but when I got back to my car, I bagged it right away. Let's see if we can get anything off it, prints, DNA, and see if it leads to anything."

Oakley took the baggie. "I'll get on it."

I picked up the pen again. "The homeless guy definitely made it sound like a man drowned Hall." I thought for a moment. "How big was Hall?"

"He was fairly tall, and thin. Not heavy."

"Then it would fit that a man killed Hall," I said. "I have a hard time thinking a woman could hold him down, especially if he was struggling like you said might've happened."

Oakley grimaced. "You know, after the press conference, we'll get flooded with tips, most of which probably won't lead anywhere."

"I know." I lowered my voice. "I sometimes don't get Follett. It seems like he has no clue what's really going on. He plays the politics well, though."

Oakley smirked. "I'll keep you posted on what comes in, if anything seems relevant."

"Great." I gestured at my computer. "I'll get cracking on your report."

Oakley got to his feet. "It just keeps getting better."

I smiled and turned to my computer. Before I could open my email, my cell phone rang. I stared at it. It was Diane. It was the middle of the day, and it surprised me to hear from her now. She's a family doctor with a thriving practice, and she typically doesn't have time to call until the evening. I was tempted to ignore the call, then thought about how I'd said I would try to do better with her, so I picked up.

"Hey," she said, her voice clipped. She always seems like she's going a mile a minute.

"Hi, Diane. How are you?" I put as much cheer in my voice as I could.

"You sound tired," she said. Her voice is low, always with a commanding edge to it.

"I guess there's no fooling you," I said. "To be honest, it's already been a long day. I started a new investigation early this morning, I've been going since about one."

"They're letting you back in the field?"

"Yes." I couldn't tell if there was something in her tone, or if it was me. I silently coached myself to stay calm and chalked it up to it being me. "It's been a month. I think I'm doing well."

"Well, I hope you know what you're doing."

Ah, there it was. And like clockwork, the same old resentments bubbled to the surface. I quickly pulled myself back to the present. "What's going on?"

"I ..." she hesitated. "I wanted you to know that I appreciate what you did that night." She cursed Carson Welch's name. "Although I wish I'd never seen that man, if you hadn't come in when you did, I don't know what would've happened."

I stared at my monitor and blinked hard a few times. This was not what I expected from her. And such odd timing.

"Thank you," I said. "You know I'm sorry about what happened, all of it. I wish I'd realized things sooner, and caught Welch earlier, before he got to you."

"Yes," she snapped, then stopped herself. "I've been seeing a therapist, in fact, I just came from her place. This whole thing hasn't been easy for me, but I realized today it hasn't been easy for you, either. I just wanted you to know that."

"Thank you," I said again.

"Let's get together. Mom says she hasn't heard from you in a while. You can't let the job get in the way."

And, with that, Diane was back to being Diane, telling me what I should or shouldn't do, that whatever I was doing was not quite right enough. But still, there seemed to be a tiny bit of progress between us.

"I'll call Mom soon," I promised.

"I've got to get back to work. I'll talk to you soon."

She ended the call, and I stared at my desk. I was stunned, surprised, and pleased. I didn't know what our relationship would be like, and I doubted we'd ever be really close, but this was a step in the right direction for both of us.

CHAPTER SEVENTEEN

I sat for a moment, feeling the drag of the day pulling on me. I'd been up all night, at first not being able to sleep, then being called out to start Nicole Lockwood's investigation. I yawned and rubbed my eyes until I saw stars, then logged into my email and found Oakley's. He had attached the report on the Hall investigation and I downloaded it, then opened it up.

I read through the initial report, how a jogger, Wendy Barnes, early on Wednesday morning last week had seen Hall's body lying partially in the Platte River. She walked partway down the slope toward the river and called out. When the man didn't respond, she got scared and dialed 911. Then she waited until the police arrived. Wendy lived in the area and ran along the bike path regularly. According to the responding officer's report, she had been shaken up at finding the body. A cyclist who happened by stayed with her until the police arrived. Neither one had seen or heard anything. As Oakley had told me at lunch, there had been no witnesses, nobody that he could find who'd seen what happened to the victim. Certainly not the old man I had run into. They canvassed the businesses in the neighborhood, and the few that had surveillance cameras didn't have a view of the Platte. Forensics had combed the area near the body and hadn't found anything they felt was significant to the crime. Oakley's report had a list of trash that was near the body. It had been found and collected, just in case it was discovered to be evidence in the future. A gas station receipt, a Coke can, a King Soopers tan plastic grocery bag, an almost empty bourbon bottle, and an empty water bottle. It was good that they had collected the stuff, but I doubted it would lead anywhere.

After some stale coffee that I beefed up with sugar and cream, I read the autopsy report. There was a lot of technical jargon, the gist being that Hall had aspirated water into his lungs, a clear indication that he had drowned. He also had twice the legal limit of alcohol in his system, and marijuana as well. I briefly pondered that. As drunk and high as Hall had been, would that have made it easier to drown him? A couple of Hall's fingernails had been broken. The autopsy report didn't speculate on when that might've happened, but I wondered if it was possibly from a struggle with an assailant. The autopsy did note bruises on the back of Hall's neck. Again, the report made no conclusions, but it was consistent with someone holding him down. Hall was underweight, had rotting teeth, and X-rays showed several prior bone fractures. He had a cut on his left leg that was infected. As I read the report, nothing besides the bruising on his neck stood out.

I studied the autopsy photos that came with the report as well. Hall had hollow cheeks, sunken eyes, and thinning brown hair. I wasn't sure how closely Oakley had studied the body when it was down on the Platte River, but the bruises could have been missed. Although Oakley may have been hasty in his initial conclusions, I could see why his preliminary impression was that it was an accidental drowning.

My cell phone vibrated, a message from Ernie saying he was

still talking to Nicole Lockwood's friends, and that he was having a ball. I smiled at the sarcasm, told him to keep at it, then moved on to Oakley's interview with Hall's family. Jonathan's mother had broken down, said only that her son had some problems, and then she left the room. Oakley resumed his interview with the lieutenant governor. Carlton Hall had been stoic, in Oakley's words. The lieutenant governor was hesitant at first to share much about his son, other than that he'd been troubled. Oakley pushed for more information, and the lieutenant governor had said that Jonathan served two tours in Iraq, that he'd always wanted a military career, that he'd gone to West Point and seemed to have a bright future in front of him. But Jonathan had come home a changed man, and Oakley noted some bitterness when the lieutenant governor had talked about his son and how different he was after Iraq. Jonathan had left the military, and the lieutenant governor had gotten him a job in his financial firm. But Jonathan had not done well. He struggled in civilian life, had been diagnosed with PTSD. The lieutenant governor didn't share details of that, only that Jonathan had issues. Jonathan eventually lost his job, then his apartment. It was difficult for the lieutenant governor to share how hurtful it had been, and Oakley got the impression that he was embarrassed about his son as well, worried what people would think. The lieutenant governor had not wanted it known that his son was homeless; that piece had never been made public knowledge.

I heard detectives talking in another room, and an argument started. I tuned it out and kept reading the report. Jonathan had two older brothers, and Oakley had talked to both of them as well, along with some of Jonathan's last known friends. No one indicated that Jonathan had any enemies, much less did anyone know of someone who wanted to kill him. None of the friends seemed to dislike Jonathan, either. Jonathan had a criminal record, some petty arrests, one DUI, and nothing else. Oakley had diligently tried to find a witness to the drowning, and the homeless people he had talked to didn't know anything or weren't saying. Oakley had concluded it was an accident.

I swiveled in my chair and stared at my monitor. Everything Oakley had concluded made sense, until the autopsy report came back. That had changed everything, as he had said, the pressure was on. I read through the report again. There wasn't a lot to go on, no physical evidence, no witnesses, nothing to point us in any particular direction. I scrolled through pictures of the crime scene again, and then my heart stopped.

Jonathan had been found wearing old jeans, a ratty T-shirt, a flannel shirt, and worn shoes. What caught my eye was a gold necklace with a red stone on it that hung on his neck.

I SWORE and stared at the screen. Nicole Lockwood had been found with a ring with a red stone in it. Now this victim had a necklace with a red stone in it. Coincidence? I didn't buy it. I let fly some other choice words, then picked up my phone and called Oakley. He answered after a couple of rings.

"Where are you?" I asked briskly.

"Just dropped the knife with forensics. What's going on?"

"I've been reading your report. You didn't say anything about the necklace found on Jonathan Hall's body."

"I put it in the report. I didn't think it was anything."

"It might be. Can you get back up here?"

Consternation leaped into his voice. "Sure, I'm on my way."

I began pacing. When Oakley walked in, I pointed at the screen. "I don't believe this."

"What's going on? Why are you so excited?"

I stopped and leaned against my desk. "My victim, Nicole

Lockwood, was found with a cheap ring with a red stone on her finger."

He stared at me and his jaw dropped. "Wait. Jonathan Hall had that cheap gold necklace around his neck. It had a red stone in it. That seems too much of a coincidence." He started to speak, then shook his head slowly. "Oh wow."

I paced again, quick steps. "What do we have here? A serial killer? I just went through that."

He digested the information. "This has just gotten more complicated."

I raked a hand through my hair and thought about it. "If that's the case, is our guy going after vulnerable people? He hit a prostitute and a homeless guy. No one will notice their deaths." I stopped and put hands on my hips.

"And the cops might dismiss their deaths," Oakley finished, with shame in his voice. He cursed. "Man, I did that."

I looked him in the eye. "Don't fault yourself, but now let's make it right by finding this guy." I waved him over to my desk. "Let's compare reports to see if we can find anything else in common."

He pulled Ernie's chair over and sat down. It didn't squeak nearly as much as when my partner sat in it. I opened the report I'd created for Nicole Lockwood.

"Let's read through this."

He nodded, and we spent several minutes comparing both murders. When we finished, I looked at him.

"We have the red jewelry and the types of victims, people no one cares about, no one sees," I said. "Did you catch anything else?"

He shook his head. "No, but those two things are significant."

I crossed my arms and nodded my head in an imaginary beat. "One is killed on West Colfax, one down by the Platte. Both in the middle of the night. With one, we have a possible witness, if I can find her, but not necessarily someone reliable."

Oakley shook his head, disgusted. "What's in common doesn't help us."

"No, it doesn't." I glanced over my shoulder. "We need to let Rizzo know this, then we need to begin researching to see if we have any other victims that fit this MO."

Oakley didn't look happy about the prospect of having to talk to Rizzo.

"It'll be fine," I said.

I stood up, and Oakley followed me into Rizzo's office. He saw us approach and waved us through the door.

"You can't have any tips just yet?" He was eating an apple, and he took one final bite and dropped the core into a trash can. He wiped his hands together and looked at his wall clock. "I can't imagine the news has run the story yet."

I shook my head and sat down. "I think we might have a serial killer operating."

Rizzo's mouth twitched. "What's going on?"

I filled him in. When I finished, he leaned his elbows on his desk. "If that's the case and we do have a serial killer out there, this is way bigger than we first thought. Follett is going to have a conniption, and I can only imagine what the lieutenant governor's going to say."

Oakley shifted from foot to foot behind me. Rizzo looked up at him. "Don't worry about it, I'll handle them." His eyes went back to me. "What's your course of action?"

"We'll start looking through records, see if we can find any other open cases that might fit this MO. We're still following up with friends of Nicole Lockwood's to see if they know anything. We also have a tip about a man that she was dating in high school, possibly a cop. He might have something to do with it."

"A cop?" Rizzo frowned. "That's not good."

I nodded agreement.

Rizzo rubbed his chin. "But what would that guy have to do with a homeless vet who was killed?"

I shrugged. "I don't know yet."

Rizzo nodded. "All right, keep me posted." He narrowed his eyes at me. "I know you want to keep on this, but you make sure you get some rest, okay?"

"Yes, sir."

He picked up the phone, and we left his office.

CHAPTER EIGHTEEN

Back at my desk, Oakley said, "I'll start looking through our records to see if I can find unsolved murders where cheap jewelry was found with the victim." The office was quiet, someone on the phone in another room, then silence. Oakley glanced at my desk, as if looking for inspiration. He wasn't going to find it there.

"Searching our records is going to be a needle in a haystack." I gestured at my laptop. "Email your contacts throughout the state to see if what we have fits with any of their unsolved cases, and I'll do the same."

Oakley was nodding his head as he went to the coffeemaker. He poured a cup and drank some, then winced. "Gawd, how long has it been sitting there?"

"Try sugar and cream."

"Nothing will save that." He tossed the cup into the trash.

"I'm not as picky, I guess."

That barely drew a smile. He was worried. "I'll do some research on the jewelry found with both victims. It looks like cheap crap, bet you can buy it at Walmart, places like that.

There's no way we'll be able to trace a purchase back to a buyer. *That's* a needle in a haystack."

"Too bad." I eyed him. "We'll get to the bottom of this. I need to follow up with Lola, the woman I saw at the Princeton Motel." I glanced at my watch. "She should be on her shift soon, so I might get a bite to eat, then head down there. Let me know what you find out about any other unsolved cases."

Oakley left, and I took a few minutes to email some contacts I had in other departments around the state. I described the details of our two cases and asked them to contact me if they had any similar murder cases. I was about to head for my car, when Ernie hurried into the room.

"You're not gonna believe this," he said as he sat down. He looked at me and wagged a finger. "Were you about to leave?"

"I was going to the Diamond Club."

"Save it for a bit."

"What? Don't keep me in suspense."

"You know the guy that Nicole Lockwood was seeing? The older man?" I nodded. He took a dramatic pause. "I got his name."

I threw up a hand. "Spill it."

"Arnold. I guess she called him Arnie." He gazed at me triumphantly. "I found out from another of Nicole's friends, Lynn Richards. She saw Nicole talking to him. He was a Commerce City cop. She saw him in his cruiser, if you can believe that, somewhere near the high school. Nicole tried to blow it off, tried to make it not a big deal, but Lynn was sure she heard Nicole call him Arnie, and she teased Nicole about him."

"You don't happen to have a last name?"

"Don't harsh my buzz," he said.

I arched an eyebrow at that. "Harsh your buzz? Is that what the kids say these days?"

He laughed. "There can't be that many Arnolds that were

working with the Commerce City Police Department a few years ago. I'll make some phone calls, see what I can find out."

"When did this happen? Could Lynn pinpoint a timeframe?"

"Springtime." He shrugged. "It was a long time ago."

I grinned at him. "Still, that's good work."

"Yeah, I get wood on the bat sometimes."

"You are just full of clichés at the moment."

That got a laugh out of him. Then he picked up the phone and dialed, and as he did, he looked up at me. "Fill me in on what you've been doing."

"Oh, there's a lot."

He held up a finger. "Hold on a second. I got a contact with the department, I'll see what he can tell me." I took a seat and listened as he talked to somebody at the Commerce City Police Department. He nodded his head a few times and jotted down some notes. Then he hung up the phone. "We're in luck. My friend says there's one cop there, Arnold Culbertson. He's been on the department for a little over five years. My friend says he's a good cop."

"We'll see about that," I said. I turned to my laptop. "Let's see what we can find on him."

"Here's his picture," Ernie said, after only a few seconds. He turned his laptop around and showed me.

"Nice looking guy."

"I'm telling Harry you said that."

"I can look," I replied. I went to my favorite people-search site. "He's married, and possibly has a couple of young daughters, based on the ages listed here. If he was seeing an underage girl ..." I left the rest unsaid.

Ernie shrugged. "We don't have any proof he knew her, let alone that he slept with her. It's not a crime until that happens."

"I know." I drummed the desk with my fingers for a minute. "It's all circumstantial. We could go talk to Arnie, see if we can stir him up and get some information. What if we're wrong, though? We could be damaging his career, or worse. Who knows what he might do."

Ernie stared across his desk at me. "We're just talking to him at this point. If we're wrong, he goes on his merry way and no one knows but him and us." I still hesitated. "I don't like thinking another cop would do this, but we have to check it out. What if he was seeing Nicole back then, and now he's worried that someone found out, and he does away with her to keep the secret?"

It took me a moment to answer. "I guess I better go talk to him, and I can head to the strip club later."

He stood up and hefted up his pants. "I'm going with you. My friend said Arnie's off today, and it's about dinnertime, so maybe we catch him at home."

I checked the computer and wrote down Arnie's address. "Come on, then."

We didn't speak much on the drive to Arnie's house, a newer two-story house near Interstate 76. The neighborhood was tucked between a more rundown part of the city and the Rocky Mountain Arsenal, a wildlife refuge that was once a chemical weapons manufacturing center.

"Nice-looking house," Ernie said as I parked behind a white truck.

We heard the steady hum of traffic in the distance when we got out. As we went up the walk, we heard kids in the backyard, yelling and playing. I rang the bell and we waited. It was almost six, dinnertime for most people, and I hoped Arnie would be home. A moment later, a man with a solid build, square shoulders, and brown hair cropped short opened the door. He looked slightly older than the picture Ernie had shown me, his jaw more pronounced.

"Are you Arnold Culbertson?" Ernie asked him.

Arnie's startling blue eyes went from Ernie to me. "Yeah, what's going on?"

I introduced Ernie and myself, and we showed him our badges. His eyes narrowed.

From another room, a feminine voice called out, "Arnie? What's going on?"

"It's nothing," he called over his shoulder.

Arnie stepped onto the porch and closed the door. "Again, what's going on?" He was smart and knew that two homicide detectives coming to talk to him probably wasn't something good. Not something he wanted the woman, presumably his wife, to hear.

"Do you know Nicole Lockwood?" I asked.

He went pale, then quickly recovered himself. "Nicole who? I don't know any Nicole."

Ernie glanced at me out of the corner of his eye. He shifted slightly, to look eye to eye with Arnie, and I let him do the talking.

"Arnie, right?" Ernie asked, playing friendly to get Arnie to relax. "Are you sure about that?" Ernie played up his bemusement. "That's not the information I have."

Arnie crossed his arms, his biceps bulging, and glared at Ernie. "I'm not sure who you got your information from, but it's wrong." There was a clear challenge in his voice.

"You didn't see Nicole about three, four years ago? She would've been about sixteen. You saw her near the Adams City High School."

"Not me," Arnie said.

Ernie scratched his chin. "That's so funny. I have at least two witnesses who saw you talking to Nicole. You were in your cruiser, and it was at the end of the school day."

"Not me," Arnie repeated.

"You're sure? If it was you, it'd be better to talk to us."

Arnie's jaw clenched. "I don't know what this is about, and I don't like what you're implying. I think you need to leave now." He pointed toward the street.

I stepped in. "Nicole Lockwood was murdered last night. What do you know about that?"

Arnie wasn't giving us anything. "I don't know this Nicole, so I don't know anything about her death."

"Where were you last night?"

"I was here all night, my wife could tell you that."

"What do you know about the Princeton Motel?"

The muscles in his jaw moved. "Nothing."

"Do you know Jonathan Hall?" I started to describe him, and Arnie cut me off.

"No."

Ernie glanced toward the door. "May we talk to your wife?"

Arnie shook his head. "Get out of here." With that, he whirled around and stormed back in his house. The door banged shut.

"That went well," Ernie said.

I pondered Arnie's reaction for several seconds. "What do you think?"

"He knows her."

"That's what I think, too." I pushed his elbow. "Let's go. We have some calls to make."

CHAPTER NINETEEN

W e went back to my car and got in. Ernie squinted through the windshield. "I'll bet he's pissing his pants right now," he said. "For his sake, I hope he didn't do it. But if he did ..." He left the rest unsaid. He was angry, mad that a man, and a cop no less, could take advantage of a teenager. I was just as furious.

"What'd you think when I asked him if he knew Jonathan Hall?"

He popped a cigar in his mouth and chewed on it. "He was in robot mode. You could've asked him if the sky is blue, and he would've said no."

I nodded. "We certainly stirred things up. Now let's see where this leads." I pulled out my cell phone and looked up the Commerce City Police Department. I dialed a number and asked to speak to the chief, Ken Grafton.

"Let me call Rizzo, tell him what's up," Ernie said.

I gave him a thumbs up as I held the phone to my ear, then had to explain that I was a homicide detective from another department and that I was calling about an important matter. I was finally connected.

"I'm Homicide Detective Sarah Spillman with the Denver Police Department."

"How may I help you?" Chief Grafton spoke quickly, a man who didn't mince words.

I got right to the point as well. "I have reason to believe that an officer with your department, Arnie Culbertson, had a relationship approximately three years ago with an underage girl, who was then murdered last night."

Dead silence, and then he swore. "You're sure about this?"

I nodded as if he could see me. "I believe so. We interviewed several of the vic's friends from high school, and one says the vic was seeing a cop named Arnie. This person says she's sure he was with the Commerce City Police Department. She saw him in his cruiser."

Ernie was telling Rizzo the same thing, and I turned toward the window so Grafton wouldn't hear that conversation. I had a good view of Arnie's house. I wondered what he was doing at that moment.

"Worst case scenario is they talk to him, and it turns out to be nothing," Ernie was saying to Rizzo.

I went on with Chief Grafton. "We tried to talk to Arnie, and he clammed up. My sense is he's not telling us everything. He knows the vic, for sure."

A guttural sigh ripped through the phone. "I'll give Arnie a call as soon as we hang up. We have to get to the bottom of this right away. These are serious allegations."

"I know."

"Since this involves an investigation of yours, if you want to come down to the station and formally interview Arnie here, I'm okay with that. I'll have another detective sit in."

"Thank you, I appreciate it." I was pleased that he wasn't trying to hinder my investigation.

"I don't like these kind of allegations," he said. "Not at all. If one of my cops is dirty, I want to get it taken care of."

"I certainly understand that."

I told him that my partner and I would come down to the station soon, and I ended the call. I stared at Arnie's house.

Ernie ended his call with Rizzo and glanced at me. "Well?"

"Chief Grafton is sending someone to pick up Arnie. Things will move fast from here. What did Rizzo say? You know darn well Grafton's calling Rizzo to make sure we're on the up and up."

Ernie nodded and put an elbow on the door. "Let him. We're not the ones who messed up." I shifted to look at him, and he went on. "Rizzo is hoping we're wrong about Arnie, but he assured me that if Grafton calls him, he'll have our backs."

"Good," I said.

We watched Arnie's house for a minute. Some kids were playing in the yard across the street, and a woman walked her dog past his house. Then Arnie's garage door opened. A black truck backed out of the garage, Arnie at the wheel. He peeled away from the house, oblivious to us.

"Grafton didn't waste any time," Ernie said.

I put the key in the ignition. "I'm sure he told Arnie to report to the station pronto. And if Arnie's lying, like I think he is, he's in a full panic."

Ernie gestured at the road. "Let's get down there, too."

HALF AN HOUR LATER, Ernie, Culbertson, and another detective, Hank Wesley, were sitting with me at a rectangular table in a drab interview room at the Commerce City police station. A conspicuous camera was suspended in the corner of the room, which, by the way, smelled of disinfectant. Arnie was across from me, his hands on the table, a defiant look on his face. Tension hung like a black cloud over us.

Wesley glanced at all of us, then cleared his throat. He was heavyset, with a round face, wide eyes, his expression neutral. He noted the date and time, and who everyone was for the record, and then stated that I would be conducting the interview. He gestured for me to begin. He and Ernie stayed quiet and let me do the talking.

I looked across at Culbertson. "I really wish we didn't have to be here under these circumstances, but I'm sure we can get to the bottom of this." My try for casual wasn't working. He stared at me, expressionless. "Probably just a misunderstanding." Still nothing, so I went on. "I went to your house earlier tonight, with my partner Ernie Moore," I motioned at Ernie. "Do you recall this?"

"Yes."

"At that time, we asked you if you had any knowledge of a woman named Nicole Lockwood. Do you recall what your answer was?"

"I told you then, and I'm telling you now, I don't know who that is." Arnie had ice in his eyes.

"A few years ago, were you ever at Adams City High School?"

"Do you have a specific date?"

"Springtime."

His eyes flickered with caution. "I drive a patrol car. I'm at a lot of places at a lot of different times. I couldn't tell you if I was around the high school or not."

"So you're not denying it?" I asked.

"Nor am I confirming it," he replied.

"Do you know Lynn Richards?" I went on.

"No."

"Have you ever been to the Princeton Motel?" I asked.

"No."

"Do you own a .22?"

"No."

"Where were you early this morning, say one a.m.?"

"I was at home in bed. My wife can confirm it."

More than a yes or no answer. He was sure of that one. Or at least sure his wife could lie for him.

I kept going. "Were you on the Platte River on Wednesday night last week, anywhere between midnight and five a.m.?"

Surprise crossed his face, then disappeared. "I was at home, sleeping. Again, my wife can confirm it." He shifted in his chair, the legs scraping the tile floor with a screech.

I stared at him for a moment. He didn't blink. "Do you know Jonathan Hall?" I asked.

"No."

"Do you own any hunting knives?"

"No."

He was careful in all his answers, not giving me anything. "To reiterate, you deny knowing Nicole Lockwood or Jonathan Hall?"

"That's right."

I thought long and hard. The room was quiet. Arnie held my gaze. I finally put my hands on the table. "You know what I think?" He stared at me. "You were with Nicole when she was just a kid, and for a while, no one knew. But recently, someone discovered what happened. You're worried about your career, so you find her and take her out. Or you paid to have someone take her out. Then she can't say anything."

He blinked at me and remained silent. I thought I saw a flicker of fear in his eyes.

"Care to comment?" I asked.

"No."

I should've seen that coming.

I glanced at Ernie, and he subtly signaled he didn't have anything else to add. Arnie stared at me, his tight jaw betraying his anger. I looked over at Wesley and jerked my head toward the door.

"I'll be with you in a minute," Wesley said to Arnie. He stood up, as well as Ernie and I, and we went into the hall.

"What do you think?" Wesley asked. A detective walked past and gave a curt nod to Wesley. Wesley barely noticed.

Ernie and I exchanged a glance.

"He's a very good liar, that's what I think," Ernie blurted. "The women I talked to were certain Nicole was talking to a cop in a Commerce City squad car, and one is certain she heard Nicole call him Arnie."

I leaned my back against the wall. "He's not giving away anything, is he?"

"If he did it, his career's over," Ernie said.

Wesley looked at the interrogation room door. "Truth is, if he's lying about any of it, his career is over."

None of us said anything to that. We all knew that in law enforcement, if you lied, that was it. It didn't matter why, or about what, you were supposed to be truthful. We all also knew that Arnie Culbertson would have to take a lie detector test. If he refused, that would also end his career. There would be a criminal investigation, as well as an internal one. Ernie and I might get some information on the criminal investigation, but internal affairs wouldn't share anything they learned with us. My gut was knotted. I hoped we weren't damaging an innocent man's career. But the tied-up gut also said we were on the right track. I didn't like how Culbertson was acting, and Ernie was certain that his information was good. If that was the case, not only had Arnie traumatized Nicole Lockwood, but he may have murdered her to keep it quiet. I was going to find out.

Wesley rubbed at the back of his neck, a sure sign he was tense about what was going on. "Man oh man, what a mess." He looked back and forth the two of us. "Is there anything else you two need right now?"

I shook my head. "We appreciate your letting us talk to Culbertson."

"No problem. The last thing we need is a cop messing with underage girls. We've got to get this thing cleaned up, one way or the other." He glanced at the door again. "I wouldn't have pictured this from Arnie. And if he executed her? Man oh man," he repeated.

CHAPTER TWENTY

"The Commerce City department will be doing their own investigations on Culbertson," I said to Ernie as we ate hamburgers at a Five Guys restaurant. "But let's not wait on them. You start looking into him, okay? I'm going to see if I can talk to Lola tonight. She might know if Culbertson was seeing Nicole. Spats did say that Nicole had been seen arguing with some man."

"You got it." He licked ketchup off his finger. "You think Arnie popped Nicole so she couldn't rat him out?"

I wiped my hands with a napkin and mulled that over. "Not wanting your career ruined is a good motive to kill someone. I'd like more than circumstantial evidence, though."

"Me, too." He ate some fries. "If he did it, we'll find out."

"See if he has an interest in knives," I said.

"Oh, the knife you got from the homeless man." He nodded. "I'll check that out as well."

I paused. "I still wonder if that guy saw more than he was telling me. I'll get a picture of Culbertson and show it to him. That might get him talking."

"If you can find him."

"I got the sense he hangs around that overpass a lot."

Ernie pointed at me. "I can tell by the look in your eye that you might stop by the Platte tonight. You be careful. Things can get rough in the dark."

"Thanks for the warning, but you know me, I'll be careful."

Ernie was the protective type, and although I brushed him off, I actually appreciated his concern. He took another bite and said through the mouthful, "You think Culbertson popped Hall as well?"

I looked out a window. "I don't know. He seemed surprised when I asked him about being down on the Platte. Was he surprised because we knew about that murder, or because he didn't do it?" I looked at him. "What do you think?"

"I don't know. I'll work on his alibis. If he left his house that night, maybe someone in the neighborhood has surveillance cameras, and they'll have him on video."

"I'll talk to Oakley in the morning, and see if he knows of any connection between Culbertson and Hall. Maybe they knew each other from somewhere."

We finished our meal, and I dropped Ernie off at the station. I was heading south, on my way to the Diamond Club, when Harry called.

"How's your day going?"

"Busy," I said.

I'm sure he knew by the curt answer that I didn't have much time to talk.

"I think I can answer this," he said, "but you won't be home for dinner?"

I realized I'd been short with him. "No, hon, I'm sorry. I have one more stop, then I should be home."

I heard music in the background, and a kettle clinking. "Are you fixing dinner?"

"Yes. Some tilapia and noodles. Want me to save you some?"

"I ate, sorry."

"Then a drink and some rest. You can't push it so hard that you get sick."

"I know," I said. Just him talking about rest made me yawn. "I'll be home as soon as I can. Things are really intense right now." I told him a bit about the investigation and what was going on with Oakley's case. "I've got to track down this other prostitute."

"I understand. Be careful, okay?"

"I will."

We started to discuss some vacation plans when a call from Spats came through.

"I have to go."

"Love you," he said.

"I love you, too." I ended the call and connected with Spats.

"I've been talking to people all afternoon," he said without greeting. "My head is spinning, and I need a break. I'm going to pick things up tomorrow."

"It's been a long day. Go see your family, recharge a bit. I've got one more stop and I'll be going home for some rest, too."

"Oh, a couple of things. A few hookers I talked to knew Nicole, only no one's saying anything more than that. I mostly got asked to keep moving along so they could keep working. That and a few 'why don't I take you somewhere for some fun.' I passed on that."

I laughed. "Stick with Trissa."

"Oh, no doubt. I also talked to the bartender who worked at the Easy Bar last night. He says Steve and Madison were there for a few hours, then left about midnight. And a couple of the hookers remember seeing them sitting in a car near the Princeton."

"Selling drugs."

"Yeah. No one saw them with Nicole. So that checks out."

"We can probably cross them off our list."

"I agree. Talk to you later."

With that, he was gone.

———

THE DIAMOND CLUB parking lot was a lot more crowded now than it had been earlier in the day. I had to park on the street and walk back to the building. I felt a few curious eyes on me as I walked inside. A different bouncer was at the door. He wasn't nearly as imposing as the man I'd seen before. This guy was thin and wiry, with gold wire-rimmed glasses. His short-sleeved shirt bulged with muscles, though, and I was sure he could handle himself.

I didn't waste time showing him my badge. "I need to speak with Lola."

He hesitated. I was tired, not in the mood for any games. "Is Victor Golic here?"

"Uh, sure."

"Get him," I snarled, then muttered, "I'm not taking no for an answer."

His gaze darted around, and he seemed to quickly realize he had no choice. He called on the phone behind him, and Golic soon came to the front. He saw me and frowned.

"I know you want to talk to Lola," he said with a head shake, "but she's ... indisposed at the moment."

"And as I told this fellow," I pointed at the bouncer, "I'm not taking no for an answer. Get her for me. Now."

Golic, too, saw I wasn't going to be dissuaded, and he finally said, "Give me a minute, please." He spun around and disappeared into the club.

I stood with the bouncer and waited. A new song came on

"Kiss," by Prince. It had a great beat, and the bouncer started to subtly dance. He saw me watching him and stopped. Golic came back a moment later and gestured for me to follow him. We walked through the club, and I ignored the naked women pole-dancing on a long stage. The place smelled of greasy food, sweat, and sex. I resisted putting a finger under my nose to block the smell. On the other side of the room, we went down a tight hall-way. The music grew slightly less loud, and Golic stopped in front of a door. He tapped on it, then opened it.

CHAPTER TWENTY-ONE

"Lola, this cop would like to talk to you."

He stepped aside and I entered the room. An unpleasant mix of heavy perfume and cigarette smoke lingered in the air. Golic looked at us. I waited a beat, then said, "You can shut the door."

He frowned at me, then eyed Lola. "Don't take too long. Myra will be finished soon, and she'll need to finish her break while you go back on stage." He quietly shut the door.

Lola was sitting at a long makeup counter, one with bright lightbulbs all the way around a large mirror. She was probably in her late twenties, with long black hair, red fingernails, dark eye shadow that enhanced blue eyes, and lashes so long I didn't see how they couldn't be annoying. A scanty robe covered her nude body, her breasts of a shape and size not likely found in nature. Heavy makeup couldn't hide the scarring on her face that was more pronounced than I realized, a long, reddish spot, possibly from a burn. I made sure not to stare.

"What do you want?" she asked. Her voice was low and gravelly, forced boredom in her tone. If she was concerned that I was a cop, she wasn't showing it.

I didn't waste her time. "You know a woman named Nicole Lockwood? Pixie Dust?"

"Sure, I know her." She grabbed a pack of cigarettes from the counter and lit one, which of course is illegal. But I think she and I both knew I wasn't concerned with that at the moment.

She stared at me, one eye slightly drooped, as if daring me to mention it.

"I saw you at the Princeton Motel the other night." She didn't say anything, so I went on. "Tell me what you know about Nicole Lockwood's death." The music from the club pounded, and we spoke loudly to be heard over it.

"I don't know what you're talking about." Her voice shook slightly.

A rickety chair sat in the corner, and I pulled it close to her and sat down. "Lola, I'm sure you're scared, but I need you to tell me the truth. Someone shot Nicole, execution-style, and I don't think this was just somebody who was mad at her. This was something more."

Her bottom lip trembled. She smoked, stared at the floor, and whispered, "She was my friend."

I nodded. "She didn't deserve what happened to her."

She shook her head. "It all happened so fast." I waited, and she finally looked up. "I don't want to get in any trouble."

"You won't. Not from me. What did you see?"

"I was in a room at the motel, you know?" She left the rest unsaid. "We – me and the guy – had just finished, and we were about to leave the room. I opened the door, and then we saw the car." She drew in a breath, let it out slowly. "Someone pushed Nicole out, and she just tumbled to the ground." She squeezed her eyes shut, as if picturing it. "Then the car drove away." She paused. "I didn't know what to do at first. I thought maybe

Nicole had been beaten up. She didn't move, and we went outside and looked at her. Then I knew she was dead." She stopped talking.

"What happened next?"

Her mouth moved, but no words came out.

"It's okay," I said gently.

She took a drag from the cigarette and blew smoke away from me. "Ch –" She stopped before she said the john's name. "I said we should call the police, and he said no way, he wasn't going to get involved. He's terrified that his wife will find out that he sees prostitutes. He ran off and left me there. I didn't want to get in any trouble, either, so I went down the street to a gas station and used their phone to call the police."

"Then you went back to the motel and watched for the police to arrive."

She nodded. "I didn't know what else to do. I was scared, and I didn't know if someone had been looking for any prostitute, or just Nicole. I didn't want anything to happen to her until the police got there, so I watched."

"Did anybody else do anything to the body?"

She shook her head. "No. It didn't take that long for the police to arrive, and I only saw that guy Steve, the one who sells drugs with his girlfriend Madison. They were watching the parking lot, and I think they were going to see if Nicole had any money on her, but then the cops showed up, and they ran away and came back later, right before you chased me."

"Tell me about the car."

She thought for a second. "It was black."

"Did you see the license plates?"

"No."

"You're sure?"

She smoked. "I don't pay attention to stuff like that."

"What make of car? The model?

She shrugged. "I don't know. I'm not good with cars. I was so surprised about what happened, I didn't really pay attention."

"Was it two-door or four-door?"

She closed her eyes, as if trying to picture it. "Four-door, I think."

"Was it a fancy car, or an SUV, or just an ordinary sedan?"

She frowned. "I'm sorry, I just don't know."

"Do you think the guy you were with would know?"

A hand went to her mouth. "You can't talk to him. He would get in so much trouble, and he'd be pissed that I said anything. He's a good customer of mine. Nice."

I leaned forward. "Don't you want to find out who killed Nicole?"

The trembling lip grew more pronounced and a tear rolled down her cheek. "Yes, but I need the work." She glanced into the mirror. "You know how hard it is when you look like this?"

I nodded slowly. I could only imagine, but I still needed to find the man she'd been with. "I'll be discreet."

We waited. The music pounded through the walls. She crushed her cigarette out in an ashtray.

"His name is Chuck," she finally said. "I don't know his last name."

It was something. "You've got to help me find him," I pressed her.

She bit her lip. "He goes to a coffee shop on Colfax, near Wadsworth, to work. He does some kind of freelance writing and editing. Not early, though. He joked about how he hates to get up before seven, so he's there later in the morning, then sometimes meets his wife for lunch. I only know that because one time after, well, you know, we were talking, and he told me that he liked to work with people around there, and that he was there a lot."

"What does he look like?"

"He's kind of average height, a little heavy around the middle. His hair is thinning some."

"What color?"

"Brown."

"His eyes?"

"They're brown, too."

"What kind of car does he drive?"

"A white Hyundai, an SUV."

"Anything else you can tell me?" I pressed her. "You just described a lot of men. Any tattoos?"

"Yeah, on his back. But you can't see it unless his shirt's off."

"What else?"

She pointed to her left hand. "His wedding ring. It's not a band, but more like a class ring."

"That's something," I said. "Did Nicole ever talk about an older man that she dated in high school?"

She shook her head. "All I know is she had kind of a rough time, didn't get along with her mother, and her father died. I think that crushed her, and she was always looking for a way out. Unfortunately, it didn't work out the way she had hoped. She always said that she wanted to be a singer, but she really didn't have the drive, or the talent."

"Can you think of anybody who would've wanted to kill her?"

"No, she was cool. Popular with the guys."

"Did you hear about her having a fight with a man last week? They were shouting at each other."

"I hadn't seen her in a few days, so I don't know about that. You think that guy might've done this to her?"

"It's a possibility."

She shook her head slowly. "I just don't know. It's terrible, though."

I locked eyes with her. "You're telling the truth?"

"Yes, of course."

"If what you're telling me is true, you know this guy is your alibi. And you're his."

A hand shot to her throat. "You don't think I did that to Nicole, do you?"

"I have to check everything." The reality was I didn't think she did it, but I had to check everything, including her alibi. "May I see your ID? Just routine."

Lola hesitated, then reached down under the counter and pulled out a small purse. She got out her ID and showed it to me.

"Lola is your real name," I said.

She smiled, slightly crooked due to the scarring on her face. "Lola, like the song by the Kinks. My parents loved that song, and the Kinks. I got so sick of hearing them."

"The Kinks. That's going back a ways."

She nodded. "Yeah, it is. Personally, I hate the song."

"I liked 'You Really Got Me' better."

She shrugged. She probably hadn't listened to a Kinks song in a long time.

A knock on the door interrupted us, and Golic stuck his head in. "Lola, you need to get back on stage." He looked at me, and his eyes narrowed, daring me to challenge him.

"Lola," I said, "Thanks for your time."

Golic shut the door, and she glared. "Man, I hate him. I wish I didn't have to be here. He thinks he owns me," she muttered.

I didn't have a response to that. I stood up and put a business card on the counter. "Call me if you think of anything important, something that might lead me to Nicole's killer."

I left the dressing room, ignored stares as I exited the club, and drove down Santa Fe to Mississippi. I parked and walked to the overpass. I googled Culbertson's picture on my phone, then got on the bike path. It was dark, and the sounds of Sante Fe made it hard to hear anyone or anything on the path. I looked where I had seen the homeless man, but he wasn't around. I walked north and came across a homeless woman in tattered clothes. I showed her Culbertson's picture, and she shook her head and asked for money. I gave her some cash and moved on. After ten minutes, my efforts produced nothing, so I gave up, walked back to my car, and drove home.

THE KITCHEN WAS quiet when I walked in the door. I kicked off my shoes and padded through the house. I found Harry in his home office. It's sparse, white walls with one black-and-white picture of the mountains above his desk, a file cabinet in the corner, one bookcase with business books. He's a big '70s music fan, and Foreigner was playing. I stood in the doorway and watched him for a second. He was concentrating, staring at the monitor, and he didn't hear me. I love the way his eyes look when he's thinking, the crow's feet around the edges. For some reason, it's sexy to me.

"Hey there," I said.

He jumped and spun around in the chair. "I didn't hear you come in."

I nodded. "You look like you're concentrating hard."

"I'm glad you're home." He turned the music off. "Just some contracts for work. It's nothing."

Harry owns his own consulting company, and he sometimes keeps long hours. He stood up and walked over to me. He gave me a gentle kiss, then said, "You look tired." He wrapped his arms around me and squeezed, then whispered in my ear, "I missed you."

I let him hold me for a second, then stepped back. "It was a crazy day."

"Yeah, for me, too."

"I'm beat." I pointed at his desk. "You finish whatever you need to. I'm going to bed."

He waved a hand at the computer. "It can wait."

We went into the bedroom, undressed, and crawled under the covers. I laid on my side, and he wrapped an arm around me. My mind still raced.

"Diane called today."

"Oh?"

I told him about the call.

"Wow, she actually said all that?" he said.

"Yes. It surprised me."

He moved his arm and rubbed my neck. "I'd say that's a really positive thing. She's making some effort."

"Did you have anything to do with that? Did you talk to her?"

He chuckled. "No, I didn't. That was all on her own."

I shifted my head on the pillow. "It was good to hear. I needed that."

"Yeah, you did. You don't need to blame yourself."

"I guess you're right."

He kept rubbing my neck. Exhaustion finally set in, and I was soon asleep. I didn't have any nightmares.

CHAPTER TWENTY-TWO

Marilyn had been poking around another clandestine chatroom when she noticed there was a message from the group. That was odd, because contact was limited, and since they had met earlier in the day about her deed, she didn't expect to hear anything until tomorrow at the earliest. For Teddy to make contact now, it must be something important. She checked the message, and was told to be in the chat room at eleven p.m. That would be easy to do. Her husband wouldn't be suspicious; she was a night owl and was on the internet a lot when she couldn't sleep. He'd be in bed, oblivious to what she was doing. That seemed to be their way. She thought about her husband for a moment. They had been in love, once. Not anymore. But they kept up appearances, and they did occasionally have fun together. She shook her head to clear away those thoughts and left her office.

She spent the evening wondering what had happened, what was going on in the group to prompt a special meeting. As she ate dinner, she puzzled through options and landed on one she hadn't dared allow herself before. What if Teddy said they all could kill again? She'd been pondering whether she could do it again. She went back to last night. The exhilaration she'd felt had been astonishing. She had tried to compare it to something. She'd gotten high back when she was in high school, so long ago. Marijuana was okay, and she'd even tried cocaine. She enjoyed the feeling, the rush, but this was a thousand times better than that. Another deed, though? It would be a huge risk. Was she willing to take it? She'd been careful the other night, but what about a second time? So much was running through her head that even her husband noticed she was distracted. She brushed him off and went back to thinking about her deed. She'd never allowed herself to think about doing it again.

Could she?

After dinner, she watched TV for a while. Her husband was early to bed and early to rise, and he retired to their bedroom by nine. Marilyn fixed a Scotch and went into the study. For once, she wasn't on the internet. She sat in her chair, listened to Mozart, and stared into space. At eleven o'clock, she logged into the chat room.

Teddy: *The Guild will now come to order.*

Teddy asked everyone to adhere to the rules of the group. A round of agreement from all the members. Marilyn stared at the screen and waited for Teddy's next move.

Teddy: *Did any of you watch the news channels this evening?*

Everyone said no, except for Brad Pitt.

Brad: *Yes, I saw Channel Four.*

Teddy: *Did you see the story about Jonathan Hall?*

Marilyn sipped her drink. The name meant nothing to her.

Brad: *Yes, he's the son of Carlton Hall.*

That name Marilyn knew. He was the lieutenant governor of Colorado, and she'd met him and his family. She set down her glass. What did this have to do with the group?

Teddy: *Correct. Jonathan Hall, Carlton's son, was killed down*

on the South Platte. He was homeless. This was a certain someone's deed.

He was careful in how he phrased things. The chat stayed
silent for a moment. Marilyn stared at the blinking cursor. Then
someone spoke up.

Joe: *Daffy, how could you be so careless???*

Marilyn could almost feel his anger. No one was supposed to
kill a high-profile person.

Daffy Duck: *He was a homeless guy! How was I to know that
he was the son of the lieutenant governor? It's not like he had that
written on his clothes, and I didn't search for an ID.*

Pete: *Didn't you research your victim at all?*

Daffy Duck: *Of course I did. I watched homeless people for a
while, watched where they hung out and where they went. I spied
on that guy for a week or two. Trust me, he was never with anyone
except other homeless guys. There was no way I could've known
who he was.*

Marilyn watched the screen, her Scotch in her hand. She
didn't realize her hand was trembling. Brad Pitt and Daffy Duck
began arguing, Brad's comments littered with swearing. Marilyn
had never been fond of so much swearing.

Teddy: *Please stop, all of you. This is not how we conduct
ourselves.*

Marilyn had long ago put a voice to his typing, and to her he
sounded sophisticated, with the trace of a British accent. Even
now, the way he worded things. So calm, and yet so in control.

Teddy: *The police are now calling Hall's death suspicious,
and they are asking for the public's help. They are treating this
case very seriously. Daffy, are you sure there were no witnesses, no
one that could trace anything back to you?*

Daffy Duck: *I'm positive. I didn't make any mistakes.*

Pete: *You'd better be damn sure. This could bring us all down.
And you know what, I won't let that happen.*

Marilyn didn't know what that threat meant. Even though she had plans for what she would do if things got too close to her, she'd never really thought seriously about it. Would she have to actually implement her plans?

Brad Pitt and Daffy Duck began arguing again.

Teddy: *Stop, before someone reveals something they shouldn't. Regardless of how we got here, this situation can only be resolved in one way. The Guild is now terminated. We will all go our separate ways, and no one must speak about this again.*

Joe: *Wait a minute. I haven't had my turn.*

Teddy: *I do apologize, but it has to be this way. We cannot risk anyone getting caught, and now, with police involvement in Daffy's deed, we cannot proceed.*

Joe: *That's not fair! Others got their turn, and I listened to them talk about how great it was. I want my chance. I'm finally ready to act, and I have to do it.*

Teddy: *No.*

Joe: *You got to experience this, now it's my turn.*

Brad: *Joe, get over it. You can't jeopardize everyone.*

Joe: *Shut up, Brad. You got your turn.*

Teddy: *This discussion is over. Please adhere to the group rules. This group shall go no further, and I will be shutting down this chat room. I wish you all the best. It's time to sign off.*

Marilyn saw that Joe Smith tried to say something else, but then the chat ended. She sat back and stared at her monitor. This was a stunning turn of events. She felt for Joe, not being able to experience what she had. And she'd wondered about him. He was, in her opinion, brash. He came across impulsive. What would he do? He had sworn to the Guild rules, but he was so upset about not getting his turn. Would he adhere to those rules? Another thought crossed her mind: Did Teddy secretly know who they all were, and would he be able to stop Joe, or any of them, if they acted irrationally? Marilyn realized she would never know.

As she listened to the music, she felt a sudden sense of loss. Even though she had never met any of these people, had no idea if they were men or women, they had become like friends to her. She looked forward to their discussions, and to hearing how things had gone for them. She wondered if the others felt the same about her. She was sad to see it all end.

She picked up her Scotch glass and drained it, then shut down her laptop and went into the kitchen. She left her glass there and went to bed.

CHAPTER TWENTY-THREE

On my way to the office the next morning, I stopped at the apartment on Race Street to see Rachel Ingalls. It was early, and when I rang the apartment, no one answered. I kept at it until someone buzzed me in. When I went upstairs, Rachel answered, her hair askew, face drawn.

"What do you want?" she muttered.

"Are Misty Chandler and Gwen Pruitt here?"

She didn't have any fight in her. "Yeah, hold on."

A minute later, two young women, both in T-shirts and shorts, plodded to the door. I introduced myself, and they stared at me. Both looked worn out.

"You both know Nicole Lockwood?"

"Yeah," both said.

I went through the same questions I had with Rachel the previous day, and the only extra information I got was that Misty knew the same guy, Chuck, that Lola did.

"Do you have a last name?" I asked.

She shook her head. "They don't give last name, you know?"

"What does he look like?"

"I don't know, kind of heavy, thinning hair."

"Average," I said.

"Yeah."

I pushed them a bit, but they didn't have any more information. I left, at least knowing Misty had confirmed what Lola had said. I drove to the station and was sitting at my desk when Oakley walked in with the folding knife in his hand. He held it up, and had a hopeful look on his face.

"What did you find out?" I asked him. I'd caught up on a little sleep, but still felt I was dragging a bit, and the coffee I was drinking was fresh and black.

"Forensics did some overtime work on this one, since it has to do with the lieutenant governor's son. They said there's DNA from a couple of different sources, and none of it belongs to Jonathan Hall."

I tapped a staccato beat on my desk with a pen. "If the vic owned the knife, wouldn't we expect his DNA on the knife?"

"I would think so."

"Me, too."

Oakley studied the knife through the baggie. "There's traces of human blood on it. None of the DNA samples match to anything in the databases."

I held out my hand and he handed me the bag. I twirled the knife around. "It's fancy, but I know next to nothing about knives. Can you get something like this at a Walmart?"

He shook his head. "No, you can't. This is a custom-made knife." He put his hands to his face and drew his fingers down over his mouth. "I worked on that last night, searched the internet, made a lot of phone calls, learned more than I ever care to know about knives."

"How can you tell it's custom-made?"

He held up a hand. "The blade is hand-forged, the handle is made from something special, although I don't know what. I was going crossed-eyed from looking at all the variations, so I stopped researching. One thing I did discover." He nodded toward the knife. "If you look on the bottom end of the blade, near the handle, there's a little mark on the metal."

I peered closely through the plastic and saw a tiny symbol. "What's this? A couple of 'P's?"

"Something the person making the knife put in when he forged the blade. It took me a while to track down the symbol, but there's a guy here in town who makes knives: Pete Palmer. He owns a small hunting and fishing supply store on the corner of Zuni and Alameda. It opens at ten. Unfortunately, I have a meeting with the chief and the lieutenant governor this morning." He scrunched up his face unhappily. "Can you believe this? They're pushing me hard now, want to know in less than twenty-four hours what kind of progress we've made." He snorted. "Hall thinks because we had a press conference, things are going to magically turn around on this. All we've gotten from the tip line so far is a bunch of stupid rumors, everything from a guy reporting his neighbor as the killer to, I kid you not, a Russian conspiracy. And of course we have to check out everything, because there might be something that really is a good lead."

"Nothing good?"

He shook his head with a wry smile. "Not so far. It's taken a hell of a lot of extra time, though."

"Yes," I sympathized with him. "Been there, done that. If only people understood how investigations really went."

That brought a laugh. I continued to twirl the bag between my hands. "I got a name of the john who was with Lola."

"The hooker from the motel who reported the murder?"

"Yes, that one." I told him about my conversation with her. "Tell you what. I need to stop at a coffee shop, see if I can find this guy, and then I'll go by Palmer's shop." I set the knife down. "I want to know what's going on with this."

"That'd be great. What have you found out on your investigation?"

I gnawed my lip. "We managed to track down a guy that Nicole was seeing when she was underage. Get this, he's a cop."

He rubbed his hands over his face again. "Man, with everything going on these days, that's not good."

I nodded. "You got that right."

"You think someone found out about them, so he offed her?"

I thought about that. "I'm not sure. We interviewed him last night, and I've got Ernie looking into him more. We need to canvas the area around the Platte again, take his picture and see if anyone recognizes him. That homeless guy might know more than he's saying, and a picture might help."

"If you can find him."

"I looked for him last night, but no luck."

"I'll get some detectives on it today. What's he look like?"

I described the old man, then said, "I emailed you Culbertson's picture. And I gave Ernie and Spats the rundown a little bit ago. Spats went to West Colfax to see if he can find anyone who saw Culbertson there the other night. If we could place him around the motel, let him know someone saw him ..."

"He might cave and confess?" Oakley finished as he went over to the coffeemaker in the corner and returned with a cup of coffee. "I didn't get a ton of sleep last night, and I'm sure that's going to be the case until I can get this resolved."

"I'm right with you."

"Do you figure this cop offed Jonathan Hall?"

"I don't know. I'd ask Hall if he knows Culbertson, or if he thinks Jonathan knew him. Maybe Culbertson had a beef with Jonathan and killed him."

"I'll ask him, and ask around, too, to see if I can find a connection between Culbertson and the Hall's son." He didn't look happy. "I appreciate the help, even if I didn't seem like it yesterday. I don't want this to ruin *my* career."

I brushed that off. "Get prepared for your meeting with the chief, tell them that you're tracking down all the leads from the tip line, but don't tell them you're wasting a bunch of time on it. That'll only make them angry. I'll follow up on this," I pointed at the knife, "and let you know what I find out."

"Thanks." With that, he left.

Lola Tyndale had said that Chuck, the man she was with when they saw Nicole dumped in the motel parking lot, hung out at a coffee shop near Colfax and Wadsworth. My research showed a Starbucks nearby, and I stopped there for coffee and watched for a man she described: average height, a little heavy, with thinning brown hair and brown eyes. Nicole had said Chuck wouldn't be getting coffee too early, so I thought I'd spend what time I could there. Whenever I saw a man like that, I paid attention to his left fourth finger to see if he wore something like a class ring. No one fit the bill, so I finally left. On my way to the hunting and fishing shop, I called the station and asked for surveillance on the shop. That way, I could channel my resources elsewhere.

Sharply at ten, I was at the hunting and fishing shop Oakley had told me about. I had no idea of the shop's name, as the sign above the door read, "Supply." I walked in, and a man with light hair and a goatee stood behind a counter at the back. The shop was packed with all sorts of hunting and fishing supplies, rods, nets, camping equipment. I smelled leather and oil.

I walked up to the counter, and he looked at me curiously. "May I help you?"

I showed him my badge and introduced myself. Before I could say more, he said, "Homicide?"

I nodded and put the bagged knife down on the counter. "Do you know anything about this knife?"

He stared at the bag for a moment as if it might bite him, then finally picked it up. He turned the knife around in the bag, then nodded. "Sure, this is a specialty knife that I make."

"That's your mark on the blade?"

"Yes, my initials. Pete Palmer."

"How many of this particular style of knife have you made?"

"Not that many." He was scant on details.

"Do you keep records of the knives you make?"

"Yes." He gazed almost lovingly at the knife. "Most people just go out and buy knives, whatever they can find at a store, like here. They hunt and fish. They might be ex-military." He pointed at knives in a display case near the counter. Then he was back to the bagged knife. "But something like this? This is for someone who wanted something a little bit different, something special. They come to a blade-smith like me, and I work to their specifications. The weight of the knife, the length of the blade, the handle, all worked to perfection so the blade is like an extension of their hand. I've been making knives for ten years. People want them for hunting, collectors want them, some people just want to show off." His shoulders lifted. "There's a story behind each one."

I pointed at the knife. "This particular one, who did you make it for?"

He stepped back from the counter as if it was suddenly on fire. "I have a varied clientele, and some of my customers wouldn't want that information revealed."

I held out my hand and he returned the knife. "That would make me think you deal with criminals."

His laugh was a few short, hesitant breaths. "I'm not saying that. And I'm not saying that I do anything illegal. Everything I do is on the up-and-up."

I smiled pleasantly. "I'm sure that's the case. I'm in the middle of a murder investigation, and I need to know who you made this knife for."

He shook his head slowly. "I'm afraid I can't tell you. That's confidential."

"I can't be the first cop that's come here wanting to know about a knife that you made for someone."

"No, and I'll tell you what I told the others. If you want that information, you're going to have to get a warrant." He wasn't smug, just matter-of-fact.

I tried for nice. "You're sure we can't avoid that? Time is precious, and having to track down a judge will delay things."

He shook his head slowly. "A warrant, or I don't say anything."

My instincts don't fail me often, but they did then. I couldn't tell if he knew more than he was saying, or if he only had the confidentiality of his customers in mind, and knew his legal rights. I looked slowly around the store, then back at him. His gaze held the same determination as before. Sometimes, I would point out that a warrant would bring extra scrutiny to the store, and to the owner. In this case, he seemed so sure of himself, I figured I would be wasting my breath.

"Okay," I said. "A warrant it is."

He didn't respond, so I turned around and left.

CHAPTER TWENTY-FOUR

"How'd your talk with Follett go?" I asked Oakley. I could hear office sounds in the background, someone carrying on a loud conversation. After my visit to the hunting and fishing shop, I was on Colfax, headed back to the station.

"Oh, he's irritated," Oakley said. "I told him we were handling things, going through all the evidence, checking all the tips, but it didn't seem to be enough." He sounded discouraged.

"Maybe this will get your spirits up." I told him about my conversation with Pete Palmer at the hunting and fishing shop.

"Do you think he's hiding something?"

"Like who owns that knife?" I stopped at a traffic light at Broadway and stared at the car in front of me. "Could be. He certainly wasn't going to be pushed into giving me the information."

"I'll get on a warrant right away."

Ernie was calling, so I told Oakley I would catch up with him later.

"I've been doing some research on Arnie Culbertson," Ernie

began. "You're not going to believe this. We saw him drive a truck last night, but his wife drives a four-door Ford Fusion. A sedan."

I thought back to my conversation with Lola. "She said that the car she saw was a dark sedan."

"Yep. The Culbertson car is black. What if Arnie took his wife's car over to the motel and took care of Nicole?"

"You think he'd be that stupid? If somebody saw him, they'd be able to trace the car back to him, just like you did."

Ernie grunted. "I don't know, maybe he panicked. Or he thought he could get away with it. He was stupid enough to be seen in his cruiser hitting on an underage girl, maybe he's stupid enough to screw up her murder."

Traffic can get snarled up near Broadway, and I crept through the light, only to be stopped at Lincoln Avenue. "What else have you found out?"

"I ran a background check, too. Culbertson's clean, nothing to note. Finances look good. He owns a Glock *and* a .22."

"Wait. I specifically asked him if he owned a .22, and he said no."

"I remember. I called Wesley at the Commerce City department, told him they should double-check with Culbertson on that."

"Culbertson'll say he sold the gun, or it was stolen."

"Uh-huh. How many people bother with the registration when they sell a gun?"

"Same thing if it was stolen," I said sarcastically. "No way to trace it." I finally turned onto Lincoln. "Could you tell if Culbertson owns any specialty knives?"

"Not so far. I've talked to a couple of his friends, they've never seen him with the kind of knife you got from the homeless guy."

"Did you try to talk to his wife?"

" 'Tried' being the operative word. I went by Culbertson's

house and lucked out. She answered the door, but when I started asking questions, she slammed it in my face."

"I'm not surprised. Culbertson probably told her he was being investigated, but not for what."

"I'm a nice guy, she could've talked to me." He was mock hurt.

I laughed. "Be careful. Culbertson knows he's being investigated, and if he's guilty of what we think he is, he might kill again."

"Don't worry about me."

I pulled into a parking place at the station, cut the engine, and sat for a moment. "I'm still back to this, though. If he killed Jonathan Hall, why?"

"I've been noodling on that one, too. Culbertson's a vet. What if they knew each other, and Hall also knew that Arnie liked underage girls?"

"Oakley's digging into that to see if he can find a connection between the two men. I'm telling you, just when I feel like we may be getting closer to something ..."

"It's a marathon, not a sprint."

"There you go with the clichés."

"If the shoe fits ..."

I laughed again. "Stop it! And keep me posted."

He ended the call. I was about to get out of the car when Spats called.

"Speelmahn," he greeted me. "What are you up to?"

I gave him a rundown on my morning. "I have pieces, nothing concrete."

"Maybe this'll cheer you up," he said, sounding eerily like me talking to Oakley. "I finally found some surveillance video of the motel. It's a 7-Eleven that's just down the block and across the street from the Princeton. The manager ran back the video for me. The 911 call came in around one a.m., correct?"

"Yes, that's true."

"Good. Around that time, two cars drove out of the motel lot, both of them four-door sedans, like Lola said. And get this, I was able to get license plates on both."

"Really? The 7-11 must have good cameras."

"Yeah," Spats said. "Apparently the old ones recently crapped out, and the owner put new ones in. These new cameras can pick up so much more, it's incredible."

"Good for us, bad for the criminals. What are the license plate numbers?"

Spats rattled them off, and I wrote them down. "I just got to the station," I said. "Why don't you head back here as well? We can track down these plate numbers and talk to the owners."

"I'll see you there soon."

"So the first one is Mike Densmore," I said to Spats when he walked into the room.

"Hold on." He went to his desk and sat down. He was back to his fashionable self today, in a dark suit, pinstripe tie, and perfectly polished shoes. He looked great. "Have you researched him?"

"Not yet."

"I'll run a check on him."

"The second one is Robert Herrera," I said. "I'll check him."

"Michael Densmore." He hummed as he typed on the computer.

"You're cheery," I said.

He looked up and smiled tentatively. "You know how things have been a little ... tense ... with Trissa?"

"Yes."

He pondered what he was going to say. "We had a good talk

last night. It was late, I was dead tired, and yet ..." He searched for the right words. "Maybe that made me a little more 'vulnerable.' Her words. I was just sharing how hard this job can be, and how I see such crap on the streets, and I come home to her and it's all okay. You know?"

I nodded. "I do." I felt that way with Harry. He's my rock. I didn't know how I would've gotten through the aftermath of the Welch shooting without him.

"Yeah, you know," Spats said, reading my face. He shrugged. "It was good. We're close. I'm not sure how to explain it."

"You don't have to."

He smiled and turned back to his laptop. After a moment, he said, "Densmore is forty years old, he's had two DUIs, but other than that, his arrest record is clean. Let me check LinkedIn and some social media sites, see what else I can find out."

While he did that, I looked at Robert Herrera. "My guy doesn't have an arrest record at all. And his name is common enough, I'm not sure who the right one is. I got a driver's license photo, but there's so many Robert Herreras on LinkedIn and social media, it could take forever to find the correct Herrera."

Spats gave me a look, feeling my pain. "Densmore works at some kind of tech company downtown. Looks like he's a programmer. All this stuff listed on his profile is Greek to me. My guess would be he wouldn't want anybody to know he's been to a sleazy motel on West Colfax."

My desk phone rang and I picked it up.

"It's Jack Jamison. I have the autopsy results on Nicole Lockwood."

"How are you?" I asked. I knew better than to start asking him any substantive questions yet. He'd tell me what he knew when he was ready, not a moment sooner.

"I'll be sending you the report later today or tomorrow, but I hear there might be some heat on this investigation, so I thought I'd call."

"Thanks, I appreciate it."

"As I'm sure you surmised, she died from two shots to the back of her skull. I didn't find signs of other trauma, but she did have some postmortem cuts and bruises on her knees. Tests show no signs of poisons, although she did have marijuana in her system. We'll get a full toxicology, but as you know, that will take a while. She had needle marks on her arms, so I would conclude she used harder drugs recently." He read some technical jargon.

"So it doesn't appear she was somehow subdued, either physically or with harder drugs, before she was shot."

"You know I can't make conclusions."

"Come on, Jack, give me your gut feeling."

He sighed. "I would doubt it, but I wouldn't say that in court."

"Thanks, Jack, I appreciate it."

I hung up the phone and told Spats what Jamison had said.

"So basically he told us what we already knew," he said.

I nodded. "Yeah, not that helpful."

He stood up and adjusted his tie. "I think I'll go have a little chat with Mike Densmore in person. Take him by surprise, so he doesn't have time to think up any lies. I'll let you know what I find out."

"I can't find anything on this guy." I stood up as well. "I'll drop by his house and see if he's around."

"What if he's at work?" Spats asked.

I frowned. "I don't know. I'll cross that bridge when I come to it." I'd had too much time at my desk the last month, and I didn't want to sit around staring at the computer any more than I had to. I needed to be moving, doing something active.

We both headed downstairs to our cars, and I drove west again. I soon parked in front of a small home in a neighborhood near the Princeton Motel. The yard was tiny, the lawn a late September dry. Two rickety barrel planters on either side of the porch steps were bare of flowers. I went up the steps and rapped on the door. My energy belied my mood. I felt like we were doing a lot, just not getting anywhere.

"Hey." The woman who answered the door said. She wore shorts, and she was wiping something off a yellow T-shirt. Somewhere in the house, a toddler wailed.

"Is Robert Herrera available?"

"He's at work." She glanced over her shoulder, flustered. "You want to give me your name, and I'll have him call you? Or you can stop by later."

I showed her my badge. "I need to talk to him about an open investigation."

"What's this about?" Now she was apprehensive. "Bob's not in some kind of trouble?" The toddler's protestations reached a high pitch. "Hold on a second."

She spun around and shut the door. I could still hear the baby, then the crying suddenly stopped. The door opened again, and the woman had a small girl propped on her hip. "What's going on?" the woman asked.

I held back telling her anything. "I'm afraid I can't divulge the details, but I do need to speak to Robert."

"He goes by Bob, and he's at work."

"Where's that?"

The little girl fussed a bit, but stayed relatively quiet. "He works at Byers Industries in Golden. He's in IT. I don't know the address. It's near the Coors plant."

"I'm sure I can find it," I said. "Thank you for your time."

I turned around before she could ask more, and hurried to my car. I knew she'd be on the phone with Bob right away, and I needed to get to his workplace before he had a chance to dodge me.

CHAPTER TWENTY-FIVE

Bob Herrera worked a block off of Washington Street, the main street in downtown Golden. As I got out of the car, the hops smell from the nearby Coors Brewery assaulted my nostrils. I'm not much of a beer drinker, and I didn't find the smell appealing. Cirrus clouds swept a blue sky as I strolled into the office building, a two-story reddish box with lots of windows to take in the view of the mesas and foothills that surrounded the town. I didn't see stairs, so I took an elevator, the old thing groaning as it deposited me up one floor. Byers Industries was on the right, the lobby done in bright blue and white, almost garish. I walked up to a counter where a receptionist was working at a computer, her forehead pinched in concentration. I asked for Bob Herrera, and she called back to him, then went back to whatever project was causing her such consternation, making no attempt to muffle unhappy sounds.

I was sure that Bob's wife – I'm assuming that's who the woman with the toddler was – had called ahead, so Bob would be expecting me. I took it as a good sign that he hadn't left the office. I bounced on the balls of my feet until a tall, twenty-something man with a thin mustache hurried into the reception area. Before I could say anything, he pointed at the doors.

"Let's go outside." His voice was deep and tinged with irritation. He'd definitely heard from his wife.

I followed him into the hall. A couple came out of the elevator, and Bob nodded at them, then hurried around a corner to a stairwell. He didn't say a word to me. We went outside and sat at a metal bench near the building entrance. A tall tree blocked the sun's rays, and it was pleasant.

"Are you the cop that stopped by the house?" he asked. I nodded and introduced myself. He paused to tug at his shirtsleeve, worked to calm himself down, then pasted a smile on his baby face. "What's going on? I haven't done anything wrong. Why didn't you tell my wife anything?" The questions came fast, his voice a nervous jangle.

"Are you sure you would want me asking questions around your wife?"

He put an arm up on the side of the bench and turned toward me, the face now full of bewilderment. "Yes. I haven't done anything wrong."

I matched his casual stance. "We have a video camera showing a car with your license plates leaving the Princeton Motel around one a.m. yesterday morning."

His eyes narrowed. "The Princeton Motel? Isn't that that dive on Colfax? I pass it all the time, but I've never been there."

He was either an incredibly good liar, or he was telling the truth. Now I was puzzled. "You've never been there?"

He shook his head and scowled. "Never. Why would I go there? I can imagine what those rooms are like, and I'm sure you know hookers use that place all the time, and the drug use. And," he paused and held up a finger, "oh ... my license plates were stolen the other night. Someone must've put my plates on their car."

I considered what he said. "Your license plates were stolen." I couldn't help repeating him, not expecting this turn in the conversation.

He nodded his head vigorously. "Yeah, and I can prove it. I have a doorbell cam, and you can see a car stop near mine. Someone gets out and takes the plates."

"Did you get a good look at the person? Man or woman?"

"I don't know. He wore a dark hoodie. What's this about?"

I deflected the question. "I need to see that video."

He nodded. "Sure, I can get it for you any time. I have access to the video online."

He didn't really mean any time, but I did. "I'm on an active murder investigation, and I need to see it right away."

He glanced up at his building. "Oh my god. Okay, I guess I could show it to you on my work computer. I just need to clear it with my boss."

I stood up. "If you could do that, please. This is very important."

"Sure." He stood up and gestured at me. "Come on."

We went back inside the building and up to the second floor. On the way, he said, "Let me talk to my boss. I'm supposed to be in a meeting soon."

"I can talk to him if you want."

He shook his head. "Not necessary."

I followed him into a large room full of cubicles to an office that faced north, with a view of townhomes. Bob poked his head inside and said, "Hey, Frank."

Frank stopped typing and looked up. "You going to be in that meeting? I –" Bob stepped into the office and gestured for me to join him. Frank looked at me, then at Bob, waiting for an explanation. Bob told him who I was and what I needed.

"Is it okay if I take her into a conference room and show her the video?"

Frank eyed me carefully. "Sure, do whatever you need to. We're happy to help."

I walked with Bob to his cubicle where he got his laptop. A woman across the aisle stared, and he said something about coming back soon, and we went into a small conference room dominated by a round table too big for the space. He rolled back a chair, sat down, and opened up his laptop. "Just give me a second to log into the app. I can pull up the footage from anywhere."

I stood and looked over his shoulder as he typed, then a black and white image appeared on the screen. It showed his front yard, with the planters on either side of the porch, some cars parked along the street.

"This happened a little before one," he said.

That fit with the timing of Nicole Lockwood's murder, I thought. And Spats had seen two cars leaving the motel parking lot not too long after that. My mind raced. Someone steals the license plates and switches them out with their car, picks up Nicole, takes her somewhere nearby and shoots her, then returns to the motel to dump the body. About twenty minutes or so.

He tapped the monitor. "See, that's my car right there."

"What's the make?"

"It's an Acura TLX. Nice car."

I took his word for it. He fast-forwarded the video. There was no activity on the street until the time he had said. He hit a button and the video resumed normal playback. The street was quiet for a moment, then a dark car pulled up near his car.

"See?" He pointed at the screen.

As we watched, we saw movement, and a dark figure in a hoodie came around the front of the stopped car.

"No dome light came on," he said.

I nodded. "They probably disabled it. That person's a bit on the slender side."

"Yeah."

The figure walked carefully to Bob's car, bent down, and quickly took off the license plate. Then the figure hurried to the front of the car, and took the front plate as well. With that, the figure hurried back to the stopped car, hopped in, and the car drove off.

Bob swiveled in the chair and looked at me. "See? My plates were stolen. And as I told you before, I've never been to the Princeton Motel. Did you check the register?"

"A place like that doesn't keep records," I said.

He frowned. "That's probably true. Nobody wants to get caught there."

"Let me see the video again," I ordered.

He backed up the video and replayed it. I moved close to the screen. "I can almost make out the plates on that other car. Can you zoom in?"

"Sure."

He pushed some buttons to focus on the car, but the quality was diminished.

"Is that a BMW?"

"It's hard to say."

I stood straight. "Can you give me that recording?"

He turned back to the computer. "Yeah, no problem. I'll just download the whole night and I can send it to you. Do you have an email?"

I told him my email, and I watched as he opened up his email, typed it in. Then he said, "There you go. Just sent it to you." He pushed back his chair and stood up. "I hope this helps you. And I hope you believe me that I was never at that motel."

"At least not at that time," I said with a wry smile.

He laughed. "Good point, but trust me, I wouldn't want to be there. Ever."

He grabbed his laptop and walked me back to the lobby. I thanked him for his time and gave him a business card, in case he thought of anything else. And I told him that if we recovered his license plates, I would return them.

"Don't bother, I already got new ones. I guess you know what the fine is if you get caught without plates."

"I know it's a lot."

"You got that right," he said with a shake of the head.

I left him, and as I hurried to my car, I called Spats. "The license plates were stolen." I said.

"Hold on, Sarah, not so fast."

As I got in my car, I told him what I'd learned. "I'm headed back to the station now. I want someone to enhance this video quick. I think we might be able to get the plate number off of the car that drove up to Bob's car. I'm going to get some detectives to canvas the neighborhood again, see if anyone saw the BMW."

"That's great. By the way, the conversation with Densmore didn't help. He admitted to being at the motel and said he'd been with a hooker named Janie for about an hour. I'll try to track her down, but I'm leaning toward this guy telling the truth."

"It may not matter, depending on where things go with this video," I said.

"Let me know what you find out, okay?"

"You got it."

Not too long ago, I felt we weren't getting anywhere. Now my nerves rang with anticipation. We were on to something. I broke every speeding law on my way to Thirteenth and Cherokee.

CHAPTER TWENTY-SIX

"James Hackenberg."

I stared at Spats, who had just walked in. When I'd returned to the office, I'd had Tara Dahl, one of the department's tech specialists, enhance the video I'd gotten from Bob Herrera's doorbell camera, and we were able to get a license plate number from the vehicle that had stopped near his car. I'd just looked up the owner.

"Who's he?" Spats asked.

"The real owner of the BMW." I told him about Herrera's doorbell camera footage.

He sat down and typed on his computer. "Let's find out what we can on Jimmy."

"Jimmy?"

He chuckled. "He might go by that. James is so formal."

I typed Hackenberg's name into a search engine as well. "I want to go in there with as much information on him as we can. No surprises." After a moment of searching, I said, "He's fifty-five, married, with an adult son. There's another woman listed on this people search site, maybe a daughter-in-law."

Spats nodded. "He doesn't have an arrest record. Nothing, not even a DUI or a parking ticket."

We lapsed into silence as we kept looking. I didn't find anything on social media for him, but I did find something else. "Look at this," I said. "Hackenberg is big in the financial realm. He's been written up in several articles, about how he sold his hedge fund several years ago for an insane amount of money."

Spats whistled. "Man, I'd like a little slice of that."

"You and me both. He went to Princeton, no joke." Spats tilted his head, disbelieving. "He worked in New York for several years, then moved out here. They live in Cherry Hills. Of course. You have millions, you live with the millionaires."

I looked up Hackenberg's address on googlemaps. "It's a nice big lot, has a swimming pool and tennis courts."

"Of course," he repeated.

He sat back and tapped a pencil on the desk. "So what's a guy like that doing at a sleazy motel on West Colfax? With the kind of money he has, you'd think he'd be smarter than that, or at least use more expensive hookers."

I shrugged. "Maybe it's the thrill of being down there. You know, the sleazier the place, the more fun it is."

"I guess so."

"I think he'd go by James, too. Not Jimmy."

"You think?"

"Let me look up the wife." Spats typed a bit. "Her name is Mary. Looks like she comes from a good family in New York. She's active in a couple of local charities. Oh, and here's something about his running a charity for the homeless. The charity has a gala downtown every fall. Here are some pics of a past event. Hang on." He studied the screen for a moment. "There are some VIP's there, sports figures, the Coors family, some local politicians."

"The lieutenant governor?"

He shook his head. "The mayor." He rested his chin on his hands, then looked at me. "We have to be careful with this one. If we're wrong, this guy could make trouble for us."

I stood up. "Yes, he could." We read stuff about Hackenberg for a bit longer, then I signaled him. "Let's go talk to him together, a united front."

"Works for me, but let's see if he's home." He picked up his desk phone. "I hate to give him advance notice, but if we drive down there and he's not home, we'd be wasting a lot of time."

"Right."

Spats held up a finger, then spoke into the phone "Is this James Hackenberg? No? Is he home?" He winked at me. "I'm a friend of his." A pause. "He's golfing, but he should be home for lunch soon. No, no message." He hung up the phone, the corners of his mouth twisting into a wicked smile.

"You lie far too easily."

He stood up. "I do what I have to do. Come on, let's catch Jimmy – I mean, James – while he's eating lunch."

JAMES HACKENBERG LIVED in a gated neighborhood near University Boulevard and Hampden Avenue, an area known for multi-million-dollar homes where several local celebrities lived, including some of Denver's prominent sports figures. I turned onto Hampden and drove up to a gate. A guard in a booth glanced at my Ford Escape, disinterested.

"We're here to see James Hackenberg." I held out my badge and now he was attentive. "He's expecting us."

"You lie so well," Spats murmured from the passenger seat.

I tried not to smile. The guard reached down and pressed a

hidden button, and the gate swung open. I drove through and let the GPS guide us through the neighborhood to a large two-story estate with white pillars in the front, and huge oaks that shaded a vast lawn and kept prying eyes from seeing the house. I wound around a long drive lined with perfectly sculpted bushes and red and yellow flowers, then parked near a four-car garage. One bay door was open, revealing a gleaming yellow Lamborghini. As we got out, Spats whistled again.

"Man oh man, this is some house."

I gestured at him. "Wipe the drool off your mouth."

We walked up stone steps between the white pillars to a large front porch. I was about to knock with a huge cast iron door-knocker, when Spats saw a doorbell and pushed it.

"I'll bet the knocker is just for show."

I smiled at him. Loud chimes sounded behind the white door.

"Loud enough to be heard throughout the house," Spats said.

We waited so long Spats was about to ring again, and then the door slowly swung inward. A butler in a dark suit and tie looked at us without expression. "May I help you?" If he was surprised at visitors, he didn't show it. I wondered whether the guard at the gate had called to announce us. I showed him my badge and asked to see Hackenberg.

"I'll see if he's available. Would you wait here?" He stepped back and opened the door wider. We entered a large foyer with a round staircase and a huge chandelier. He nodded at us politely, then disappeared down a long hallway.

"This is my next home," Spats murmured to me.

"You couldn't afford the taxes, let alone the mortgage."

He snickered at that. We were both admiring what had to be expensive paintings and sculptures around the foyer when the butler reappeared.

"Mr. Hackenberg will see you now."

He turned and we followed him down the hallway, through

another hall. He opened double doors and stepped aside. We walked into a large two-story office with bookcases and a second-story walkway lined with more bookcases. Floor-to-ceiling windows looked out onto a huge green lawn and a pool. Sitting behind a long mahogany desk was a man with dark hair going gray, bushy eyebrows, and piercing blue eyes. He stood up and came around the desk. He wore tan shorts, a white polo shirt, and leather loafers. He was fond of gold, from his wristwatch to a thick bracelet and a pinky ring. He held out a hand, and I got a whiff of cologne. "I'm James Hackenberg," he said. "And you are?"

"Detective Spillman." His handshake was firm. I introduced Spats. "Thank you for taking the time to see us."

"Of course. Although I am puzzled as to what this is about." He gestured for us to take seats at leather couches near the windows. He took a wingback chair and crossed one leg over the other. "I just returned from golf and am about to eat lunch." It seemed a subtle way to tell us we shouldn't take a lot of his time.

"Do you go by James, or Jim?" I began, trying to get him relaxed.

"James." He looked at me curiously.

"You have a beautiful home."

"Thank you." He glanced at his watch.

"James, we're here because your BMW was seen about one a.m. Wednesday morning outside the Princeton Motel on West Colfax."

His brow furrowed. "That can't be. I couldn't tell you the last time I was on West Colfax, let alone at a motel." Just a hint of disdain in his voice.

My hand was on the couch, and I subtly signaled for Spats.

"Before that, a car with your license plates was also seen in a neighborhood near the motel. The car stopped, someone got out and stole the license plates from a parked car, then drove away."

Hackenberg stared at him. "I don't know whose car you saw, but it was not mine."

"We're certain it was your car," Spats said.

Hackenberg tapped the arm of his chair. "Is this some kind of joke?"

I shook my head. "It certainly isn't. This is part of an active murder investigation."

"Who was murdered?" he asked.

"You don't know?" Spats said.

Hackenberg looked at him with annoyance. "Again, is this some kind of joke? Not only do I not have any idea what you're talking about, I wasn't even in the country early Wednesday morning. I just returned from New York last night." He seemed very sure of himself.

I glanced at Spats. If Hackenberg was to be believed, that meant he wasn't in town when Jonathan Hall had been murdered, either. "Can someone verify that?" I asked.

He nodded. "I have a private jet, we had a registered flight plan from New York, my pilot as well as my wife were on board, and I'm sure other people at the airport could verify seeing us. Our driver then picked us up and brought us here."

That would be a lot of people to lie for him. "We'll need that information," I said.

He got up and went to his desk and jotted down some notes. I glanced at Spats. The look on his face matched what I was feeling: confusion. If Hackenberg wasn't driving his car early Wednesday morning, then who was?

Hackenberg came over and handed me a piece of paper. "Call any of them. You're implying I might be a murderer, and I assure you, nothing is further from the truth."

I looked at the list of names and numbers. I handed it to Spats, then said, "This is puzzling because we have video of your car, just like we said. We clearly saw your car, your license plates."

He sat back down and held up his hands. "I don't know what to tell you. My car would've been in the garage the whole time I was gone."

"Do you have a security system?" Spats asked.

"Yes, but I personally don't pay that much attention to it. We have alarms on the doors, some cameras outside. I'm told I can access it from my computer, but I never do."

"Could we get access to the video?" I asked.

He pursed his lips. "I suppose I can get that for you. I'll have to make some calls. I'm not sure what you'll see. The cameras are focused on the drive, and the front and back doors. Not the garage."

"We'd like to see them anyway," I said.

"You're sure no one took your BMW?" Spats went on.

Now Hackenberg hesitated. "I don't know anybody that would take it."

"But it's possible?" I asked.

"I guess." He wasn't sure of his answer.

"Who might have access to your house and cars while you're gone?" Spats asked.

"A gardener comes in to check on the plants. She has a lock-box code. Her husband mows the lawn, does the outside work. And my son and daughter-in-law. They have a key to the house."

I took over the questioning. "What about cleaning staff?"

He shook his head. "They only come when we're here."

"And the butler?"

"Fred? He had the time off."

"But he has access to the lock box? He could get into the house?"

He frowned and let out an audible sigh. "Yes, but I trust them all completely. You can talk to Fred now, as well as Carol. She's the gardener."

"That would be helpful," I said. "Would they have keys to your car?"

"I keep extra keys in a drawer in the kitchen." He went back to tapping the armrest. "I suppose any of them could take the car. I never even thought about it." He considered that. "I don't see why my son or daughter-in-law, or the help, for that matter, would take the car."

"Is there anyone else that could come in your house while you're gone?"

"A couple of our neighbors keep an eye on the house."

"Their names?" I asked.

"Eve and Tom Godwin. They live across the street. Julia and Niles Nelson live next door to the north. You'll want their numbers as well?"

Both Spats and I nodded. Hackenberg pulled out his cell phone and scrolled through it. Then he gave us the numbers. I jotted them down on the piece of paper Hackenberg had given me.

I thought for a second. "And all of these people you mentioned know the code to disarm the security system?"

He frowned. "Yes."

"This is complicated," I said. He didn't reply.

"Could we get your son and daughter-in-law's contact info?" Spats asked politely.

Hackenberg sighed again. "Of course." He gave us that information as well. "I don't see how this is possible, though," he said. "All the cars were in the garage, just as I left them."

"How long were you in New York?" I asked.

"A month. My wife and I go there to see friends, and I have some business."

Spats stared at him. "Would your son borrow your car?"

186

His eyes narrowed. "To commit murder? Of course not. My son has never been in trouble." His leg twitched. He was irritated by that.

"Anyone else?"

"No." He stood up. "I'm afraid I'm going to have to cut this short. I'll let you talk to Carol and Fred, and then I do need to go. I have an engagement this afternoon that I need to get ready for."

CHAPTER TWENTY-SEVEN

"May we talk to your gardener and butler now?" I asked Hackenberg.

"Of course."

He led us out of the office and found Fred, the butler. Spats began talking to him, and Hackenberg and I walked back through the house. We passed a huge dining area, a kitchen done in copper, and a den with the biggest TV I'd ever seen. Hackenberg opened French doors and I followed him through a patio area arranged with two glass tables, a bar with granite countertops, and two barbecue grills. More oak trees shaded one side of the back yard. A large pool filled a sunnier area. Past the pool were several beautiful flower gardens. I followed Hackenberg around the pool, and we walked down a path to a sitting area near the gardens. A woman with long, dirty-blond hair was kneeling down at a flower bed, pulling weeds and dead flowers. Hackenberg approached, and she looked up with a smile.

"Hello, Mr. Hackenberg. I should be done with this area today."

Hackenberg smiled at her. "I'm sorry to bother you, Carol,

but this homicide detective would like to speak to you for a moment."

She wore gloves, and she brushed sweat off her brow with the back of her wrist. "Whew, it's hot today," she said as she stood up. She was about my height, but with longer legs and a shorter torso. She had on baggy shorts and a sleeveless blouse. I wish I could look that good when I was out doing yardwork.

"Sure," Carol said. "A homicide detective? What can I help you with?"

I began. "Mr. Hackenberg says you have access to the house when he's on vacation."

"Yes, that's true." She blew a strand of hair out of her face. "I need to get into the house to water the plants, and when the Hackenbergs are returning, I put vases with fresh flowers around the house. Mrs. Hackenberg likes that. Plus, I take care of the gardens."

"What were you doing early yesterday morning?" I asked her.

Hackenberg was listening for her answer as closely as I was.

"I was home, in bed." She was baffled. "My husband can verify that."

I didn't answer. "What about a week ago? Tuesday overnight?"

"The same," she said. "In bed with my husband."

"Does your husband have access to the house as well?" I asked.

She shook her head. "I have the combination to a lock box that's on the front door when Mr. Hackenberg is out of town." She glanced at him, now nervous. "I've never told my husband the combination. He mows the lawn and does the outside work, so he doesn't need it."

"Is there anybody else at your house besides your husband?" I asked.

"No, my kids are grown, and they don't live at home." Her

brow furrowed. "What's this about? Wait, are you questioning what I've told you?"

"No, I'm not." I smiled to keep her calm. "My questions are routine. However, I'd like to talk to your husband, if I could."

"Of course. His number is ..." She pulled out her cell phone and forced a laugh. "I never dial his number, so I don't remember it." She looked it up and gave it to me, and I wrote it down.

I held my pen at the ready. "And your last name is?"

"Manning," she said.

"Do you know Nicole Lockwood or Jonathan Hall?" I went on.

She shook her head. "No, should I?"

I studied her closely. She seemed relaxed, not bothered by my questions. "Do you ever use the Hackenbergs' cars when they're out of town?"

"Of course not." She was indignant and looked to Hackenberg for validation.

"I don't believe you ever have." He came to her defense.

I smiled at Carol again. "Thank you for your time."

"You can't tell me what this is about?" she asked again.

I shook my head. "I'm afraid not."

She shrugged, carefully dabbed her brow again, and turned back to the garden. Hackenberg walked me back into the house.

"Are you satisfied with our answers?" he asked as he led me through the house to the foyer, where Spats was waiting.

I ignored that. "Thank you for your time, Mr. Hackenberg."

He stared at us, bemused but also a little perturbed. "I do hope you find your answers. I am at a loss as to who might've taken my car. It's just preposterous, and I think you're looking in the wrong direction."

I smiled, and Spats nodded curtly. Hackenberg watched as we walked to my car.

"What'd the butler say?" I asked Spats.

"He was in and out of the house, right after the Hackenbergs left, and shortly before they came home. He was impassive, says he knows nothing, he was home when Nicole and Jonathan were murdered. I'll check with the wife, but I don't buy him as a killer."

I nodded. "I'll park on the street," I said as I drove down the driveway. "We need to talk to the neighbors. You take the Nelsons, see what you can find out. I'll tackle the Godwins."

He nodded toward Hackenberg's mansion. "What'd you think?"

I turned onto the street and pulled over. "I don't know. He has enough money, he could pay people to lie for him."

"You don't buy it, though." He frowned. "Me, neither."

"Did he let someone borrow his car?"

He had his hand on the door handle. "I don't know."

We got out. "That leaves us with a lot of people to talk to. If he's telling the truth, someone used his car to drive to the Princeton Motel."

"Meet you back here," he said.

He headed down the street to the Nelson's mansion, while I went across the street to the Godwin house. Or mansion, as it looked to be almost as big as Hackenberg's, but in a Tudor style with well-manicured evergreens on either side of the porch. My phone rang, and I stopped to answer.

"It's Chad Lattimore," he said. "I'm at the Starbucks. I have orders to watch for a man who's average height, a little heavy, with thinning brown hair. And a class ring on his left hand."

"Yes."

"He's come in the coffee shop."

I smiled grimly. "What's he doing?"

"He skipped coffee, went to a table."

"Does he have his laptop with him?"

"Yes."

I looked toward the street. Spats was engaged, and I needed to talk to the Godwins. I couldn't get away yet. "Stick with him. I'm tied up, but I'll connect with you soon."

"You got it."

I slipped my phone in my pocket, rang the bell, and waited. A moment later a taller woman with long, grayish hair opened the door.

"Yes?"

"Are you Mrs. Godwin?"

She pinched her mouth. "Yes. What can I do for you?"

I showed her my badge and introduced myself. "I just had a conversation with your neighbor, Mr. Hackenberg."

"James?" She looked past me, as if she could see his house through the trees. "What's going on?" She quickly frowned. "Where are my manners? Would you like to come inside? It's hot today."

I thanked her, then followed her inside to a foyer smaller than Hackenberg's. She led me around the corner to a warm, comfortable living room with wood-paneled walls and beamed ceiling. She gestured to an upholstered sofa, where I took a seat, and she went to a love seat across from me. She rested her hands on her knees. "Oh, my manners again. May I get you anything? I have an assistant, but it's her day off. I can't make you what I'm drinking, but I could get you something out of the refrigerator."

I shook my head. "No, thank you. I'm in the middle of a homicide investigation, and your name came up." I felt as if I'd seen her before, but couldn't place where.

"Well, since you said you're a homicide detective, this is about a murder?" I didn't answer, and she said, "Go ahead and ask your questions."

"Thank you. Mr. Hackenberg says that you and your husband have access to his house while he's gone."

"That's correct. When James and Mary go on vacation, they

want us to keep an eye out on the house, even though they have a security system and we're in a gated community."

"Have you or your husband been to their house recently?"

She thought about that. "I went over to their house once while they were gone. I needed to drop off some mail. You'd think our mailman could get it right, but no. Why?"

"What about your husband?"

"I don't think he went over there. I don't know why he would."

"Have you or your husband ever borrowed the Hackenbergs' BMW?"

She shook her head and laughed a little. "No, we have our own cars, why would we borrow his? Did someone say we did?"

"I'm just trying to gather some information," I said.

She held up a hand. "I'm afraid I can't help you so far."

I asked her about Nicole Lockwood and Jonathan Hall. She denied knowing either of them, and said I'd have to ask her husband whether he knew them.

"What about the Princeton Motel?" I asked.

"I don't know it. Where is it?"

"On West Colfax."

Her face wrinkled in distaste. "I've never been there, and I'm sure my husband hasn't."

"Do either of you go down to the Platte River?"

She looked perplexed at this question. "Never."

"Where were you and your husband around one a.m. yesterday morning?"

"We were home, of course. Earlier that evening, my husband and I had gone to a dinner with some friends, and then we were home for the rest of the night."

"What about a week ago, on Wednesday? What were you doing that night?"

She thought for a second. "We were home all evening."

"Would anyone else besides your husband be able to verify your whereabouts yesterday and last week?"

"I don't think so," she repeated.

"I'd like to talk to your husband. Is he here?"

"He's at work right now. I'm sure he could talk to you later, but I know he's tied up in meetings all afternoon."

"I'd still like his number, please."

"Of course." She got up and went into another room, then returned with a piece of paper. "That's his office number." She remained standing. "Is there anything else you need?"

I got up as well. "Not at this time. I appreciate your talking to me."

"Of course," she repeated. She led me to the door and I went outside.

As I got to the street, Spats was leaning against the Escape, looking as dapper as ever, even after half a day's work. He was just finishing a call, and he slid his phone into his pocket.

"Well?" I asked him as I unlocked the car and we got in.

He tipped his head, thinking. "Julia's a nice lady. Petite, and a spitfire. I get the impression she's not too fond of Hackenberg, that the friendship is mostly between the husbands. She says they popped over once to the Hackenbergs' house while they were in New York, just to check on things, and they've never touched the BMW. They were home both nights of our murders, and only her spouse can verify that."

"You believe her?" I jammed the key in the ignition.

Spats adjusted his vent so the cool air would blow on him. "Yeah, I do. She told me where her husband works, and I just got off the phone with his office. He wasn't available. The receptionist said I'd have to try tomorrow. So I will." He fiddled with the vent. "What about the Godwins?"

"I talked to the wife. She seems nice enough, but her husband was at work. I'd like to talk to him before I eliminate them from my list." I scowled. "I feel like I know her from somewhere, but I can't place her."

"It'll come to you."

"I hope so. Those things bug me. I'll drop you by the station so you can get your car. Can you tackle Hackenberg's son and daughter-in-law, too? I'm going to see if I can talk to Eve Godwin's husband."

"Sure." He fiddled with the vent. "You know Hackenberg's on the phone with his kid right now, asking him if he borrowed the old man's car."

I nodded. "If he's the one, he'll have time to cook up a lie."

"Yep." He felt the air. "Nothing we can do about that."

"We also need to talk to the security firm for the neighborhood. If there's a guard at the gate, would he or she remember the Hackenberg BMW coming and going early Wednesday morning?"

"I'll check that as soon as I can."

I was silent for a moment, then wondered aloud, "Someone drove Hackenberg's BMW to the Princeton Motel. Who is it?"

CHAPTER TWENTY-EIGHT

Marilyn stood in her kitchen and stared out the window. She had been surprised when the detective had come to the door. She wondered what the police knew. She couldn't tell from the conversation, and had wanted to ask more, but she didn't dare look too curious.

She wasn't worried about her husband lying for her. He was gullible, had been their entire marriage. She performed certain sexual favors, and he did anything she wanted. He would do so now, too.

As soon as the detective had walked out of the house, she'd called his office and talked to him. She told him to make himself unavailable for the afternoon, and that if a homicide detective called to talk to him, to say that she had been home with him early yesterday morning. He only objected to the lying a little, then said he'd do as she asked. He had been out of town on business until last night, had no clue what she had done while he was away. She also knew that he saw women when he was gone. He wouldn't want anybody to know *that* information, so he would lie not only to cover up his indiscretions, but because she would make promises to him when he got home. His sexual appetites were insatiable, whether it was with her or someone else. It was his downfall. She moved away from the window, fixed a drink, and thought through her short conversation with the detective. Had she made any mistakes? She didn't think so. She'd stayed calm, and hadn't revealed anything. She was certain that there was no way she could be caught.

Another thought occurred to her. Should she try to contact Teddy Roosevelt? Would he want to know that the police were asking questions, not only about her deed, but about Daffy Duck's as well? She shook her head. No, she would stay silent. Her deed had been flawless, and even if she could reach Teddy, all he would likely do was worry. Besides, the group had been shut down, and Teddy had said no one should have contact with each other anymore.

Marilyn downed the rest of her drink, dismissed any doubts she had, and went into her office.

CHAPTER TWENTY-NINE

By the time I reached the station, Lattimore called again.
"What's going on?" I asked.

"The subject stayed at the table for a little while, and he kept looking at his watch, like he's waiting for someone. No one showed up, though, and then he left. He looked kind of mad."

"Where are you now?"

"He went south on Wadsworth. Now he's sitting outside an office building near Belmar."

Belmar is a newer shopping and urban neighborhood, in what was formerly downtown Lakewood. It had replaced an old shopping mall, and now included several blocks of restaurants, bars, stores, and a movie theater, along with nearby office buildings, condos, and townhomes. I knew the area, had been to an outdoor skating rink there with Harry last winter.

"Keep watching him," I said. "I'm headed that way now." I ended the call with a victorious smile.

"What?" Spats asked.

"We found Chuck, the guy Lola was with. I'm going to see if

I can talk to him now. You follow up with Hackenberg's family. And make some calls, see if his alibi does check out."

He tapped a finger to his forehead in salute. I left him at his car and sped west on Sixth Avenue, then south on Wadsworth. At a stop light, I looked at the piece of paper Eve Godwin had given me and called her husband's office.

"Mr. Godwin is tied up all afternoon," the receptionist told me. "May I take a message? He may not be able to return your call until tomorrow."

"No message," I murmured and ended the call.

Traffic was thick, and I was worried I'd miss my chance to talk to Chuck. I sped around a semi, and as I neared Belmar, I ran a yellow light. I did not want to lose an opportunity to talk to Chuck. As I waited at a light at Wadsworth and Alameda, I called Lattimore.

"Where are you parked?"

"I'm near the FirstBank, right by the Chick-Fil-A. Your guy is parked in a white Hyundai near the doors to the office building."

As I pulled into the parking lot, I saw the car he meant. I could see someone inside. I also saw another man sitting in a nondescript car at the other side of the lot.

"Watch me, okay?" I said to Lattimore. "I'm going to go talk to him."

"I've got your back."

I ended the call and parked in a space nearby, where I could watch the Hyundai. The man inside had his window rolled down, and rested his elbow on the door. He appeared to be waiting for someone, alternately doing something on his phone and watching the building entrance. I watched for a minute, didn't feel that he was a threat, so I got out and approached the car. I heard rock music coming from the vehicle as I neared.

"Chuck?" I asked.

His head jerked around, and he squinted into the sun. "Do I know you?" He hit a button and the music died.

I stood by the side of his car and showed him my badge. "Detective Spillman, Denver homicide."

His gaze went to the badge, then to the gun on my hip. His jaw dropped, then he looked back toward the building. He started to put his right hand down and I said, "Put your hands where I can see them, on the steering wheel."

"I wasn't doing anything." His voice warbled as he did as instructed.

"Let's just play it safe. What's your last name?"

"I don't have to tell you that."

"Okay, then we'll go down to the station."

"No, I can't! It's Ames."

I gestured at him. "Let's see your license."

He held up one hand. "May I?" I nodded, and he carefully reached in his back pocket and pulled out his wallet. His hand shook as he handed me his license.

I confirmed his name and quickly memorized his address. I handed it back.

"What's this about?" He dropped his wallet in his lap and put his hand back on the steering wheel. His jaw locked tight.

"Tell me about the woman at the Princeton Motel."

He glanced at me. "Man, my wife is coming out soon. I'm supposed to take her to lunch."

I leaned against the car. "You better start talking then. Or, if you'd rather, we could go downtown and talk there."

He shook his head quickly. "I don't know anything."

The lie was lame, not to mention unimaginative, and he so obviously looked guilty.

"The clock is ticking," I said. "What's going to happen if your wife comes outside?"

"Okay, okay." He threw up his hands, realized what he'd

done and placed them back on the steering wheel. "I was with a girl, you know, the other night." His face went red with embarrassment. "After we had, you know, we were leaving the room and we saw a car stop and dump that girl's body out. I didn't want to get involved, so I left."

"You left Lola to deal with it." I couldn't hide the contempt in my voice.

"I can't let my wife find out," he said. "It'll destroy my marriage."

"You think?"

He peered through the windshield at the office entrance. "What else do you want to know? Please, I can't get caught."

"You're telling me the truth? How do I know you and Lola didn't cook up something and kill Nicole?"

"Nicole?" He looked puzzled. "Oh, the hooker. It's preposterous that I would do that. Someone would've seen us."

I tended to believe him. "Tell me about the car you saw."

"It was a black BMW, four doors. It looked newer, a nice car. That's it."

"License plates?"

He shook his head. "It happened too fast, I didn't see anything."

"What else?"

He thought for a second. "Someone reached over to close the door, after the body was pushed out. I swear the person I saw was wearing a wig because it kind of got caught in their hoodie, and I saw long gray hair underneath."

"What color wig?" I fired the questions at him, not giving him time to think.

"Black, and curly."

"A hoodie?"

"Yeah, a black one. I didn't see his face."

"What else?"

"I don't know, it was dark."

"Was he wearing gloves?"

He nodded. "Yes. Gloves, that's right. And I think maybe sunglasses, although I can't be sure."

"You saw his face?"

"No, just a brief glimpse."

"Did you see the interior of the car?"

He stared at the office building entrance and thought. "There might have been seat covers on it. Like the dashboard was black, the interior of the door was black, but the passenger seat was white. It didn't fit." He looked as if that had just occurred to him, and I couldn't disagree with his logic. Tires screeched, and a horn honked somewhere. Chuck shifted to look at me.

"Did anybody else see you leave the motel?" I asked.

"I don't know, maybe the manager. I was parked on the side of the motel, so he might've seen me."

I made a mental note to check with Spats to see if he remembered the white Hyundai in any surveillance video.

"Did you know the dead woman?"

He shook his head. "I think I've seen her around once or twice, but I was never with her. I never talked to her."

"Did you see her having an argument last week with another man, shouting and yelling at each other?"

"No."

I crossed my arms and stared at him. "You left Lola to take care of things."

He blushed with humiliation. "I know, it was a crappy thing to do. I can't get caught." He turned, then gasped. "My wife's coming," he hissed.

A tall slender woman in a gray pant suit emerged from the office building. She had short hair styled to perfection, dangling earrings sparkling in the sun.

I glanced at Chuck. "Why would you be seeing hookers when your wife looks like that?"

"Looks aren't everything," he muttered. "Can you leave me alone now? I don't have anything else to tell you."

The woman walked up to the car and looked over at me curiously. "Hi," she said hesitantly.

I smiled pleasantly at her. "I was just talking to your husband," I said.

"Oh." She opened the car door and glanced inside.

"I'm sorry. I thought I knew him from high school," I said. I looked down at Chuck. "I guess I was wrong."

"Yeah, guess so." Chuck didn't return my gaze.

His wife returned my smile. "That happens."

I nodded. "Well, sorry to have bothered you."

"I doubt it," he said quickly. He started the car, and I waited as he backed out. As he drove off, I heard something about, "... no idea who she is."

I waited until he drove out of the parking lot, then walked over to Lattimore's car. His wide face and dark eyebrows were easy to recognize. I'd seen him around the station before.

He nodded in greeting. "How'd it go?"

"I'm not sure," I said. "He says he didn't see the killer."

"I don't know much about your investigation, so I can't speak to that," he said gruffly.

"I know." I was thinking through the conversation, of Chuck's description of the driver. Things were coming together. The street sounds faded away.

"What's going on?" Lattimore stared at me. "You okay?"

I turned back to where the Hyundai had been parked. "He said something about a wig, and long gray hair." I stood for a moment.

"Spillman?"

I looked at him. "I need to go."

CHAPTER THIRTY

M arilyn logged onto the internet, but her mind was elsewhere. She didn't hear the classical music she had playing, and she didn't pay attention to the Scotch that sat on a coaster on the desk. She wasn't happy that the detective had come to talk to her. That wasn't a good sign. She stared at the screen, her mind on her deed. She thought through the other night. Had she missed something?

Once she had decided on a prostitute, she spent time figuring out where specifically in the Denver metro area you could be sure to find one. Everyone knew they hung around parts of Colfax Avenue, but she'd never checked that out in person. Late one night, when her husband was gone, she decided to find out. She went to a stretch of Colfax east of the Capitol where women seemed to linger around. Women of the night, as the expression went. As she studied the women, a Beethoven sonata played. After watching the street for a while, she determined it was too crowded, too many people around besides the hookers. That wouldn't do. So she'd gone west on Colfax until she passed the Princeton Motel and the Easy Bar. There she saw women that she was sure were working in the sex trade, and even a few men and boys. They lingered on the sidewalks, walked up and down the street in revealing clothes. Some men approached them on foot, and they'd talk. Sometimes the couple would go to the motel, other times they would walk off. Cars also stopped, and the prostitutes would bend down and talk through the passenger window. *Bartering for what they would do*, Marilyn thought. Then some would get in the car, and the car would drive away. Others would turn and walk away. Marilyn also saw a few drug transactions, and one fight between two women. There was no shortage of drama, so different from her life. She didn't know who she would pick, though.

⁻ She parked and watched. A couple of hours passed, and no one paid any attention to her. Traffic and business for the prostitutes died down. She nodded in satisfaction. This would be a good time and a good area to pick up her victim. She drove home and got on the internet. She was careful in her research, but knew her research couldn't implicate her; it wasn't a crime to look at things on the internet.

She learned what she could about prostitution. It was amazing what people would pay for, and how little some sexual favors cost. She also learned that a lot of prostitutes were drug addicts. In Marilyn's social circle, this was nothing they talked about. All this was new to her. She'd only seen things in the movies, she had no idea what it was like in real life. It was fascinating. As she read stories and articles about prostitutes, she felt no pity for them. As far as she was concerned, they didn't have to be doing what they were doing. They'd done something to get themselves in those situations. It was their own fault.

She went back to the same area of West Colfax several more times and watched the action. Then she'd seen the woman she decided to use. She was young and blond, with a thin nose and way too much make-up. Her slinky clothes hung on skin and bones. *Who knows when her last good meal was,* Marilyn thought. As per the rules, Marilyn had no idea who the prostitute was. She briefly wondered about her background. Where was she from? What had she done to end up in this kind of life? She was too young for it, for that kind of degradation. Marilyn slowly came to the idea that she would be rescuing the girl from a future filled with nothing good. Another thought occurred to her. Would a prostitute hop in the car when she realized a woman was driving? Marilyn wasn't sure, but she'd have to try. Money would be a powerful lure. It would work. That night, after Marilyn decided on her victim, she felt such a satisfaction, she could hardly describe it.

After that, she put the rest of her plan into place. She could pick up the prostitute in a car, just like so many of the johns did. She had to be absolutely certain the crime could not be traced back to her, so she knew she couldn't use her own car. She'd thought about renting a car, but knew that wouldn't work. Too easy to be traced back to her. Same with buying a cheap car. She couldn't take a taxi or Uber, that could again lead back to her. She'd have to borrow a car. But whose? She'd have to figure that out.

The other thing she had to think about was the gun. Her father had been a gun collector, and she'd been to gun ranges herself. She needed a small weapon, a .22 or something similar, but how to find one that was untraceable? That piece resolved itself when she saw something on the news about illegal guns. She learned enough, and then with the help of the internet and some chat rooms, she found a contact in downtown who got her a gun. It had cost her a decent amount of money, but it was worth it. The gun was untraceable.

She googled the area around the Princeton Motel and found a nearby park that was surrounded by some office buildings and a few houses. One night she spent hours watching the park. It remained quiet the entire time. It would work for her purposes. She bought cheap clothes and a black hoodie, along with a black wig, dark glasses, and black gloves.

She wanted to tell the Guild she was ready, but she hadn't resolved the car situation. She hadn't been sure what to do about that, and then the solution presented itself. Her neighbor mentioned that they would be out of town for a month. While they were gone, she had access to their house, could check on things for them. She knew from going out with them that they kept the car keys in the kitchen. She could borrow the car, take off the license plates, and then afterwards she could clean it and bring it back to their house. No one would be the wiser. Once they had left, it was perfect. Her husband was out of town as well, so she had volunteered to do the next deed.

Once the time came, her deed had gone without a hitch. She sneaked through the gate that separated her backyard from her neighbor's. Both yards had a lot of tall trees, and she didn't think anyone in nearby houses would see her. If, on the off chance someone did, what did Marilyn have to do with it? She was already in her disguise, so a police report would describe only someone in a hoodie. She let herself in the back door of the neighbor's house. She had gone into the house earlier that evening, after all help was gone, and disabled the alarms. If anyone asked, she would say she forgot to re-arm the system. She got the BMW keys and went into the garage. She had purchased seat covers, and she put them on. She couldn't figure out how to disable the dome light, so she put tape over it. Then she drove her neighbor's car out of the garage. No one was on the street as she left the neighborhood. The guard at the gate was glued to his phone, as she'd often observed, and didn't even notice her leaving.

She drove west toward the Princeton Motel, and as she approached it, she saw the young blond walking down the street. Now that she knew the girl was working that night, Marilyn drove into a nearby neighborhood and stole the license plates off a parked car. She drove several blocks away, stopped, and switched the BMW plates with the stolen ones. Then she headed back toward the motel.

Marilyn pulled slowly to the curb and rolled down the window. The girl had looked in, her eyes widening when she saw it was a woman. But just as Marilyn had surmised, when Marilyn had offered her a hundred dollars, the girl had accepted. She'd gotten in, and Marilyn had driven off. The street was empty, and the only other prostitute was a block away.

As per her plan, she drove to the park. The girl didn't seem to care. The park was empty, the neighborhood quiet and dark. Marilyn parked and the girl asked what she wanted to do. Marilyn asked her to turn away. When she did, Marilyn pulled the .22 from her hoodie pocket. Her heart was racing, and her breaths came in little gasps. She smelled the woman's body odor. Marilyn quickly pressed the gun to the girl's skull and pulled the trigger. Then for good measure, she shot again. The girl slumped down, her head resting on the dashboard. There had been little blood from the shots, but if there was any splatter, the seat covers would help. Marilyn sucked in a huge breath and glanced around. She didn't see anyone. Her body was a mix of exhilaration and fear. The girl didn't move, didn't appear to be breathing. Marilyn wanted to check her pulse, but she didn't want to touch the girl's wrist because she'd read somewhere that they might be able to get fingerprints from the body. Before she could think or feel more, Marilyn put the rest of her plan into motion. She drove carefully out of the park and back toward the Princeton. She figured it would be better to leave the body somewhere besides the park, that this might throw off the police. And she wanted to make sure the body would be found soon.

Marilyn stopped once to slip a ring with a fake ruby onto the girl's finger. She's bought the ring with cash at a Walmart far from her house. There was no way to trace it back to her. Then she drove into the parking lot behind the motel and slowed to a stop. She quickly reached across the dead woman's body and opened the passenger door, then pushed her out. She shut the door, and drove out of the parking lot. She saw no one. It had taken seconds.

She headed east on Colfax. When she was a good distance from the motel, she turned down a side street, parked, and quickly put the BMW license plates back on. She drove to a different neighborhood and took off the seat covers, then pulled off the hoodie and the wig, sunglasses, and gloves. She headed down an alley and tossed the gun into a dumpster, then a little farther on, the seat covers and hoodie into another. Then she drove east toward her house. On the way, she dropped the sunglasses out the window. Finally, she turned down another alley and dumped the stolen license plates, wig, and gloves in other dumpsters. She saw a few cars, but was sure no one could possibly know anything about what she'd done. She passed the guard at the gate, just gave him a quick wave with her head turned away. Past experience told her he would recognize the car and open the gate. If he bothered to think about it, he'd think the Hackenbergs were coming home late.

When she drove down her neighbor's street, she turned off the headlights. She knew her neighbors well enough to know that no one would be up now. She pulled into her neighbor's drive and parked the car in the garage. She went in the house, got paper towels and cleaner, then wiped out the car and took the tape off the dome light. She was certain there were no traces of her deed. She pocketed the used towels and put back the cleaner, then left the keys where she'd found them. She sneaked out of the house and back through the gate to her house. She put her clothes in the washer and donned a robe. Then she tore up the used towels and flushed them down the toilet, the last piece of evidence that could be tied to her.

She continued to stare at the screen. Then she shook her head. It was a perfect crime. And yet the police had come around, asking questions. What had she missed?

CHAPTER THIRTY-ONE

I raced to my car, my mind still putting things into place. Chuck had said the person he'd seen had long gray hair. It hadn't clicked for me right then, but when I was talking to Lattimore, I thought about the doorbell cam video. That figure had seemed a bit on the slender side, not a strong person. The whole time, I'd been assuming the killer was a man. More than likely a man would have been with a prostitute, not a certainty, but the odds were high. But what if it had been a woman? I thought about the people we had interviewed, the ones with access to James Hackenberg's car. I peeled out of the parking lot and headed north. I called Ernie, but he didn't answer. I left him a message to call me back. Then I tried Spats. He answered right away.

"After you dropped me off, I made some calls, and James Hackenberg's alibi checks out. There's no way he could've driven his BMW to the motel."

"Good work. One thing about Julia Nelson. Tell me about her hair."

"Her hair?" he repeated. "It's short brown. Why?"

"Eve Godwin has long gray hair." I told him about my conversation with Chuck Ames, including his mention of what he thought was long gray hair. "All along, I've been assuming the killer was a man, but what if a woman murdered Nicole Lockwood? What if a woman pulled her hair back into a ponytail and tucked it under a wig, but the wig slips when she was dumping the body out of the car, and her gray hair falls out? Is that a stretch in my logic?"

"There's some sound logic there. But if we now think the killer might be a woman, could it be Hackenberg's daughter-in-law? Sounds like she would've had access to his car, too."

"Yeah, maybe. Does she have gray hair?"

"I'm going to speak to them now. You find out what you can from Eve Godwin, and let's see where that leads us."

"All right," I said. "I'll call you back soon."

I ended the call and raced back to the Cherry Hills neighborhood. This time I flashed my badge at him and told him I had another appointment with Hackenberg. He hesitated, and I forcefully told him to let me in. I hoped if he called Hackenberg, by then I'd be at Eve Godwin's house. I drove through the neighborhood and pulled into her drive. My heart raced as I rang the doorbell and waited. What seemed an eternity later, Eve opened the door and looked at me with surprise.

"Detective ... I'm sorry, I don't remember your name." She smiled sheepishly.

"Spillman."

She nodded once, perfunctorily. "Yes. That's right." She held the door and didn't invite me inside.

"Do you have a few minutes?" I asked. "I have a few follow-up questions."

"So soon?" She glanced past me, seemed to search for words, then sighed impatiently. "I suppose I could spare a little time. I do have a meeting to get to."

"May I come inside?"

She paused, then opened the door wider. "I guess."

Her earlier friendliness was gone. She led me back into the living room, and we sat in the same places as before. She put her hands in her lap and looked at me. She didn't offer me a drink. I glanced around the room, fully took it in this time. A few pieces of abstract artwork hung on the dark, wood-paneled walls, and some sculptures adorned shelves on either side of a large fireplace.

"You have some beautiful pieces of art," I said, trying to put her at ease.

"Thank you. My husband and I have attended some auctions in New York. We particularly like Michele Vargas." She gestured at a painting in dark blues and greens.

"It's quite stunning," I said. I took another moment to look at the paintings, and saw her breathing slow down. I started with an easy question. "When I was here before, you said you were home Tuesday overnight," I said.

"That's right. My husband can confirm that. Have you talked to him?"

I shook my head. "When I called his office, he was unavailable."

"He'll corroborate what I said."

"I hate to say this, but he could lie for you."

"Why would he do that?" The reply came a little too fast.

"You're sure no one else can verify your whereabouts overnight Tuesday?"

"No."

I nodded thoughtfully. "And you visited the Hackenberg house once while they were gone?"

"Yes, Detective, to drop off some mail. That's what I told you." A little snippy.

"What day was that?"

"Um, it must've been Thursday."

"You don't sound sure."

She sighed. "I'm sorry, I don't remember for sure."

"Do you know the Princeton Motel?"

Something flickered in her eyes. "No, I do not. Princeton. Isn't that in New Jersey?"

"No, it's a motel on West Colfax."

"Detective, we went over this." She let out an exasperated sigh. "I couldn't tell you the last time I was on that side of town. It's not anywhere I would go."

We stared at each other. The house was eerily quiet, almost spooky. My gut was churning, telling me I was on the right track.

"Mrs. Godwin, before we go further, I need to advise you of your rights."

Her brow furrowed. "What?"

"I'm sorry, but I have to do this. You have the right to remain silent ..." I continued to recite her Miranda rights. "Do you understand these rights as I've explained them to you?"

"Yes, of course." Her look was cautious.

I went on. "Do you own any guns?"

"I do not. What are all these questions about, Detective?"

I slid to the edge of the couch, tense. "We're looking into the murder of a prostitute. She was killed at the Princeton Motel. In the process of our investigation, we have video from a nearby surveillance camera, placing Mr. Hackenberg's car at the scene. Only he couldn't have been there. He was out of town." I paused, and she stared at me. "It would appear someone borrowed his car and used it in a crime."

She rested her palms on her thighs. "And?"

"We also have footage from a doorbell camera from a house in the neighborhood near the motel. It shows someone in a BMW with Hackenberg's license plates stop on the street, and someone gets out and steals plates from another car. I watched the video. The person could've been a woman."

"Detective, this is all fascinating, but what does it have to do with me?"

I went for it. "Did you use Hackenberg's car, switch the plates, then go to the Princeton Motel and kill Nicole Lockwood?"

She stayed cool. "What a preposterous suggestion."

Something about her manner hit me, and it suddenly dawned on me where I'd seen her. At the community meeting a week ago. She'd asked me questions about homicide investigations. Looking for information to help her commit the perfect crime? My blood turned cold, and I went on high alert.

"You were at the DPD community meeting last week," I said. "You were full of questions."

"I don't recall that."

I nodded. "Yes, I'm sure it was you."

She studied me for a minute, her lips a thin line. "Would you excuse me for a moment?" she suddenly said. "I need to use the bathroom." She stood up and hurried out of the room.

"Mrs. Godwin?" I called after her. I hesitated, waited and listened. The house remained still, the windows buttoned up so tightly I couldn't hear anything outside. I glanced at my watch. Had she just gone to the bathroom, or was she using the phone? I put my hand on the butt of my gun, stood up, and called out to her. No answer. I called again and got no reply. Blood pounded in my ears. I walked toward the front entrance and glanced into the foyer. I heard nothing, and saw no one. She'd said she was going to the bathroom, but I found a powder room off the foyer, and she wasn't there.

Where had she gone?

The night I'd rushed into Diane's house flashed in my mind, racing through her house, wondering where she was. I felt the same apprehension now as I had then. I quickly brushed that aside. I had to do my job. I pulled out my gun, then called out again and walked carefully toward the kitchen. I saw nothing but my own fuzzy reflection in the stainless steel refrigerator. I quickly canvassed the rest of the first floor, eyes and ears alert. I didn't see Eve or anyone else. I went to the stairs, called out, then walked up to the second floor. I stood on the landing and called her name yet again.

Silence.

I headed down a wide hallway in search of the master bedroom. I passed several smaller rooms, glanced in each one, and determined they were empty. I finally found the master bedroom, a huge suite dominated by a king-size, four-poster bed.

"Mrs. Godwin?"

I raised my gun and moved into the room. I walked past a chest, a large dresser, and double doors that were open, exposing a huge closet. Another nearby door was closed. I went to it and knocked.

"Mrs. Godwin? Open the door."

At this point, I didn't expect an answer. My breathing was short, nerves on edge. I put my hand on the knob, raised my gun, and twisted the knob. I pushed the door open and glanced inside.

CHAPTER THIRTY-TWO

E ve hurried upstairs and went into the bathroom. Acid roiled in her stomach as she shut the door. Her breathing came in short gasps, and she fought not to be sick. She walked to a large counter, rested her hands on the edge of the sink, and stared into the mirror.

How could she have been so stupid not to think of a doorbell camera? And one that picked up the license plate number from Hackenberg's BMW. She had never considered a doorbell camera for her house. It was set so far back from the road, in a gated community. Why would she? But others did. She shook her head as she stared at herself. She was so certain she'd thought of everything, but not that.

Eve had always thought she'd never get caught. She'd had the courage to go through with her deed. Now she had to have the courage to carry out her back-up plan, the one she'd assumed she would never need. Thoughts of her husband ran through her mind. He was a dullard, but he'd provided her with a lot. She didn't feel love for him, but she did hope that he wouldn't get in too much trouble, although he deserved it, after cheating on her so routinely. He didn't have a clue what she'd done, so he should be safe. She wondered if he'd miss her. Probably not too much.

No more time to reminisce, she thought. The detective would come looking for her soon.

Eve crouched down and opened the bottom cabinet drawer. She rummaged around in the back until she found a small package tucked under facial supplies. She pulled out the envelope, tore it open, and shook out a small baggie. Cyanide. Daffy Duck had told her where to buy it online, but she never *really* thought she'd have to use it. She had read up on different types of poisons, how fast they acted, and where she could get them. She chose cyanide in part because, if inhaled, it could kill within minutes. She opened the baggie, and with a trembling hand, poured some of the powder on the countertop, then took the envelope and cut a couple of lines as she'd seen people cut lines of cocaine in the movies. She kept a hundred dollar bill with the envelope, and she quickly rolled it up. She swallowed hard, bent down, and before she questioned herself, she snorted the two lines of powder. There was a second of nothing. Then she felt it. She fell to the floor and gasped. Her lungs fought for air, to no avail. She stared at the ceiling and thought, *So this is what death feels like.*

CHAPTER THIRTY-THREE

When I entered the bathroom, Mrs. Godwin was lying on the floor, facing the vanity cabinet.

"Mrs. Godwin! Eve!" My gun was still on her. I moved carefully to where I could see her face, keeping a distance so she couldn't trip me. Her eyes were wide and glassy, her mouth open, some spittle at the corners. I nudged her and she didn't move. Then I saw a baggie with powder on the counter.

"What the hell?"

I holstered my gun, bent down, and grabbed her. "Mrs. Godwin!" I shook her and tried to get her attention. Her eyes rolled up into the back of her head. Then her body quivered and was still. I felt for a pulse, but she was gone. I didn't know what she'd ingested or how, so I was not going to perform CPR. The process of helping her could kill me.

I stood back and quickly dialed 911. I identified myself, and asked for backup and an ambulance. The dispatcher said she'd send emergency personnel right away. I ended the call and glanced around the room. I didn't see any signs of other poisons or pills that she might've taken, but I wasn't going to check drawers. I suspected Eve had killed Nicole Lockwood, and I wanted everything properly documented. I smelled lavender, felt a crushing silence. I had been too late. I gave her one last look, then went downstairs and onto the porch. While I waited, I called Spats. He didn't answer, and I suspected he was still talking to Hackenberg's son and daughter-in-law. I tried Ernie next, and when he picked up, I told him what happened.

"Are you okay?" he asked.

"Yes, I'm fine." The truth was, I wasn't sure. I wasn't going to admit that.

"I'm on my way," he said, then was gone.

I stared at the Godwins' perfectly manicured front lawn, my mind momentarily tortured. I still didn't want things to end this way. My nerves were on edge, the danger I'd felt looking for Eve Godwin reminding me of that night at Diane's house and chasing Welch. I closed my eyes and gulped in a few breaths. A minute later, I heard sirens, and soon two squad cars and an ambulance arrived. I shoved my regret aside and trotted down the driveway.

"Detective Spillman, Denver Homicide," I said to the first officer, a short, muscular man. A taller woman with braided hair hurried up beside him. I showed them my badge and told them the situation. "I'll be joined by one of my partners soon."

After that, I let the officers take over. We were in Cherry Hills, which was not my jurisdiction. I followed them upstairs and showed them Eve Godwin's body, and the EMTs confirmed that she was dead. I explained in detail to the uniforms what had transpired, and by the time I finished, two detectives from their department had shown up. They took charge and began working the crime scene, and I went back downstairs to the foyer, where I saw Ernie at the front door.

"That's my partner," he said to the Cherry Hills cop at the front door. Once his identity had been verified, Ernie strode over and stared at me. "How ya doin'?"

I hesitated, then nodded. "I'm ..."

"What?" he asked in a low voice.

"She told me she had to go to the bathroom. Maybe if I had followed her ..."

"Don't go down that road again," he said. "You have to stop second-guessing yourself." He put hands on my shoulders and looked me in the eye. "You hear me?"

"Yes." I took a deep breath and focused on the task at hand.

"Go over everything again." I did, and he nodded his head when I finished. "I would've played it the exact same way."

"Yeah?"

He nodded. "Yeah."

Spats called, and I told him what had happened. He swore when I finished.

"All I was going to tell you was that Hackenberg's son and daughter-in-law have a good alibi for Tuesday night. They spent the night in Vail, plenty of witnesses. I guess that doesn't matter now."

I heard a commotion out front. "Spats, I need to go."

"You want me down there?"

"No, Ernie and I aren't doing much. I'll see you at the station later."

"See you there. I'll give Rizzo an update."

I thanked him, and Ernie and I headed to the front door.

"It's my house! Let me in." A tall man in a dark suit fitted to perfection was standing at the door, arguing with the police officer.

"Are you Mr. Godwin?" I asked.

"Yes. This is my house. Who are you?" Godwin was average height, with a thick head of gray hair, square shoulders, and an air about him. "What is going on? Where's my wife?"

Ernie and I led him onto the front porch.

"Just a moment," I said.

The policeman was already rushing inside and returned with one of the Cherry Hills detectives, a woman named Cotton. Her long brown hair was pulled into a ponytail, and her nails were bright red, a touch of lipstick. Godwin was flustered and kept asking what was going on. Cotton stepped in, put a hand gently on his arm, and introduced herself.

"Detective Grace Cotton," she said. Ernie and I stepped aside and listened. "You are Mr. Godwin? May I see your ID?"

"My ID? Well ..." He was flustered as he took out his wallet and showed her his ID.

"Thank you. I'm sorry to tell you this, Mr. Godwin," she went on, "but your wife is dead."

His eyes darted back and forth, then his jaw dropped. "What? I don't understand. I just talked to her a little bit ago."

"It would appear she poisoned herself." Cotton told him what happened. "I also have to inform you that these detectives," she gestured at Ernie and me, "believe she's a suspect in the murder of a woman on West Colfax."

He stared at me. "I don't understand."

I glanced at Ernie. I'm sure he was wondering the same thing I was: why wasn't Godwin protesting more? Cotton looked at me, then back at Godwin.

"I'd like for you to identify your wife, and then would it be all right with you if these detectives ask you a few questions?" she said.

Godwin's jaw tensed. "Yes, anything to clear this up."

Cotton took him upstairs, and they returned a few minutes later. Godwin was pale. Cotton moved back and listened as I took over the conversation.

"Where was your wife Tuesday overnight?"

"She ..." he hesitated. "We were home all night."

I pursed my lips and crinkled up my face sadly. "Mr.

Godwin, I know this is difficult, but I need you to tell me the truth."

He looked shaky, and he reached out until his hand found the porch railing. He backed up and leaned against it. "This is all so crazy."

"Please, Mr. Godwin," I said mildly.

"She called me earlier today and asked me to lie for her. I didn't know why, and I didn't ask." He was sheepish. "I was in Boston Tuesday night. I just got back home this morning."

"Why would you lie for her?" Ernie asked.

He looked at Ernie, his face defeated. "You have to understand Eve. She could be very manipulative, and very persuasive. We have an understanding: I do what she wants, and she does ... what I want. I figured she had been out late, maybe had too much to drink and wrecked her car, drove away from the scene, something like that. That actually happened one time a while back. I've learned over the years not to ask Eve too many questions."

"And you were home a week ago Tuesday, overnight?" I made eye contact again, didn't let him dodge me. "That's the truth?"

Another hesitation. "Mr. Godwin," I prodded him.

"She was out for a while and came home late, around two. She came to bed and ... I didn't ask questions." For the first time, he seemed slightly embarrassed at this admission.

I glanced at Ernie and he gave me a look as if he wasn't sure he believed Godwin. I wasn't sure, either.

"Was she wearing a hoodie?" I asked.

"A what? When she comes to bed? No, of course not."

"Do you own any guns?" I went on.

"We have some guns that belonged to Eve's father. She was a gun person because of him."

"What about a .22?"

"I don't think so." He shook his head. "This is just unbelievable."

"Would you show us where you keep your guns?" Cotton asked him.

"Yes."

He led us through the house to a basement door. We went downstairs to a small room with a gun safe. He tapped a keypad to open it, and let us inventory all the guns. "They're all here," he said.

"Nothing's missing?" Cotton asked.

He double-checked. "All accounted for."

There wasn't a .22. Cotton nodded, and we all traipsed back upstairs.

"Mr. Godwin," I said. "Do you know a reason why your wife would want to kill this woman, and possibly others?"

"I don't know," he snapped. "This is preposterous." He ran a hand over his face, then pointed toward the hall stairs. "What's going to happen next? Can I see my wife?"

Cotton glanced at me, and I signaled I was through with my questions.

She stepped forward and touched Godwin's arm. "I'd like you to come down to the station for a more formal interview," she said. "Would you be willing to do that?"

"I ... uh ... yes." His face twisted in confusion, the shock setting in. "I just don't understand."

She walked with him toward another detective, who then drove off with Godwin. Then she joined us again, and we went back into the house.

"I GUESS THAT WRAPS THINGS UP," Oakley said.

"I don't know." I was sitting at my desk, twirling a pen in my fingers. "We worked with the Cherry Hills detectives and searched through the rest of the house, and didn't find any evidence that Eve Godwin murdered Jonathan Hall."

"But her husband said she'd been out the night he was killed," Spats said. He was sitting at his desk, working on a report.

I thought about that. "I don't know. I'd like to have it solid. Just because she was out ..." I left the rest unsaid.

"I don't know that we'll get that," Ernie said. "He says she came home late, and he was in bed. She could've been out, drowned Jonathan Hall, and then came home. He would never have been the wiser."

I looked at them all. "What about the homeless guy who said he was certain Hall's killer was a man?"

Oakley shrugged. "He could have been wrong."

I pondered that, and didn't like the conclusions I came up with. "Do you see Eve Godwin as a serial killer?"

"I'll admit, female serial killers are rare," he went on.

"Yeah, but killing Hall? Drowning him would be hard for her, wouldn't it?"

"I don't know."

"How did Eve go about killing the prostitute?" Oakley asked.

"We don't know for sure," Ernie said. "She must've gotten a gun from somewhere, borrowed Hackenberg's car, went to the motel, and picked up Nicole."

"Then took her somewhere, shot her, and dumped her back in the parking lot, like we've suspected," I said.

"And she gets rid of everything she wore, and the gun, some-where, returns Hackenberg's car, and sneaks back into her house," Ernie finished.

I snapped my fingers. "We still need to get Hackenberg's surveillance video. That might clear up part of this. And we need to search his car."

"I'm working with the Cherry Hills detectives. They're

getting a warrant for the Godwins' electronics," Ernie said. "I think they'll share the data with us. Then we can see what Eve had on her computer, and if that leads us to anything. Maybe she has a diary somewhere, something that might tell us what she was thinking."

"We'll also follow up with other family and friends," Spats said. "Maybe she talked to friends, gave them hints as to what she was doing."

"You're probably right." I yawned and stretched. "It's seven o'clock already? I never even had lunch."

"It's been a long thirty-six hours," Spats said.

I nodded. "Oh, when you looked at surveillance video from places around the Princeton Motel the night Nicole Lockwood was murdered, did you notice a white Hyundai parked in front, or somewhere nearby?"

"No. I could see if I could look at the videos again," he said.

"No, it's probably a moot point." I smiled wanly at both of them. "Everybody go home and get a good night's sleep, and we'll pick this up tomorrow."

Ernie heaved himself out of his chair. "That sounds good to me."

Spats and Oakley agreed. They left, and I sat at my desk for a minute, bothered about the investigation. Things didn't add up for me. I couldn't see Eve Godwin as a multiple murderer. Then I shook my head. For the moment, I needed to let that go. I needed rest, and I wanted Harry.

WHEN I WALKED through the door, Harry was in the kitchen, preparing pasta and a salad. I had called him on the way home to tell him what had happened, and he said he'd fixed dinner for us.

"Hey, honey." He gave me a kiss. "Let me get you some wine." As he poured me a glass, he said, "Tell me all about it."

One of the things I love about Harry is that he listens to me talk about my investigations. He seems to know that it helps me figure things out. He handed me the glass. I took a sip and began, then helped him finish the dinner.

"It's crazy how fast this all happened," he said when I'd told him everything. "Do you have a motive for why this woman killed the prostitute?"

I shook my head. "No, that keeps bothering me."

He drained the pasta, put it in a bowl, and went to the table. Then he frowned. "What's wrong?"

"Everyone thinks this woman killed the homeless man, too. I don't know about that. I feel like we've missed something."

He studied me. "What else?"

I sat down, sipped wine, and chose my words carefully. "When I was going through the house, looking for Mrs. Godwin, I kept having flashes back to the night with Diane." I paused. "I mean, I know that this woman is a murderer, and she did herself in, but it's ... still hard to explain, I still have a feeling like I should've been there to stop her. I couldn't save her."

He reached across the table and took my hand. "The difference is, you couldn't save her from herself. You did everything you could, just like Ernie said. You know that, right?" He searched my eyes. "Okay?"

I squeezed his hand. "You're probably right."

"No, I'm not probably right. In this case, I am definitely right. Come on, let's get something to eat." He sat down. "I know your brain will still be thinking it over, but try to let it go for a bit, okay? You've been going for almost two days straight. After we eat, we can watch something mindless on TV. That shouldn't be too hard to find, right?"

I looked up at him and smiled. "What would I do without you?"

"Wilt away like a water-starved flower and die."

I burst out laughing. "You think so?"

He grinned, then served himself some salad. He pushed the bowl across to me. "I do."

We chatted about other things while we ate, and when we finished, we watched some sitcoms. I kept thinking about Eve Godwin and the homeless man on the Platte. The TV show ended and Harry put his hand on my leg. Then he leaned over and kissed me, long and lingering. His lips made their way down my neck.

"Let's go to the bed," he murmured.

His hand worked its way under my shirt.

"Yes," I said suddenly feeling more energetic than I had only a few minutes ago.

We stood up, and barely made it into the bedroom.

CHAPTER THIRTY-FOUR

I was at my desk the next morning, writing up a report on Eve Godwin's suicide, when my desk phone rang.

"Spillman," I barked into the phone.

"This is Rick Yamamoto," the even voice said. "Aurora Homicide. I got your email about any unsolved investigations with cheap jewelry as an MO."

My ears perked up. "You have a case like that?"

"I didn't, but I thought you'd want to know we have a sixteen-year-old victim, Olivia Childress, found early this morning in a park by a guy walking his dog. The dog sniffed out the body under a bridge. The vic had on a bracelet, and it's costume jewelry, with a fake red stone. The family didn't recognize it."

I swore as I jotted down notes. "That fits what I have. How'd she die?"

"Strangulation. I don't think she was sexually assaulted, but we won't know for sure until the autopsy is performed."

"When was she killed?"

"The coroner thinks sometime after dark last night. But we won't know for sure until we get the autopsy results."

My jaw clenched. "Wait a minute. That would mean my killer couldn't have strangled your victim."

"I don't see how."

"You're sure on the timeframe? No way the body was there longer than that?"

"Pretty sure." He grunted. "We've been at it all night. No witnesses so far. She was at a friend's house and was walking home. Her mom works, doesn't pay a lot of attention to her, and figured she'd spent the night at her friend's house. Didn't know anything until we showed up to deliver the news."

"That's rough."

"Yes. I can let you know what we come up with."

"If it's okay, I'll send someone there. I'd like to get as much information on this as I can." I gave him the details about my investigation. "Now that my suspect is dead, I'm not sure what we're up against."

His sigh was audible. "I hear that. And we'll share everything we have."

The dial tone sounded loud in my ear. I hung up the phone. Ernie was staring at me.

"What's up?" he asked.

"We have another victim."

"Huh?" Spats looked up.

"Where's Oakley?" I got up and went into the other room. He was at his desk, and I motioned him over. I told them about my phone call with Yamamoto, then got Rizzo from his office.

He looked at all our grim faces. "What's going on?"

We all exchanged glances, and I spoke up. "We have a problem. A sixteen-year-old girl was strangled last night. A plastic bracelet with a red stone was found on her body."

Rizzo's brow pinched as he processed the information. "And that's the same kind of jewelry that was found on the other two victims?"

"That's right," Spats said.

I took over the conversation, glanced at my notes, and told Rizzo everything. "The coroner thinks she was killed last night, and he doesn't think she was sexually assaulted." I thought fast. "We need to track Eve Godwin's activities yesterday, find out what she did, and if she was out killing that teenager, Olivia Childress. Although I doubt that's the case."

Rizzo thought for a minute. "What about her husband? Could he be in on the killings?"

"I'll see what Cherry Hills knows," Spats said. "They might be keeping tabs on him."

Rizzo stared at me. "What do you think? Is her husband involved?"

I considered that. "I doubt it. But I'm still shaking my head that she was involved. She came from a good family back East, she went to Smith College. She had money, was a country club member."

"Maybe she was bored," Ernie said.

"Do you think she killed Jonathan Hall?" Rizzo asked. "What's the evidence say?"

We exchanged glances again.

"I wondered that, but I tend to doubt it now," Oakley said.

"We don't have concrete evidence that she killed the prostitute yet, correct?" Rizzo went on.

I shook my head. "No. I was able to get the Cherry Hills department to share the data they got from the Godwins' electronics. We have our people analyzing it now. With that, we might find something to definitely tie Eve Godwin to Nicole's murder."

Rizzo mulled that over, then looked at Ernie. "What about the cop?"

"Arnold Culbertson?" Ernie said. "His wife is his alibi for the first two murders. I'll see what he was doing last night, and if he has an alibi."

Rizzo turned to Oakley. "What about the knife found at your crime scene?"

"It took a little time, but I've got a warrant for the hunting shop."

"Good work," I said. "I'd like to go with you when you talk to Palmer."

"The man who makes those knives?" Ernie asked.

I nodded.

"That's a good idea," Rizzo said. "You can see what his reaction is now that he has to give you information on the knives." He looked around the room at all of us. "Keep me posted."

"Let me check on the Godwins' electronics, and then we can go to the gun shop," I said to Oakley.

"That'll work," he replied. "I've got a little paperwork to do on the warrant anyway."

Spats picked up his phone. "I'll talk to the Cherry Hills department about Eve's husband, to see what more we can find out about Eve Godwin's family and friends. You'd think someone would know what she was up to."

"If they got any DNA from Hall, see if it matches with Eve Godwin," I said.

"I'm on it," he said.

I looked at Ernie. "Ernie, connect with Yamamoto, get everything you can about his crime scene. I want all the details."

He pushed himself out of his chair. "I'm on it."

"Give me a few minutes," I said to Oakley.

TARA DAHL, one of the department's best IT investigators, was sitting at her desk, earbuds in, oblivious to anything around her.

She's a technical wizard, and I knew if there was something on the Godwins' electronics that might definitely tie Eve Godwin to Nicole Lockwood's murder, Tara would find it.

I tapped her shoulder. "Hello," I said loudly.

She jumped and took out the earbuds. "Don't say anything about the music, Mom."

"You know I don't like those metal bands." I grinned. "Are you staying out of trouble?"

"But those bands are the best." She returned a smile. "What's up?"

"Are you staying out of trouble?" I repeated.

She grabbed a cup of coffee and pushed back from her chair. "Never. You'd have to ground me before I stopped."

I leaned a hip against her desk. "Did you get the electronics data for Eve Godwin?"

"Yeah, I've been going through it since last night. What's the hurry on this? I heard this woman committed suicide."

"Things just got more interesting." I told her about the murder investigations Oakley and I were working on. "We've just learned about another murder that happened earlier this morning with a similar MO, a bracelet with a red stone discovered on the victim's body."

She sipped coffee. "Hmm. Eve Godwin couldn't have done that one, could she? You think Godwin's husband is in on it?" Tara asked.

"That's a good question, but I doubt it. Spats is checking on that." I shrugged. "We're waiting on the teenager's autopsy results so we can get a better idea of time of death."

"If Godwin didn't murder her, and you don't think her husband was in on it ..." She didn't finish.

I didn't want to say anything, either. It appeared we had another killer on the loose.

"Another killer, but with the same MO?" she asked. "What's going on?"

I sighed, then pointed at her computer. "Tell me what you got on the Godwins' electronics."

She put her cup down. "I'm glad I got on this right away." She pulled her chair forward and started typing. "I've gone through a lot of her internet history. She was one interesting woman."

"How so?"

"She had a fascination with killing and serial killers. Tons and tons of research on them. She looked at Bundy, John Wayne Gacy, the Green River Killer."

"Looking at how they committed the crimes and how they got caught, the mistakes they made?" I asked. "I had to speak at a community meeting the other evening, and she was there. She even talked to me, asked me as much as she could about murder investigations. Pretty bold to talk to the police like that."

"Typical serial-killer arrogance. They think they're never going to get caught."

I sighed. "Yes, but they usually slip up."

Tara went on. "Her search history shows she was researching what would be the best method to kill a person, what poisons would kill a person, and ..."

I interrupted her. "What poisons would kill a person?"

She nodded. "Yeah. She'd found all kinds of exotic poisons. Looks like she wanted to know how fast the poisons would kill."

I looked at the monitor. "What about cyanide?"

"Yeah, that shows up as well."

"She killed herself with cyanide. What about a .22? Any research on that?"

"Nothing specifically." She pulled up another screen. "She did a lot of research on forensics and crime-scene evidence. It sure seems obvious, based on what you've told me, that she was trying to make sure she didn't slip up in any way."

"She hadn't counted on the doorbell cam."

Tara shook her head derisively. "Yeah, that's tripping up more and more people."

"What about drowning?" I asked. "Did Eve want to know what happens when a person drowns?"

"No, nothing on that so far, but I'll keep looking."

I pursed my lips. "Maybe she assumed a drowning death would be easy, not traceable," I said, trying to convince myself that Eve murdered Jonathan Hall. It wasn't working very well. I couldn't see her being able to hold down a big man like Hall. I continued to look at Tara's monitor. "What else have you discovered?"

"I'm still working on it. It looks like she belonged to some various chat groups. A couple of them are pretty secretive. It'll take me some time to see if I can get any chat history."

I nodded. "I'd like to know who she was talking to, interview them to see if she'd said anything about her activities."

"I'll let you know if I find anything."

"I don't suppose she kept some kind of online diary, or anything that documented what she was doing?"

Tara shook her head. "No, we're not that lucky. Apparently, she knew that her internet search history couldn't convict her, right? It's considered circumstantial evidence."

I nodded. "Yeah. It doesn't prove anything. But if she wrote down what she was doing, that's a different thing."

I stared at Tara. "What am I missing?"

She didn't reply.

CHAPTER THIRTY-FIVE

I left Tara with her research and circled back with Oakley. "Let's take separate cars to the hunting shop, in case we need to split up later. And bring the knife." Oakley nodded at me, and we headed out of the room. Twenty minutes later, I parked behind his Chrysler sedan in front of the hunting and fishing store. I joined him on the sidewalk.

"You're going to take this?" he asked as he took off his sunglasses. "Since you talked to him before?"

I nodded, took the warrant from him, and he politely opened the door for me and we went inside. Palmer was with a customer at the back counter. He looked up at us, his face neutral. "I'll be with you in a moment."

We stood off to the side and browsed while he chatted with the other customer, a burly man with a beard. They were discussing rods and reels, and Palmer was in no hurry to move him along. The man finally decided on a particular rod, paid for it, and left. We approached the counter. I reintroduced myself and held out the envelope with the warrant.

"What's that?" he asked.

"It's a warrant. For the list of people you made that particular folding knife for."

Oakley held out the baggie with the knife inside. "This one."

Palmer glanced through the warrant, then stared at him. "I know which knife you mean." He didn't look pleased now. "My customers aren't going to like this."

"You'd think they would be happy to help, if they're helping us track down a killer," I said.

"Give me a moment." Palmer moved to the end of the counter where a computer and monitor sat. He perched on a barstool and began typing. "I'll print you a list. There are six people I made that particular knife for." His printer croaked to life, then spat out a piece of paper. He handed it to me. "That has the customer names. Those are the addresses they gave me when they paid. As you can see, two of them are out of state."

I scanned the list. "You shipped the knives to those two?"

"Yes."

"What can you tell me about these customers?" I asked.

He shrugged. "I deal with a lot of people, so I don't know."

Oakley took a step toward the counter, subtly threatening. "Nothing stands out about them?"

Palmer shook his head. "Sorry."

Apparently, Oakley's attempt at subtle intimidation hadn't worked. Palmer had given us the customer names, and even if he did know more, he wasn't going to tell us. And the warrant didn't specify that he had to. He frowned, his face saying he was already feeling bad that he'd had to divulge the information he had. Oakley glanced at me, and I signaled to him that we should go.

"Thanks for your time," I said to Palmer. "If we need anything else, I can assure you we'll be back."

Palmer had his hands on the counter, and didn't respond. We walked out of the building. Outside, Oakley donned sunglasses. "How do you want to handle this?"

I stared at the list. "There's four men who live locally. Let's go back to the station, find out what we can about each one, and we'll split up and talk to them," I said.

He glanced at his phone. "I have another update with the chief later. I hope this leads to something."

"Me, too."

AN HOUR LATER, I was headed to speak to one of the men on the list, Clive Worchester. At the station, I'd done some research on him, along with another individual, Quinton Myers. I'd called Ernie, and he was going to talk to Myers. Oakley was on the hunt for the other two local names on the list from the hunting shop.

Clive Worchester, age thirty, came from a wealthy family who lived in the Cherry Creek neighborhood. Clive had graduated from Yale, and from what I could tell, had been at the same job since graduating. He lived in a pricey, high-rise condominium in north Denver. I called his employer and was told Clive had called in sick.

I parked behind a sleek blue Mercedes, then walked up the street to Clive's building. The lobby was large, with a waiting area, large art pieces on the walls. A young doorman stared at me as I approached his desk. I showed him my badge. He'd been trained well: his expression didn't change.

"How can I help you?" He acted more casual, his demeanor not like James Hackenberg's butler.

"I need to talk to Clive Worchester. Is he available?"

"All visitors must be announced," the doorman said.

"No problem." I smiled at him as he picked up a phone on the desk. He dialed, spoke for a moment, then hung up. He pointed to the elevators at the far end of the lobby. "He's on the eleventh floor, unit B."

I thanked him and strode to the elevators. The ride was quiet and smooth. I barely noticed I was moving. On the eleventh floor, I went to unit B and knocked. A moment later, a man with a shock of blond hair opened the door.

"You're Detective Spillman? Did I get that right?" He smiled politely. He wore blue shorts and a white shirt.

I nodded. "Yes. I was wondering if I could take a few minutes of your time."

"What's this about?"

"I'm in the middle of a murder investigation and you may have information pertinent to the case."

He frowned. "That's bizarre. I'll help anyway I can, but I think you're wasting your time."

He stepped back and opened the door wider. The condo was a typical, modern open floor plan, with steps down from the door into a huge living room with glass windows that looked out on the Rocky Mountains. The room was sleek, with black leather furniture, modern coffee and end tables, metal lamps, none of it cheap IKEA. His cologne lingered in the air, and rock music played from another room.

He gestured for me to sit at a couch, and he took the love seat. He crossed one leg over the other and looked at me. "What can I do for you?"

"I called your office. They said you were sick."

He touched his forehead. "A bit of a headache. I took some medication, and I'm feeling better."

I'd taken a picture of the knife before I'd left the station, and I handed it to him. "Does this knife look familiar to you?"

"Yes, it does. I had a knife like that."

"Had?"

He handed the paper back to me. "Yes. I gave it to a friend of mine."

"That's a custom-made knife."

He stared at me, blue eyes indifferent. "Yes, that's true. I used it a time or two, and didn't like it as much as I thought I would. So I had something different made for me. My friend had commented that he liked the knife, so I gave it to him."

"Did Pete Palmer make the other knife for you?"

He shook his head. "No, I went somewhere else."

"When did you buy the knife?"

"About a year ago."

That matched the information Palmer had given me. "And you gave the knife to?"

"Bryce Mueller."

"When did you give Mueller the knife?"

Now he cupped his hands around his knee. "A few months back, something like that."

"What's Mueller's contact info?"

"You really need to talk to him?"

"Yes."

He stared at me, then pulled out his phone. "Here's his number. He works downtown, at the Denver Financial Center. He should be at work now."

I wrote that down, then flicked a finger at the paper. "What is this knife used for?"

"Hunting, fishing."

I glanced at my surroundings. "You hunt and fish?" I was trying not to judge, but he didn't look the type.

"Yes, I do. Not as much as I would like, but I try to get out occasionally."

"Which one do you like more?"

He stood up and went to the windows, hands clasped behind his back. "Either one. It's a chance to get away. I went with my grandfather, when he was alive. My father detests hunting, but I love it."

"Do you ever go down to the Platte River?"

He turned, his face showing nothing. "No. If I fish, I head out west, get into the mountains."

"What can you tell me about Jonathan Hall?"

"Who?"

"The name means nothing to you?"

"I'm afraid not."

"Where were you a week ago, Tuesday overnight?"

He gave that thought. "I would've been with Bryce. We went out, I had too much to drink, and I crashed at his place."

"What about last night?"

His eyes narrowed. "Again, with Bryce, until very late. Then I was here, alone."

"What about Olivia Childress?"

"Never heard of her."

"Tell me what you know about Nicole Lockwood."

"I don't know who that is."

"Have you been to the Princeton Motel?"

"No." He stared at me. "Detective, what is this about?"

"I'm afraid I can't share the details."

He nodded thoughtfully. "I see. I'm afraid you're looking in the wrong direction. I don't know the people you mentioned, and I've not been to the Platte. As I told you, I gave that knife to my friend."

"You didn't get the knife back?"

"No."

I couldn't think of anything else to ask him, so I stood up and thanked him for his time. He led me to the door and let me out without another word.

CHAPTER THIRTY-SIX

Clive had said that Bryce Mueller worked at the Denver Financial Center, two high-rises on Lincoln and Sherman Streets. It didn't take me too long to get there, and I parked in a lot across the street from Tower One, a large structure with reflective windows. I called Mueller's office, found out he was there, and disconnected before the receptionist put the call through. I wanted to take him by surprise, as much as I could, assuming Clive had called him.

The elevator was crowded and made multiple stops, and I was impatient by the time I got off on the twentieth floor. Freedom Financial Consulting took up the entire floor, and I hurried to the receptionist and asked for Mueller's supervisor. I wanted that person to clear me to talk to him. The receptionist eyed me curiously as she reached for the phone, then stopped when a man about Clive's age strode into the lobby.

"Bryce," she said. "This woman wants to talk to you."

Mueller was in a dark, three-piece suit, striped tie askew. He kept going, and the receptionist called out louder. He turned around, mumbled something about not hearing her, and looked at me warily. "I'm headed out for a quick bite. Can you walk with me?"

"Of course." I hurried to the elevator with him. On the ride down, he said, "Clive told me you'd be calling. I really don't have much to say to you."

"Sure, I understand. I'd still like to ask you a few questions."

"Okay, but you're wasting your time."

The elevator stopped a few times on the way down, and Bryce clamped his mouth shut. When the doors opened at the lobby, he practically bolted out. I have long legs, but I was having trouble keeping up with him. We went through revolving doors and out into the sunshine. A breeze whipped up, ruffling his dark hair.

"Clive said he gave you a folding hunting knife," I began.

"That's right. Maybe a few months back."

That matched what Clive had said. I pulled a strand of hair out of my face. We stood at the corner of Sherman and Eighteenth and waited for the light.

"Do you have the knife now?" I asked.

He hesitated. "Sure. Well, not with me *now*. It's at my apartment."

"Could you get it for me?"

"What's this about? He gave me a knife, big deal.'"

The light changed, and we hurried across the street.

"When exactly did he give you the knife?" I went on.

"Like I said, a while back. I don't remember the exact night. We went out to eat, and he gave it to me."

"What restaurant?"

"I don't know. Do you remember exactly what you were doing months ago?"

We kept walking down Sherman, and he dodged people headed for lunch.

"Why do you need that kind of knife?" I asked.

"Because I hunt," he said.

"Oh, where?"

"Sometimes in the mountains, but usually out of state. You sure are nosy."

I took no offense at that. "It's a pretty nice knife; did you pay for it?"

"He gave it to me."

I switched topics, trying not to give him time to think. "What were you doing last night?"

"I hung out with Clive, and then I went home."

"Alone?"

"My girlfriend was there."

"What about a week ago? Tuesday overnight?"

"Clive and I went out, and then he crashed at my place."

"Was your girlfriend there?"

He hesitated. "Yes."

"Can she verify that?"

"You're not going to bother her with questions."

"So you won't let me talk to her."

"No."

"Where did you and Clive go?"

"The Palm. Do you know it?" he asked skeptically.

"Yes, actually I do, at the Westin Hotel. I've been there a time or two. You're sure that was the restaurant?"

"Yes." He appraised me. "Okay, so you have your answer."

We crossed Broadway and he stopped in front of the Brown Palace Hotel. "I have to meet somebody for lunch." He put one hand in his pocket and stared at me. "I don't know what these questions are all about. Clive said something about a murder investigation. But you're barking up the wrong tree. I didn't have anything to do with any murder. I don't know a Jonathan Hall or an Olivia Childress, and I haven't been to the Platte." He sneered. "Yeah, Clive told me all about it. Like I said, you're not getting anything from me." He took a step back. "I don't have anything else to say to you. I need to meet my friends for lunch."

With that, he spun around and walked into the hotel. I had a feeling he was lying to me, so I went around the corner of the building, then peeked back at the entrance. Sure enough, a minute later, Bryce walked back out of the hotel and headed in the opposite direction. I ran after him, and as I drew close, I yelled. He whirled around, saw me, and swore.

"What do you want?"

I jerked a thumb at the hotel. "You lied to me."

"Get off my back, okay? I don't have anything more to say to you."

"If you're lying about meeting someone for lunch, what else would you be lying about?"

He glared at me. "You want anything else from me, you'll have to do it through my lawyer."

He whirled around and walked away. I watched until he disappeared down the next block, then went back to my car.

"You THINK this guy Bryce Mueller is a killer?" Ernie asked me.

"I don't know. He's an A-1 asshole, that's for sure, and acted guilty as hell, but I don't know much about him. And of course, we're back to motive."

I was back at my desk. Ernie had just returned from talking to Detective Yamamoto, and he'd been to Olivia Childress's crime scene. It was still too early in their investigation, and Ernie didn't have a lot of details, other than that Yamamoto and his team were combing the neighborhood near the park where the girl had been found, talking to everyone they could, and looking for anyone who had surveillance cameras. Oakley had also returned, and we were going over all our information about the knife owners, trying to put things together to find a killer.

Spats walked in. "Eve Godwin's husband says there's no way Eve would've killed that teenager, Olivia Childress," he announced.

"You believe him?" I asked. "I just want to be sure we can eliminate Eve from this killing."

"The husband covered for her before," Ernie added.

"Good point." Spats paced around our desks. "So Eve killed Nicole Lockwood, and then she killed Childress sometime before Sarah talked to her, but nobody discovered the body?"

Oakley held up a hand. "Or do we have another killer, someone who owned this knife?" He held up the baggie with the folding knife.

I looked at him. "The two men you talked to still had their knives?"

"Yep, I saw both knives," Oakley said.

I turned to Ernie. "And Quinton Myers, the man you talked to, said that he lost his knife several months ago."

He nodded. "Yes, and he didn't have an alibi for last night, or for the night that Jonathan Hall was killed. He was home alone in bed. How can he prove that?"

"And my guy, Clive Worchester," I said as I looked at all of them, "says he gave his knife to his friend." I'd told them about my conversation with Bryce Mueller. "He was cagey, and he lied to me about meeting friends for lunch. He's holding something back. I want to figure out who his girlfriend is and talk to her."

"Someone's lying, that's for sure," Ernie said.

We batted around all we had, arguing points, tossing theories out, rejecting them.

"I don't know about Eve Godwin," I said. "I still come back to the homeless man. He was so certain he'd seen a man. That would eliminate her as Jonathan Hall's killer."

Ernie crossed his hands over his middle. "A tossup between Worchester and Mueller?"

Before I could answer, Tara Dahl rushed into the room. She saw all of us and stopped.

"What kind of meeting of the minds is this?" she asked.

Spats stopped pacing and said, "The brightest minds around."

Ernie snorted.

Tara walked over to me with some papers. "I thought you'd want to see this."

"What's that?" I took the pages from her.

"It's an online conversation that I took off Eve Godwin's laptop." Tara leaned over my shoulder and pointed. "She belonged to a very secretive chat group. The site is designed to keep conversations private." She smiled. "However, I managed to get into it, anyway." There was a note of pride in her tone, and I felt it, too. Tara is really good.

"There's a whole group of them that have anonymous names," she said.

"How do you know they're aliases?" Oakley asked.

Tara smiled at him. "Because of their names: Marilyn Monroe. Teddy Roosevelt, Brad Pitt, Joe Smith, Pete Rose, Daffy Duck."

"Oh, how clever," Ernie said.

"But here's the kicker. They keep talking about doing a 'deed. '" Tara stood straight and looked at everyone. "One conversation occurred a week ago Wednesday."

Oakley stared at Tara. "That's the day after Jonathan Hall was killed."

Tara nodded. "And another conversation occurred last Wednesday."

Spats put his hands on the desk and leaned over toward mine "That's after Nicole Lockwood was killed."

I was reading through the conversations. "Listen to this. They talk about their 'deeds,' how it felt to do it. It sounds like they're talking about killing. They want to know what it feels like."

Tara held up a cautious hand. "But they're careful not to say that. They know what they're doing; they don't want anything to implicate them. They even say that in one of the conversations, how they can't do anything to get caught."

"Multiple killers?" Oakley asked, incredulous.

"A killing group." Spats shook his head in a mix of awe and disgust. "Really?"

"That's what we need to find out." I said.

"Is there a leader?" Ernie asked.

"From what I can tell, Teddy Roosevelt," Tara said.

"Isn't that fitting," I muttered. "A president."

"One known for his hunting," Oakley observed.

I laid the papers on my desk. "This is great, but it doesn't help me build my case."

Tara grabbed the pages and shuffled through them. "No, but this does. I did a lot of internet work and managed to track down two of the people on the list. Joe Smith is Alan Oswald, and Daffy Duck is some guy named Clive Worchester."

My jaw dropped. "Give me those papers." I stared at them.

"I'm working on the others," she said. "I'll give whoever set up this chat group credit, they're making it really hard to figure out identities. I'll see what I can find out."

"That's great work, Tara," Ernie said.

She shrugged shyly. "Thanks. I'll leave you bright minds to figure it out."

As she left the room, I said to Oakley and Ernie, "You two talk to Yamamoto. Let him know what's going on, and find Alan Oswald. Spats, you come with me. We're going to talk to Clive Worchester again. I think we've found our killers."

CHAPTER THIRTY-SEVEN

While Ernie and Oakley got in touch with Detective Yamamoto from the Aurora Police Department, Spats and I went back to visit Clive Worchester, unannounced. When we walked into his building, the doorman stared at us, his face again blank. I walked past him, Spats on my heels.

"Excuse me," the doorman called out. "You need to be announced."

"So announce us," I snapped.

He looked confused, but reached for the phone, and Spats and I strode to the elevator and got in. The elevator stopped on the eleventh floor, and Spats and I got out and walked quickly down to Clive Worchester's door. Before we got there, it opened.

"Detectives," Clive said, his voice smooth, a cool edge to it. "I didn't think I would see you again so soon."

"A moment of your time?" I said, matching his faux politeness.

He nodded without a word, stepped back, and let us into the condo. "To what do I owe this pleasure?" he asked as he went to a

253

long bar along one wall. He began fixing a drink. "Oh, may I offer you to anything?"

Spats and I both shook our heads. He turned around, took a long pull on his drink, then walked carefully over to a loveseat and sat down. Then he gestured for us. "Sit, please."

I edged over to the back of the couch across from him and perched on the edge. Spats stayed where he was. Clive took a drink and gazed at me.

"I do have more questions," I said, "but before I begin, I would like to read you your rights. That way we've covered our bases."

He arched an eyebrow. "That sounds ominous."

"It protects both of us." I smiled, then before he could object, read him his rights.

"I understand my rights," he said when I finished. He swirled his drink.

"Thank you." I dispensed with any niceties. I held up the piece of paper that Tara had given me with some of the names of the online chat group members. I tapped it. "We found out something interesting about you."

Spats put his arms at his sides and let me talk, but his muscles tensed, one hand near his gun, ready for anything.

"Oh?" Clive's hand stopped for just a moment, then resumed. "What might that be?"

"Teddy Roosevelt, Daffy Duck, Brad Pitt, Joe Smith, Marilyn Monroe, Pete Rose." I glanced at him as I read off the names.

He stared at me, forcing bemusement. "That's an interesting list of names."

"These are names from an online chat group. We've managed to track down a few of the people behind the pseudonyms. You're one of them."

"Really?" His face was neutral, but his eyes held venom.

Then he said, "You talked to Bryce? He told you I was with him last night, and a week ago."

"Where did you go?"

"The Chophouse. I love that restaurant. Great steaks."

His eyes flickered at the same time mine did. We both knew he'd just lied.

"Your friend said you were at The Palm," I said.

He tipped his head. "Are you sure about that?"

I nodded. "One hundred percent."

"Maybe he's lying."

"Why would he do that?" He didn't answer, so I said, "Maybe you're lying."

He suddenly swore. "Bryce insisted on saying it was the Palm, but I hate that restaurant and never go there." He shook his head and softly cursed his friend. He drained his glass and set it on the coffee table with a loud clink. Then he stared at me. I was wary, wondering what his next move would be. He finally said, "Well, Detective, you caught me."

I was taken aback. "Excuse me?"

He smiled, but his perfect white teeth couldn't hide the smarmy oiliness. "The game is over, the jig is up." He leaned back casually and laid an arm over the back of the loveseat. "It was the perfect crime. A homeless man, someone that nobody knew or cared about, the deed done late at night." He pondered that for a second. "I watched the homeless people for days, knew that most of them were too high or confused to notice much that went on. I saw fights, disputes over their territory or belongings. And the drug use." He sneered. "No one around would've ever noticed anything between me and another homeless guy. And the man I chose, he was a wreck. I talked to him once. It seemed as if he barely knew his name. I knew drowning him would be easy. I'd wear gloves, dark clothes, a hoodie. In the middle of the night, down on the Platte, who would notice me?"

"A homeless man did," I said.

He smiled haughtily. "Yes, but did he know it was me?"

I shook my head. "No, he didn't see your face."

"Even if he had, I disguised myself. He wouldn't have been able to describe me." He went on, talking as if he'd been playing ball with someone, not committing murder. "That night, I went down to the Platte. That man was there, as he usually was. He was half drunk, maybe high. I made sure no one was around. Except, I guess, for the homeless man you mentioned." His laugh was casual, dismissive. "But how could I have known he was there? Anyway," he waved a hand, "I chatted with the man I'd chosen, walked him down to the river, and hit him in the stomach. I pushed him down into the river, and it was easy to hold his head under. He fought a little, but then he was gone. I walked back up the bike path to my car, and no one was the wiser." He held up a hand before I could say anything. "Oh, I know, you're going to say the other homeless man saw me, but again, what does that matter?"

The room was quiet. I heard Spats, trying to keep his breathing even. I waited on Clive. He wanted to talk, and I wasn't going to stop him.

"Then," Clive went on, "imagine my surprise when I find out my victim is the son of the lieutenant governor." He lifted his shoulders in a slight shrug. "The rest of the group thought I should've known, but how do you know who a homeless person is? They're, by nature, seemingly anonymous. And I couldn't very well talk to him at length, risk witnesses seeing me with him. The one time I did speak to him, he didn't give me his real name. Shooter. What kind of a dumb nickname is that?"

"And the knife?" I asked.

Another slight uptick in the shoulders. He smiled. "Yes, that didn't go well, did it? The knife dropped out of my pocket, and I didn't notice it was gone until I got home. At that point, I worried that if I did go back to the Platte, someone might see me. I had to leave it, hoping that if it was found, it wouldn't lead back to me. As it turns out, that was my downfall."

He was so smug, so arrogant. My stomach was a knot. "Why'd you take it with you?"

"For protection, and in case the guy fought me. I didn't want to use a gun, too much noise." He scratched his chin. "Turns out, it wasn't necessary."

"What about Olivia Childress?"

"I don't know her," he said.

"Your friend Bryce wasn't involved at all, except as an alibi?" I asked.

"After you left a while ago, I called him and asked him to lie for me." He shook his head. "He couldn't even do that right."

"You thought you had it all planned out." I said, "You never thought you'd get caught, so you wouldn't need an alibi."

He didn't argue. His conceit was astounding.

"Why tell me all this?" I asked.

His face went pensive. "When you questioned me earlier, I was dodging your questions, trying to keep from getting caught. That's why we're in the Guild, so we can talk to each other about our deeds. But it's such a small group, and we don't know each other. I want people to *know* what I did. I want *you* to know."

"The Guild?" This from Spats.

Clive nodded eagerly. "Yes, the Guild. A group for people who want to know what it's like to kill."

A chill went through me. "How many of you have killed?"

He shook his head, a sly look on his face. "Now, now, I can't tell you that. It's part of the Guild rules. I'll tell you about mine, but no one else's."

"What about Marilyn Monroe? Who'd she kill?" I tried to get him to reveal something, anyway.

Another headshake. "No," Clive said. "You won't get anything about anyone else from me."

"You've never met the other Guild members?" I asked.

He shook his head. "No, it's anonymous. One of the rules."

"How did it get started?"

He wagged a finger at me. "I can't tell you. Again, part of the rules."

"You killed for sport?" Spats asked.

Clive looked at him. "Not for sport, for science, for intellectual curiosity. To know what it was like. And you know what?" Neither Spats nor I seemed to be able to say anything. Clive went on. "It was wonderful, awe-inspiring. To have that kind of power and control over someone else."

"That's sick," I finally said.

He glared at me. "You've killed, Detective. I read about you in the paper. You didn't feel a thrill?" he whispered.

I stared at him, doing my best to control my anger. "No, I didn't."

"That's too bad," he said.

"No, it's not." I snapped.

Spats cleared his throat. I drew in a breath to calm myself. I stood up and stared at him. Spats moved to block the door, his hand now on the butt of his gun. Clive remained seated.

"Clive Worchester, you're under arrest for the murder of Jonathan Hall."

CHAPTER THIRTY-EIGHT

A few hours later, I was sitting at my desk when Ernie walked in.

"You are not going to believe this," he said.

"That seems to be your catchphrase."

He guffawed, a big belly laugh that made me smile.

"You're in a good mood," I said. "That must mean something good happened."

He nodded as he sat down. "Yamamoto made an arrest for Olivia Childress's murder. It was Alan Oswald, aka Joe Smith from that chat group."

My nod was pure satisfaction. "And," I paused dramatically, "you're not going to believe this."

He arched an eyebrow. "You got Clive Worchester?"

I nodded and called Clive an unflattering name, then told Ernie what had happened. "It was amazing. We talked to him, and he told us everything. In fact, it seemed like he wanted to talk about it. He wanted his moment of glory, wanted people to know what he did. The arrogance of that guy." I pointed toward the door. "Spats is with him now, getting a full confession on tape. I was at his condo with forensics. We'll get a warrant for his electronics as well, see what evidence he left behind. I doubt there'll be much, but I hope something concrete. I'll be talking to Mueller to see if he knows more than he's telling."

Ernie rubbed a hand over his mouth. "Mine didn't go quite like that. We went to Oswald's house, he saw us, and he ran out the back door. We chased him ..." He held up a hand to shush me. "Yeah, I know, I wasn't the one doing the chasing. Anyway, we caught up to him and the little turd actually fought us. Oakley might have a shiner."

"Wow."

"Once we had him subdued, Oswald dodged everything, tried to lie his way out of his crime. He's a whiny little twenty-something, plenty of family money, doesn't even work. The only thing is, he isn't very smart. He left a trail of evidence you could see from the moon. The Aurora detectives found some surveillance video that caught his car with his license plates near the park, and they found the girl's backpack in a dumpster near his building. You'd think he would've gotten rid of that somewhere far away, but no. And she apparently fought some, and there might be some of her DNA in his car as well. Plus, we have the chat room conversations to build motive."

"I can fill that in some for you. There apparently is a 'murder guild,' " I said, using air quotes. "Clive Worchester confirmed what we thought. The members wanted to experience what it feels like to kill."

Ernie shook his head. "I thought maybe we were wrong about that."

"Nope." I sighed. "Who would've thought?"

"So Eve Godwin was Marilyn Monroe?" he asked. "And that was her motive? That rich woman *wanted* to kill someone?"

I nodded. "Apparently so. I've been reading through some of the conversations. The members even talk a bit about how they did their deeds. That's what they call the murders; their 'deeds.' There's some talk about Marilyn Monroe – Eve Godwin – and how she planned her crime, learned all she could about prostitutes and then picked one."

"Nicole Lockwood."

"Godwin didn't know her name, but yes. She picked up Nicole, took her to a nearby park and shot her, then dumped her body at the motel. Then she tossed all the evidence in dumpsters, took Hackenberg's car to his place and cleaned it out. We can verify this. She disabled his alarm system that afternoon so there wouldn't be a recording of her going into his house."

"Unbelievable."

I held up some pages. "I was just looking at the list of members. I don't know who everyone else is. Tara's still working on it."

Rizzo walked into the room. I had filled him in earlier on Clive Worchester's arrest, and he had an update. "I've been talking to Follett," he said. "He was short on praise, but he's still pleased. However, he wants us to make sure we can nail Clive Worchester." He looked at me. "How solid is your case? You think Worchester might change his admission?"

"We'll see what evidence we can come up with," I said. "We're getting a warrant for his building's video surveillance. My guess is we'll find him leaving and returning around the time Jonathan Hall was murdered. And I don't think he'll clam up. He seems to want to brag about what he did."

Before Rizzo could say more, Tara walked into the room, looking nervous. I waved her over.

"What's going on?" I asked. "You look shocked."

"I've got the rest of the list," she said.

Ernie looked at her curiously. "That should be good news."

She walked over to my desk and handed me another set of papers. "Look at the last name, for Teddy Roosevelt."

I did. "Lawrence Ridley?"

"That ambulance chasing attorney?" Ernie said. "The one with the cheesy commercials on TV?"

Tara nodded. "I couldn't believe it either."

"He helped start the DPD community meetings." I thumped back in my chair. "You're sure about this?" I grabbed the new pages and started reading them.

"I looked this over carefully."

Rizzo stood with an elbow crooked, his chin resting on his hand. "If that's true, we have to be very careful. Ridley is a powerful man. If we're wrong, this will go badly for us."

"How much of his conversation do you have in this chat room?" I asked Tara.

She jabbed a finger at my desk. "A lot. I've been reading through some of it. They're careful not to admit to anything. But they keep talking about their 'deeds.' "

"Well," Ernie said. "Even if Ridley never admits to a crime, we could get him on conspiracy."

Rizzo nodded. "First thing, we need to get him in here, see what he has to say." He fixed his gaze on Tara and echoed my words. "You're sure on this?"

"Yes," she said.

Rizzo went to the window and looked out on Cherokee Street. Then he turned to us. "Find out everything you can on Ridley, fast. Then interview him, see what he tells us." He turned to me. "Sarah, does he talk about a deed that *he* did?"

I shrugged. "Not really. I don't see that he performed a deed, or maybe he did his murder first. Or maybe he just pulled the group together. It'll take a bit to go through all of this."

"What do we know about this guy?" Rizzo asked. "I just see his commercials on television."

I quickly got on the computer and typed in Ridley's name. "He's fifty-six years old, married, with a couple of kids."

Ernie was typing as well. "He went to Ohio State, then law school in California. A big house in east Denver. You know he's got a lot of money."

"So far, all our potential suspects have money," I said. "They have resources they assumed keep them from being caught?"

Rizzo motioned at me. "Take Ernie and bring Ridley in for questioning."

I nodded. "We're on it."

CHAPTER THIRTY-NINE

E rnie and I pulled into the Centennial Airport parking lot an hour later. After Rizzo had left my desk, I phoned Ridley's office and was told he had left. A little more digging, and we found out from his house staff that he was headed to the airport for a sudden, unplanned trip. It appeared he might be making an escape.

"Let's get in there," Ernie said, urgency in his voice.

The small airport is one of the busiest for private flights, and we had called ahead and instructed the tower to hold Lawrence Ridley's plane. We rushed into the main building, found a security person who led us to the airport director. He was puzzled, but made some calls, and we were eventually escorted outside to the operations area. The high pitch of plane engines roared close by.

The director shielded his eyes against the late afternoon sun. "His plane is over there."

"Don't let it take off," Ernie said.

The director looked at us strangely, then walked us toward a large hanger. In front of it was a small jet, its steps lowered. The director pointed. "There's Mr. Ridley's limo now."

A black limo had just pulled up near the jet. The driver got out, opened the back door, and a man with a full head of dark hair emerged from the limo. Ernie and I walked toward him, and I raised my hand.

"Mr. Ridley?" I called out.

He turned to look at me, and the slightest of frowns appeared on his face.

"Yes?" he asked as we drew close.

"I'm Detective Spillman, and this is Detective Moore. We're with the Denver Police Department."

"You've caught me at a bad time."

I forged ahead. "We have reason to believe that you may be an accessory to a series of murders."

He glanced toward the limo driver and to his wife, a blond in a skirt and high heels, who had just gotten out. "I'm afraid you must be mistaken." His voice was like his commercials, a touch too much sincerity.

Ernie stared at him "We'd like to take you in for questioning."

He glanced toward the plane. "Impossible. We're about to leave town."

I didn't have enough to charge him with murder, but I hoped to scare him enough that he'd talk with us. "If you'd like, we can charge you with conspiracy to commit murder, or you can voluntarily talk to us. Take your pick. You come to the station with us, or we'll bring charges against you. Then it gets ugly."

He considered that, then turned to his wife, muttered something I couldn't hear, and kissed her cheek. Then he looked at Ernie and me.

"Let's go."

LAWRENCE RIDLEY GLANCED around the interrogation room. His tailored suit, gold watch, and commanding demeanor was out of place in the drab room with its stark white walls, antiseptic smells, and cheap metal table. He eyed video equipment in an upper corner of the room. Ernie was sitting at one end of the table, and I sat opposite Ridley. I noted the time, who was present, and read him his rights for the record. He stated he understood his rights, and I began.

"Do you want a lawyer present?" I asked.

He shook his head, arrogance in his eyes.

"During the course of a murder investigation," I said, "we discovered our suspect was part of an online chat room whose purpose was to discuss murders that the members commit. One of the members used the name Teddy Roosevelt. We traced that user back to you."

Ridley placed his hands on the table. "That's very interesting." His expression revealed nothing.

Ernie leaned his chair back and crossed his legs, looking the laid-back observer.

"Are you the user Teddy Roosevelt?" I asked Ridley.

"That's a very interesting pseudonym to pick," he said. "An aristocrat, a powerful man, a president who was a great statesman."

I nodded. "Yes, definitely a leader, but not a murderer."

He blinked. "I'm not sure what this has to do with me."

"I just told you," I said. "The apparent leader of this online group is you."

"How do you know anyone in this group has actually committed murder?"

I stared at him. "I think you know that, because you were headed to the airport to escape."

"I had a trip planned."

"A last-minute trip." He didn't say anything, and I went on.

"What do you know about Eve Godwin, Clive Worchester, and Alan Oswald?"

"Nothing," Ridley said.

Ernie's chair legs dropped to the floor with a bang. Ridley jerked his head at the noise. "Those three, and two others, wanted to experience what it was like to kill," Ernie said, no longer the laid-back observer. He leaned toward Ridley. "They said they had a safe place to share what their plans were, and what it felt like, a private little group. Teddy organized it all."

Ernie was now pushing Ridley, hoping he would cave. We stared at him, and I wondered what we would get from him. He had resources to fight this, was too smart to leave a trail of evidence that would convict him. But I also knew, if he was at all like the others in the Guild, he wanted to share, *needed* to share. I played off that.

I got more comfortable in my chair, took a casual pose, and looked at Ridley. "Let me ask this. How would one go about organizing a guild like this? It's not part of the norm."

A gleam appeared in his eye. I was right, he wanted to talk.

He mulled for a moment. "Purely from a hypothetical standpoint," he began, his manner refined. "What if you did have people who wanted to know what it was like to take another human being's life?"

I smiled easily. "What if? How would you find people who wanted that, let alone get that group together?"

"Someone with a lot of resources, a lot of money, can do whatever they want." He turned his chair away from the table and crossed one leg over the other. Then he smoothed his pant leg. "Let's just say, again purely hypothetical, that there was someone, a little old lady, who had bothered a certain lawyer's family for years. She was an annoying friend of the family, and terribly jealous of the success the lawyer had."

"She didn't like that you're rich," Ernie said.

"Not me, the lawyer." Ridley stared at him. "And for the sake of the story, yes. She was a shrew, and her nagging got to be too much. Around that time, the lawyer had taken on a case, a murder trial. The client had shot a man, and he didn't seem to be remorseful, rather almost pleased about how he had taken a life." He waved a casual hand in the air. "Mind you, he never said that, it was just something the lawyer surmised. And it stayed with the lawyer, and he kept thinking about this nagging relative. Wondering. Then, he began to plan how he could eliminate her. She lived in a little house, nothing like the lawyer's estate. He could go there in the middle of the night. This was before all the surveillance video and doorbell cameras and whatnot. The house would be easy to break into, and she was old, lived alone, was hard of hearing. He could go sneak through the back door, go into her bedroom, and no one would be the wiser. A pillow over the head and suffocation. Easy." His smile was cold. "Hypothetically, of course."

I glanced at Ernie. We had just heard a confession, and yet Ridley had been so careful, he could deny he was referencing himself.

I felt a pain in my stomach, the acid churning. "What did you do next?"

Ridley was again too slippery to actually admit to anything. "I didn't do anything. But the lawyer might've thought through the whole thing and realized the killing was incredible. I've heard that there can be a rush, an exhilaration, when you do something like that. Mind you, I've just heard that."

"And you wanted to see if others would want the same feeling?" Ernie asked.

Ridley nodded appreciatively. "I could see where someone would want to share the wealth, so to speak."

"How did you get the group together?" I asked.

"To do something like that, I would assume one would have

to have the resources to make sure the group would be anonymous. As for finding members, couldn't one listen to people at
parties and get-togethers, get a sense that they wanted a similar
experience? It could be a lawyer's clients who wanted revenge.
The possibilities are endless. Hypothetical conversations would
indicate interest in such a group. Then members are chosen, and
someone could gather them together and create a safe, online
place to meet. Again, it might be surprising how many people
would want this kind of experience."

"I thought the group was anonymous," I said.

"The others didn't know each other, but I had checked them
all out."

It was his first slip; he didn't qualify the statement with a
hypothetical. He seemed to know that, and he sat a little
straighter.

"How could you possibly know that you could trust them all
to keep quiet?" I asked.

"Someone who could pull a group like this together would
have the resources to vet all the members first, research them to
know they could be trusted implicitly. It would be important that
the members were local, easier to keep tabs on them. And the
members would have to agree to stringent rules. After all, no one
would want to get caught, so they wouldn't risk anything that
would jeopardize the group or themselves."

"So you knew them all, but none of them knew each other, or
you."

"That could be how it works, hypothetically speaking."

It wasn't a yes or a no, but that had to be the case.

"You still couldn't know that they would all agree to the rules
or keep the rules?" Ernie interjected.

"Someone with the resources to pull a group like this together
would have the resources to keep tabs on the members," Ridley
said with thick self-assurance.

"How did you choose your victims?" I asked.

"That's an interesting question," was all he said.

"The group rules." I consulted some notes. "From what I can gather, beyond needing the utmost secrecy, is that you picked victims you didn't know." I pointed my notes at him. "But you yourself broke those rules."

He pursed his lips. "If, as you say, the first victim was known to the killer, that would create vulnerability for the killer. He, or she, could be caught." He was still trying the subterfuge, not, technically speaking, admitting to anything. "From that point forward, if group members were to commit murders, there would need to be assurances that no one could get caught."

"So, for victims, you chose vulnerable people," Ernie said. "People society doesn't care much about."

"People that society, and the police, wouldn't miss. Where the police wouldn't work hard to find the killers," Ridley said. "That would seem a reasonable request for the group members, would it not?"

"Who killed first?" I asked.

He shrugged. "I don't know what you're talking about."

I tried a different direction. "Someone had to be first." Another glance at my notes. "Possibly Brad Pitt. Knowing that someone in the Guild you created actually committed a murder must've made you feel invincible." No reply. I went on. "Tell me about the jewelry with the red stones. A calling card?"

"One would need a way for the members to know that the deed was done."

Another slip, a small one, by using the word "deed." It was circumstantial evidence, but evidence that could nonetheless connect him to the chat room. He didn't seem aware of it.

"Then it started to go badly," I said. "Jonathan Hall's murder."

"Who?" he asked.

"He's the lieutenant governor's son."

"A homeless man, correct? I think I saw something about him in the news. He would seem to be a vulnerable person, but as it turned out, not an anonymous person." He tipped his head slightly. "Something like that certainly could complicate things. At that point, with the wrong person being chosen, it seems it might be time to shut the group down, before things crumbled."

I gave him a hard look. "But things crumbled anyway."

"It was always possible that a member could make a mistake. It would then be time to close the group."

"To stop the killing," Ernie said.

"The group leader insisted on that," I said.

Ridley nodded. "Of course. I would think if the members went on, continued to kill, it would increase their chances of exposure."

"One of your members went on," I said.

He stared at me, confusion written on his face. "Excuse me?"

"I thought you kept tabs on your members."

"I did." He stopped. "I don't know what you're talking about."

"It surprises you that one of the group members, Alan Oswald, committed a murder last night?" I asked.

He blinked hard, then said, "What's this?"

"He kidnapped a girl and strangled her," I said. I glanced at my notes again. "Alan is Joe Smith. He talks about wanting to take his turn."

Ridley uncrossed his legs. "Well, I suppose no one's perfect. A member might want to act impulsively, even though he was told strictly not to."

"This was a lot for you to pull off," I said, faux admiration in my voice, hoping that might cause him to slip again.

Even though he'd gotten carried away and blundered a time or two, he wasn't going to now. "Isn't it fun to speculate?" He smiled at me, then glanced conspicuously at his watch. "I'm afraid this interview is over. I will get my lawyers together, a top team, I assure you. If you think that I'm going to go to jail, you are mistaken. To be hypothetical, do you think I would put a group like that together without ensuring that there would be no way I could be caught?" His eyes held the purest evil I think I had ever seen. "You don't have enough to charge me, or you would have." He stood up. "It's been a pleasure speaking with you."

Ernie and I left the room with him. He walked with squared shoulders, head held high, as we escorted him outside. When we reached the sidewalk, he smiled at us one last time, then got into a limo that was waiting at the sidewalk.

CHAPTER FORTY

E rnie and I watched the limo drive away. Then he turned to me.

"Can you believe that guy?" he growled.

I shook my head slowly. "I haven't conducted an interview like that in a long time, maybe never. An entire interrogation answered in the hypothetical. That's a guy who knows how to choose his words carefully."

He stuck his hands in his pockets. "Think we can get him on conspiracy to commit murder charges?"

I thought about that. "I don't know. We need to gather up as much information as we can and take it to the DA. Let them figure out charges."

It was dark, and we couldn't see clouds, but it began to spit rain. He looked up and held out a hand. "Maybe this will cleanse me. After talking to Ridley, I feel dirty."

I smiled wryly. "Let's go back inside."

He opened the door for me, and we walked back upstairs. As we entered the detective room, Spats was sitting at his desk. He held his hands up.

"Where have you guys been?"

I went to my desk and sat down. Ernie looked into Rizzo's office and beckoned for him to join us. Spats looked at each of us.

"Are you going to spill it?" he asked. "I've been busy with Clive Worchester. What'd I miss?"

"I'll get Rizzo in here, so we only have to go over it once," Ernie said.

Rizzo approached. "Let's hear it. What happened?"

Ernie and I jointly launched into what had happened with Lawrence Ridley. Part way through, Spats raised a finger to interrupt us.

"Wait a minute," he said. "While I've been dealing with Clive Worchester, you found the leader of this guild?"

Ernie nodded. "Tara tracked him down."

I went on, filling in the last of the details, and ending with our interview of Lawrence Ridley. I was explaining how cagey he had been with his answers when Ernie's desk phone rang. He picked it up, then gestured for us to be quiet. We all waited while he talked.

"Yeah. Uh-huh." He nodded a few times as he listened. "Thanks for the update, I really appreciate it."

He cradled the receiver and looked at us. "That was Detective Wesley, from Commerce City, with an update on Arnold Culbertson. Not that we needed to know at this point, but Arnie's alibi checks out. Turns out he has his own surveillance systems, and he showed them to Wesley. He was home when Nicole Lockwood was murdered, when Jonathan Hall was murdered, and last night, when that teenage girl was taken and killed."

"What about his connection with Nicole?" I asked.

"Oh, he was guilty of that," Ernie muttered. "Once Wesley started pressing him for more information, and digging into things more, good ole Arnie caved. He admitted that he'd had a thing with Nicole, but says he didn't know she was in high school."

Spats looked at him askance. "But he saw her hanging around the high school."

Ernie nodded. "Yeah, Arnie is probably lying about that. He claims she told him she was eighteen and had dropped out of school, she was just hanging around with her friends. Ultimately, I'm not sure it matters. He initially lied about his relationship with her, and now that he's admitted to it, it's going to cost him his job. I'm not sure what they'll do about charges, but that's out of our hands."

Rizzo went to the window and looked out. Rain was coming down hard now, and lightning flashed, followed by a clap of thunder. After a few moments, he took a deep breath, turned around, and said, "Back to Worchester and Ridley. What's going on there?"

"I'll take Worchester," Spats said. He nodded at me. "Just like he did at his condo, he's admitting to the whole thing." He rolled his chair back. "I've never seen anybody quite like him. I mean, some killers want to tell you what they did, they're arrogant, but this guy ... man, talk about being proud of what he did. He thinks it's all for science, an experiment of some sort."

"Just like Ridley," I said. "It's all about the experience."

"You got a warrant for Worchester's electronics?" Rizzo asked.

"Yes, we did," Spats replied. "Tara and the tech team will take a look at it all. I'm sure we'll find the same information about the chat group as we did with Eve Godwin's computer. And he might've left another electronic trail of evidence."

"Let's hope so," Rizzo said. "Sarah, do you have anything to pin on Ridley?" Before I could answer, Rizzo stared past me with raised eyebrows. I turned around to see Chief Follett standing in the doorway. He was in a suit, his tie tight around his neck.

"Calvin here already filled me in about finding Jonathan Hall's murderer." He looked at Ernie, Spats, and me. "Good work. Make sure he doesn't get away."

It was as close as we were going to get to a thank you. We all nodded and told him we would do just that. He turned around and left, and Rizzo sighed.

"Ridley?" he asked me.

I frowned. "I hate to say it, but I think he was too smart to get caught. I don't know that we'll find anything more than circumstantial evidence. Maybe a conspiracy charge, but my guess is he'll squirm out of that."

Ernie slapped his desk and swore. "We can't let that happen."

I shrugged. "You heard him in that interview. We'll work on warrants for his house and his electronics, but I don't think we'll find anything. Whatever evidence he might have will be destroyed. We can only hope the DA might see enough for a conspiracy charge, based on tying him to the chat room. But he was so slick ..." I left the rest unsaid.

Ernie grimaced and swore again. "I hate to say it, but you're probably right."

Rizzo looked at his watch. "I need to get going. You all have had some really long days. Do what you need to now, then go home and get some rest." He went to his office, grabbed his coat, and as he left the room, he thanked us.

"This is a hell of a way to end the case," Ernie groused. "We got three of our suspects, Eve and Clive, and Alan Oswald, and yet I don't feel like we won."

"I hear you," Spats said. "After dealing with Worchester, I need a drink."

I felt as defeated as the two of them, but I tried to put on a good face. "We still did good work. And we'll keep after Ridley. We might get something on him, maybe not murder charges, but something." I looked at Spats. "Where's Worchester now?"

"Sitting in a cell," he said. "Maybe now he'll start to regret what he did."

Ernie snorted. "I doubt that."

I looked at both of them. "Why don't you guys go home? Look at things tomorrow with fresh eyes. We'll need to talk to the families of the victims as well. I'll handle that."

They both nodded and soon left. I wrapped up a report, and then headed out myself.

WHEN I GOT HOME it was late, the sun long since set. The house was quiet, just a lamp on in the living room. I looked around for Harry and noticed him on the back porch. I watched him for a moment through the kitchen window, then fixed a drink and joined him. The rain had stopped, leaving the air with a fresh, crisp smell. He was sprawled in a lawn lounge chair, and he scooted over to make room for me. I snuggled up next to him and sipped some Scotch.

"Another long day for you," he said.

"Yes, with mixed results."

"What happened?"

Images of Eve Godwin, Clive Worchester, and Lawrence Ridley rattled around in my mind. So much evil. I didn't want to think about them at that moment, or talk about the investigation.

"Not now."

"Okay." He kissed my cheek. We sat for a minute, then he said, "How are you feeling?"

I shifted to look at him. "You mean, do I blame myself for anything, do I wonder if I should have done things differently?"

"Yes."

I thought long and hard about that. "No. We all did some really good work on this one. It's good to be back. And I'm okay."

He wrapped his arms around me, and we stayed there for a long time.

Revenge is a dish best served dead

Get Deadly Revenge
The next book in the Detective Sarah Spillman
Mystery Series!

Turn the page for a Sneak Peek.

DEADLY REVENGE

CHAPTER ONE

"We have to kill them, you know."

He turned in the seat and looked at her. Her eyebrows pinched, her lips pressed into a thin, harsh line. She was beautiful when she was angry, and dangerous. He smiled to himself. That didn't mean he was attracted to her. He held up his hands and stared out the windshield.

"Who first?" he asked. He couldn't believe it had come to this, that *this* was what he was contemplating.

"You know who we have to start with," she replied.

"You've been thinking about this."

"Of course. And don't play innocent. So have you."

He *had* been thinking about it. But he'd been thinking how he could talk her out of it. Ultimately, though, he knew she was right. They had to do something. "So," he sighed. "How are we going to do it?"

She tapped her lips for a moment. He could smell her

perfume, not one he cared for. She grabbed a can of Coke from the console between the seats and took a sip.

He could smell alcohol from the can. "Have you been drinking?" he asked.

"Just enough to calm my nerves."

She held up the can and stared into it. He'd known her long enough to know that this was her way to give herself time to think.

"Can't we wait another week or so?" he asked. "Maybe she'll come around."

She swirled the can, then finally spoke.

"Could we? She goes to the gym like clockwork, every morning before work. She could be taken out there."

He was relieved that she might be willing to wait, but her suggestion was not good. He shook his head. "No, too many people around, and there could be security cameras near the gym. Count on that."

She swore. "Then we need to do it now. Tonight."

He grimaced. He should've kept his mouth shut about the gym. He ran both hands over his face as he stared out the windshield, his foot wiggling. It was *his* way of thinking. She was right, of course.

"You know I'm right," she said as if she'd heard his thoughts. "We can't let them interfere in this. If we don't act now, all our work will go down the drain." She took another sip of Coke. "Do you know how much money we're talking about?"

"Of course I do."

He stared at her, then his gaze drifted again. The street was quiet, no one around. He liked this time of night, no one to disturb him. Like death, in a way. Ironic, given what they were talking about. He looked back at her. Her eyes were slits as she watched him.

"I know everything about the money," he said. "I'm the one who got us this all set up. Don't ever forget that."

Her muscles tensed, like a feral cat waiting to pounce.

"You may have set this up," she said, "but I'm the one who got us to this point. Don't ever forget that."

He nodded slowly. "I know exactly how this has gone down; you don't need to tell me. We're both in this deep, and if anything happens, we'll both pay. Which is why we need to be very careful in how we handle this."

The cloud of anger around her suddenly dispersed. She sighed and finished the soda. Her face filled with a cool determination. "People are killed every day, for a lot less than what we're talking about. We can do this."

He leaned forward and put his hands on the dashboard. "You don't see any other way?"

She shook her head. "I've laid awake several nights trying to see if I've missed something. They're not going to go along with this anymore, and —"

"They know how much money we're talking about," he interrupted.

She shrugged. "I've tried that route. I talked to them about that until I'm blue in the face. They don't care, no matter how much it is. You know, some people just don't care."

He smirked at her. Again, she seemed to miss the irony of her comment. They were all supposed to care, right? But the money was just too good.

"I'm worried they might say something, ruin it for all of us," she said.

He'd had that thought, too. He drew in a breath and let it out slowly. He didn't see any other choice.

"How do we do this?" he asked.

"I have a gun in my purse."

He was taken aback. She was more prepared than he figured. "Where did you get it?"

She shook her head. "The less you know, the better. Don't worry. It's untraceable. We'll go to her house now. She won't do anything with a gun on her. I'll force her into her car, and we'll drive someplace, then take care of her." She stared at him, daring him to protest.

He swallowed hard and tried to think of an alternative, but he couldn't.

"Let's do this," he said.

DEADLY REVENGE
Detective Sarah Spillman Mystery Series Book 4
is available on Amazon

AFTERWORD

A long time ago, I wrote three Sarah Spillman short stories, but I never fully developed her character.

Then I moved on to the Reed Ferguson series, but by book four (*Farewell, My Deuce*), I thought it would be fun to bring Sarah, Ernie, and Spats into the Reed series.

She has appeared in every Reed book since then.

For a long time, I thought Sarah's character could be expanded, and I finally did so with *Deadly Connections*.

It has been a lot of fun to see her grow into her own, along with the other characters in the series.

I now have ideas to spin off some of those characters into their own series.

We'll see. I have so many ideas and so little time!

ACKNOWLEDGMENTS

The author gratefully acknowledges all those who helped in the writing of this book, especially: Beth Treat, Beth Higgins, and Thomas Lynch.

A special shout-out to Colonel Randy Powers, retired, Chief Deputy. Any mistakes in police procedure are mine.

To all my beta readers: I am in your debt!
Sheree Benson, Renee Boomershine, Betty Jo English, Tracy Gestewitz, Patti Gross, Barbara Hackel, Eileen Hill, Maxine Lauer, Debbie McNally, Becky Neilsen, Louise Ohman, Becky Serna, Dick Sidbury, Bev Smith, Albert Stevens, Joyce Stumpff, Jennifer Thompson, Patricia Thursby, Marlene Van Matre, Lu Wilmot

If I've forgotten anyone, please accept my apologies.

AUTHOR'S NOTE

Dear Reader,

If you enjoyed *Deadly Guild*, would you please write an honest review? You have no idea how much it warms my heart to get a new review. And this isn't just for me. Think of all the people out there who need reviews to make decisions, and you would be helping them.

You are awesome for doing so, and I am grateful to you!

ABOUT THE AUTHOR

Renée's early career as a counselor gives her a unique ability to write characters with depth and personality, and she now works as a business analyst. She lives in the mountains west of Denver, Colorado and enjoys hiking, cycling, and reading when she's not busy writing her next novel.

Renée loves to travel and has visited numerous countries around the world. She has also spent many summer days at her parents' cabin in the hills outside of Boulder, Colorado, which was the inspiration for the setting of Taylor Crossing in her novel *Nephilim*.

She is the author of the Reed Ferguson mysteries, the Dewey Webb historical mysteries, and the Sarah Spillman police procedurals. She also wrote the standalone suspense novels *The Girl in the Window* and *What's Yours is Mine, Nephilim: Genesis of Evil*, a supernatural thriller, along with children's novels and other short stories.

Visit Renée at www.reneepawlish.com.

RENÉE'S BOOKSHELF

The Sarah Spillman Mysteries:
Deadly Connections
Deadly Invasion
Deadly Guild
Deadly Revenge
Deadly Judgment
Deadly Target
Seven for Suicide
Saturday Night Special
Dance of the Macabre

Standalone Psychological Suspense:
The Girl in the Window
What's Yours Is Mine

Reed Ferguson Mysteries:
This Doesn't Happen In The Movies
Reel Estate Rip-Off
The Maltese Felon
Farewell, My Deuce
Out Of The Past
Torch Scene
The Lady Who Sang High

Sweet Smell Of Sucrets

The Third Fan

Back Story

Night of the Hunted

The Postman Always Brings Dice

Road Blocked

Small Town Focus

Nightmare Sally

The Damned Don't Die

Double Iniquity

The Lady Rambles

A Killing

Dangers on a Train

Ace in the Hole

Walk Softly, Danger

Elvis And The Sports Card Cheat

A Gun For Hire

Cool Alibi

The Big Steal

The Wrong Woman

Dewey Webb Historical Mystery Series:

Web of Deceit

Murder In Fashion

Secrets and Lies

Honor Among Thieves

Trouble Finds Her

Mob Rule

Murder At Eight

Second Chance

Double Cross

The Noah Winter Adventure

(A Young Adult Mystery Series)

The Emerald Quest

Dive into Danger

Terror On Lake Huron

Take Five Collection (Mystery Anthology)

Nephilim Genesis of Evil (Supernatural Mystery)

Codename Richard: A Ghost Story

The Taste of Blood: A Vampire Story

This War We're In (Middle-grade Historical Fiction)

Nonfiction:

The Sallie House: Exposing the Beast Within